CANNIBALS AND CARNAGE

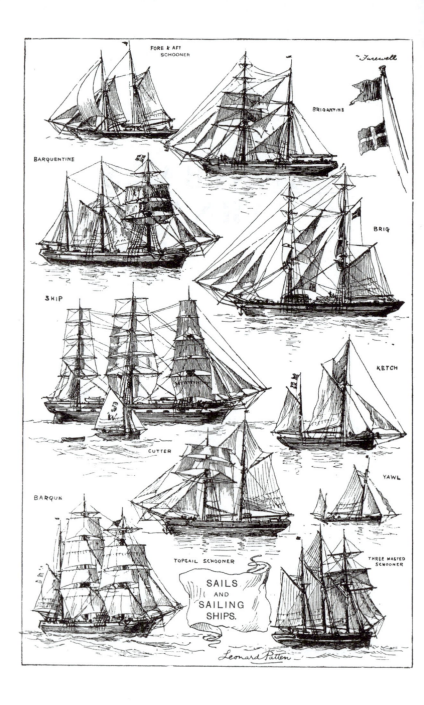

FORE & AFT
SCHOONER

"Farewell"

BRIGANTINE

BARQUENTINE

BRIG

SHIP

KETCH

CUTTER

YAWL

BARQUE

TOPSAIL SCHOONER

THREE MASTED
SCHOONER

SAILS
AND
SAILING
SHIPS.

Leonard Patten

CANNIBALS AND CARNAGE

Thrilling Tales of the Sea
Volume One

GRAHAM FAIELLA

The History Press

First published 2019

The History Press
97 St George's Place, Cheltenham,
Gloucestershire, GL50 3QB
www.thehistorypress.co.uk

British Library Cataloguing in Publication Data.
A catalogue record for this book is available from the British Library.

ISBN 978 0 7509 9084 4

Typesetting and origination by The History Press
Printed and bound in Great Britain by TJ International Ltd.

CONTENTS

PREFACE

Cannibalism and massacres by 'savages' in the nineteenth century provided a particularly salacious diet of news for the degustation of a growing number of newspaper readers. White traders and missionaries were beginning to come into regular contact with the indigenous peoples of, in particular, the Pacific Islands, as well as in Patagonia, at the southern tip of South America. Some of those tribes perpetrated aggression by the necessity for survival, cannibalism by cultural disposition, and murder by design, often for revenge.

The 'Feejees' (Fiji Islands), Solomon Islands, and the New Hebrides (now Vanuatu), as well as the archipelagos to the south-east of New Guinea in the western Pacific, were notorious for massacres and cannibalism from attacks on traders, settlers, Christian evangelists, and labour recruitment vessels (*blackbirders*). Newspapers sauced up such gruesome incidents with relish, and equally florid language, to stimulate the imagination of readers' appetites.

'The Custom of the Sea'

Primitive cannibals and 'savages' were virtually story-book characters in far-away lands, distantly removed from the everyday lives of Europeans and North Americans. Cannibalism at sea by Europeans and North Americans constituted a more kindred connection, more personal to people's revulsion of it, but with a morbid interest in it. It is hard enough to fathom the depths of desperation reached by castaways who tore into and ate the flesh of raw fish or birds (the raw liver of a turtle was highly prized, as was the liquid extracted from fish eyes), much less cutting chunks of flesh from the arms or legs (or both) of a dead comrade, to eat raw.

In 1884 the yacht *Mignonette* sank in stormy weather in the South Atlantic while she was being sailed from England to Australia by a crew of three men and a boy. After nineteen days adrift in the yacht's dingy, Thomas Dudley, the *Mignonette*'s captain, took the decision to kill the boy, Richard Parker, so that the other three, by now on the point of starvation, might cannibalise his body to survive.

This was the so-called 'custom of the sea': the cannibalisation of those killed by other shipmates, or who died of hunger, exposure or exhaustion, to sustain the life of the surviving castaways. In 1876, on the waterlogged, wrecked timber ship *Maria* in the mid-Atlantic, the starving crew members kept their collective conscience clean before falling upon their dead shipmates to feed on them to survive: 'The cannibals from necessity did not murder their companions, but waited with patience until they died.' (*Otago Witness*, 26 May 1877)

Apart from the legal niceties of whether the defence of killing another person for the necessity of survival was justifiable (the benchmark *Mignonette* legal case subsequently concluded that it was not), the public fascination with the cannibalisation of civilised people like themselves, but in dreadful circumstances of life-threatening peril, was a piquant sauce for the journalistic banquet of such reports.

Carnage

No less fascinating a subject was murder, often of a multiple quantity, on ships at sea. The killing of the captain, his wife and the second mate of the barquentine *Herbert Fuller*, in the early hours of 14 July 1896, generated the headline 'A Carnival Of Murder On The High Seas' in *The Halifax Herald* newspaper of Nova Scotia on 22 July 1896. Readers of the *Herald* and other newspapers were subsequently served up a menu of minutiae about the murders, the victims and the alleged perpetrators, illustrations of the blood-spattered murder sites, expansive coverage of the ensuing trial, and details of other high seas carnage in the past reminiscent of the *Fuller* drama. The combination of mutiny with murder only enhanced the savoury attraction and sanguinary reporting of such incidents.

As *The Sydney Morning Herald* put it, about a massacre on board the South Seas trading schooner *Marion Renny* in February 1871, the story was 'exciting and horrible enough for the plot of a sixpenny romance'.

The allure of such terrible tales of the sea was that they *were* the 'sixpenny romances' of their day. They thrilled. They happened to ordinary people in exotic places under tragic circumstances – dramas narrated by survivors of the horrors. They were *real* stories of high adventure, tinted (and tainted) by gruesome detail and sometimes sequelled by the forensic drama of court cases that recounted and examined their actions and consequences.

Those narratives, to this day, bristle with their resonance of peril.

Part I

CANNIBALS

Atlantic Ocean (North and South).

I

'THE CUSTOM OF THE SEA'

Castaways from vessels that sank at sea often ran out of food and fresh water within a matter of days ... if, that is, they had saved any provisions at all. Sometimes they caught fish or sea birds, which they ate raw, and even turtles, which they despatched to scavenge on the innards. They might catch rainwater, though this was often tainted by salt encrusted on their catching devices (such as sails or their own clothing) and undrinkable.

Unquenchable thirst and unsatisfied hunger sometimes drove men mad. Or to such desperation that they contemplated the ultimate recourse: the cannibalisation of fellow castaways in order to survive – the so-called 'custom of the sea'. Occasionally they killed another castaway outright – and sometimes more than one – to feed upon his flesh and drink his blood. More often they cut pieces of flesh from a shipmate, or shipmates, who had already died. Either way, their justification, to themselves at least, was of necessity in order to survive.

The *Mignonette*: A Landmark Case

A notorious case of the 'custom of the sea' concerned the yacht *Mignonette*, in 1884. The *Mignonette* sank in a storm in the South Atlantic. The crew of three men and a 17-year-old boy (not 19, as noted in reports) were cast adrift in a dinghy. A few weeks later, with the four on the verge of starvation, the young lad, Parker, was killed. His flesh and blood were eaten and drunk by the others. A few days later the survivors were picked up by a passing ship. During the voyage to Falmouth the men wrote their accounts of the *Mignonette*'s voyage, including the killing and cannibalisation of the boy Parker. None of them expected to be held criminally liable for the boy's death; to them it was a matter of sacrificing one person, Parker, for the rest to live. The British public, indeed, was largely sympathetic to their plight.

However, the 'custom of the sea' was just that, a custom, the law of the high seas jungle. It was not an act legally sanctioned by necessity. The *Mignonette*'s captain, Thomas Dudley, and mate, Edwin Stephens, were arrested and prosecuted for murder on the high seas. The eventual court case against the two men concluded that murder, even in the most extreme circumstances, was not justified by the perpetrators' necessity to stay alive:

The Loss of the Yacht Mignonette

The German brigantine *Montezuma* landed at Falmouth on September 6 three men named Thomas Dudley, aged 32; Edwin Stevens, 37; and Edward Brooks, 37, who voluntarily revealed to the Collector of Customs one of the most terrible stories of suffering endured at sea on record.

These three men, together with a lad named Richard Parker, 19 [*sic* – 17] years old, belonging to Southampton, were engaged to take out the yacht *Mignonette* to Sydney for Mr. J. H. Want. The yacht was yawl-rigged, 52 feet in length, 12 feet beam, and 52 tons burden. She belonged in the previous year to the Welsh and New Thames yacht clubs.

The Voyage
The yacht left Southampton on May 18 last [1884], Dudley being in command, Stevens mate, Brooks able seaman, and Parker as boy. They arrived at Madeira on June 1. The line [equator] was crossed on June 17, and, from this date trouble commenced. Dirty weather began on the 18th, lasting until June 30, when it blew a gale, which departed suddenly, for on July 2 they were becalmed. By the 3rd they were once again before the storm. In the afternoon they had to reef the mainsail and squaresail, and the captain made up his mind to heave-to and wait for better weather.

At about 4 o'clock he had the squaresail in. Stevens, the mate, was then steering. Captain Dudley heard Stevens cry 'look out,' and looking under the boom saw a great sea coming on to him. He clung to the boom until the sea swept past. Turning round, he saw that all the bulwarks aft were gone. Stevens cried out, 'My God, her side is knocked in,' and such was really the case, for looking over he saw her buttends open. Captain Dudley realised in an instant that the yacht must founder speedily, and it was therefore their first object to get the boat out.

Adrift
The punt or dingy, which was 13 feet long, and made of mahogany, was with great difficulty got out. Dudley

told Parker to pass up a beaker of fresh water, which the boy did, pitching it overboard, in the hope of picking it up again. The captain tore the binnacle compass from the deck, and got it into the boat. Stevens, Brooks, and Parker having taken their places in the boat, Dudley dropped them astern. Recollecting that there was no food in the boat, the captain rushed into the cabin, which was full of water. Seizing a chronometer and sextant, he threw them on deck. Those in the boat were then shouting out to him, 'The yacht is sinking.' He grasped some things that were supposed to be tins of preserved meat, and rushing on deck tumbled over into the boat, all but two tins slipping from his grasp.

They just managed to row the little punt a length astern when the yacht went down, only about five minutes having elapsed from the time she was struck until she finally disappeared. They searched for the beaker of water, but it could not be found, though its stand was found floating about. With those and the binnacle and bottom boards they constructed a sea anchor. Their fragile boat was taking water faster than they could bale it out. They found the leak, filled it up, and managed to bale her out with the billy and the halves of the chronometer box.

Provisions

The two tins proved to contain only preserved turnips, 1lb. each. They had not a drop of water, night was coming on fast, and the sea was raging about them. To add to their terror a shark came alongside at about midnight, knocked against the boat, but fortunately did no damage, and went away soon.

In a miserable plight they existed for four days on one tin of turnips. On the fourth day they succeeded in catching a turtle, which was floating on the water. They then finished the second tin of turnips and killed the turtle. Their thirst was fearful. They drank some of the turtle's blood, saving the remainder in the chronometer case, but it was spoilt by the salt water. Once or twice it rained a little, and they tried to catch some rain water in their oilskins. With their oilskin coats spread over their arms they waited with burning throats and stomachs, praying to the Almighty for water in their extremity, but these endeavours were defeated by the sea water getting mixed with the fresh.

Fifteen terrible days passed away without any incident to relieve the monotony. On the 15th day they set to work to make a sail out of their shirts, with an oar for the mast. On the 18th day, after having had no food of any kind for seven days, and no water for five days, and their condition having become awful, they began to discuss the advisability of casting lots as to who should be killed as food for the others.

The Killing

By this time the boy Parker was in the last stage of exhaustion. The captain and mate, who are both married men with families, discussed the advisability of killing Parker, who was evidently the nearest to death of the four; as they considered that his loss would be the least felt, inasmuch as he had no wife and family depending upon him. They communicated their views to Brooks, but he declined to be a party to such an act. The captain and the mate then decided to kill Parker. Before doing so, Dudley offered up a prayer that they might be forgiven for what they were about to do.

Parker was lying in the bottom of the boat in an almost insensible state, with his face on his arm. It was then arranged that Dudley should stab him, and that Stevens should hold him if he struggled. Brooks went to the bow of the boat, turning away his head to shut out the fearful scene with his hands. The captain said to Parker, 'Now, Dick, your hour has come.' Parker feebly replied 'What! me, sir? Oh, don't!'

Dudley then ran a penknife into Parker's jugular vein, and he died in a few seconds. They caught the flowing blood in tins and divided it amongst them, Brooks being unable to resist taking his share. They then stripped the boy and for five days subsisted on his body before they were sighted by the captain of the *Montezuma*.

Rescue

On the twenty-fourth day the joyous sight of a sail greeted Brooks's eyes while they were eating their horrible food. They all fervently prayed that the passing ship might see them, and tried with what feeble strength remained them to pull towards it. Their joy was unbounded when they discovered that they were seen, and in about an hour-and-a-half after they first sighted the sail they were alongside the German barque *Montezuma*. They were in such a state of prostration when they got alongside the ship they required to be assisted on board.

Captain Simmonsen, of the barque *Montezuma*, states that on the morning of the day they discovered the boat on looking across the horizon he thought he saw a small speck. He looked at it through his glasses, and saw that it was something floating on the water, although at the distance he could not distinguish it as a boat. As they neared it, however, they were astonished to find that it was a small punt with human beings in it. They presented a most frightful spectacle, looking like living skeletons.

On getting them on board they explained to him the history of the mangled corpse, which was even then lying in the boat.

Captain Dudley remained firm in his resolve to retain the corpse of the boy as long as possible, and in case they should fall in with a vessel to make a clean breast of the circumstances. When Dudley had explained matters to Simmonsen the putrefied and mangled remains of the victim were consigned to the deep, and the punt was taken on board the *Montezuma*. Captain Simmonsen treated the forlorn ones with every kindness, giving them food and clean raiment. They were on board the *Montezuma* for 38 days.

Dudley attributes the foundering of the *Mignonette* to her being rather old for such a voyage. She proved a good seaboat, and had she been new he considered that she would have weathered the storm.

On being landed at Falmouth the survivors were taken to the Sailors' Home and afterwards to the Customs Office, where they made their depositions. On the afternoon of September 8 they were apprehended on a warrant signed by the Mayor of Falmouth, and taken to the borough prison on a charge of murder. Their apprehension took them by surprise, as they had made arrangements for leaving Falmouth for their homes that night. The small penknife with which the act was committed is in the possession of the Falmouth police. (*The Sydney Morning Herald*, 18 October 1884)

Edwin Stevens' own account of the voyage concluded:

We had thus been in the boat from July 5, at 5 p.m., until July 29, at 1 a.m., nearly 24 days, having drifted and sailed a distance of 900 miles, viz., from latitude 27'10S [*sic* –27°10'S] longitude 9'50W [*sic* –9°50'W], to latitude 24'20 S [*sic* –24°20'S] longitude 28'25W [*sic* –28°25'W], our position when picked up.

While the men were in the dinghy Captain Dudley penned a note to his wife:

… written on the back of the certificate of the chronometer, which was saved from the *Mignonette* by Captain Dudley, [and] is in his possession. It is written in pencil, and is much defaced by the effect of the salt water. Captain Dudley wrote it while they were in the punt, in the hope that, should they succumb, it might be afterwards found:

'July 6, 1884. To my dear wife Dudley, Myrtle-road, Sutton, in Surrey, *Mignonette* foundered yesterday. Weather knocked side in. We had five minutes to get in boat, without food or water; 9th, picked up turtle. July 21. We have been here 17 days; have no food. We are all four living, hoping to get passing ship. If not, we must soon die. Mr. Thompson will put everything right if you go to him, and I am sorry, dear, I ever started on such a trip, but I was doing it for our best. Thought so at the time. You know, dear, I should so like to be spared. You would find I should lead a Christian life for the remainder of my days.

'If ever this note reaches your hands you know the last of your Tom and loving husband. I am sorry things are gone against us thus far, but I hope to meet you and all our dear children in heaven. Dear, do love them, for my sake. Dear, bless them and you all. I love you all dearly, you know; but it is God's will if I am to part from you; but have hopes of being saved. We were about

1,300 miles from Cape Town when the affair happened. Good-bye, and God bless you all, and may He provide for you all. Your loving husband, Tom Dudley.' (*The Shipping Gazette and Lloyd's List*, 13 September 1884)

Dudley and Stephens were put on trial at Exeter, Devon, early in 1885. Judge Baron Huddleston outlined the principles of the case. In doing so he suggested that many people undoubtedly felt 'the deepest compassion' for the accused men in the circumstances that compelled them to commit murder (which indeed many people did). The law, however, was the law, though 'the peculiar circumstances of this melancholy case' would suggest, he said, that an appeal to the Crown for clemency, if the men were found guilty, would not only be justified but likely upheld.

The result of the trial of Dudley and Stephens was that 'the prisoners were sentenced to death, and respited during her Majesty's pleasure, but subsequently committed to gaol for six months'. (*Grey River Argus* [New Zealand], 8 January 1885)

Within six months both men were released from gaol.

The legal proceedings of the *Mignonette* case were convoluted, controversial and complex. They ultimately concluded with a landmark decision in English criminal law that necessity was not a justifiable defence of murder, including the killing of someone – the boy Richard Parker in this case – in order, necessarily, to assure the survival of others.

The *Turley*: Mate Driven to Drink the Blood and Eat the Flesh of a Comrade

Later in 1884, the same year that the *Mignonette* sank, a small pilot boat, the *Turley*, cruised off the Delaware Capes

UNDER FULL SAIL

The crew of the yacht *Mignonette* in an open boat at sea. From sketches by Mr Stephens, mate of the *Mignonette*. (*The Graphic*, 20 September 1884)

on the American Eastern Seabord, to put a pilot on board the steamship *Philadelphia*. One of the two pilots in the *Turley*'s skiff, which was used to ferry pilots out to vessels, Jacob Marshall, and a cook, Thomas Bunting, were left on the *Philadelphia*. The other men started rowing back to the *Turley*. The weather on that freezing November day blew up. The skiff never made it back to the *Turley*.

The other pilot in the skiff, Marshall Bertrand, recounted what happened before they were rescued a few days later by the three-masted schooner *Emma F. Angell*, and brought to land at Lewes, Delaware:

Driven to Cannibalism – A Horrible Story of Suffering at Sea – Pilot Bertrand Tells How His Mate Was Driven to Drink the Blood and Eat the Flesh of a Comrade

'Early on Saturday morning we left the Pilot Boat *Turley* in a skiff 18 feet long by 5 or 6 feet wide. There was on board the boat, Pilot Jacob Marshall, Cook Thomas Bunting, Alfred Swanson, Andreas Hansen, and myself. When we left the *Turley* we were off Five Fathom Bank Lightship, 25 miles east of the Capes, and were rowing for one of the American Line steamers – I think the *Pennsylvania* [*sic –Philadelphia*], which lay a quarter of a mile from the *Turley*. We put Pilot Marshall and the cook on board the steamer, and then started, at 4:15, to row back to the *Turley*.

'It was a dark morning, with a high sea on, and a regular north-west gale blowing. We had three oars and a small paddle, the latter for steering, and we all three pulled together, but we couldn't row to windward, and soon saw we couldn't make the *Turley*. They kept flashing the light from the *Turley* for us, but we drifted astern of her, and the wind and sea were so loud that there was no use of trying to signal her by shouting. When I saw that we could not make the *Turley* I tried for the Five Fathom lightships, but the wind carried us to leeward, and I had to give that up. Then I tried for the eastern lightships, bearing north-north-east of the southern ships, but the gale drifted us to leeward, and we went further out to sea.

'When day broke we could see the *Turley* cruising about for us, but the white caps ran so high she couldn't see our little boat between the high seas. The wind cut us, and every particle of spray that struck the boat froze where it fell. I wasn't scared, and didn't give up hope, but I seemed to have twice the strength I ever had before. I pulled on one side of the boat against both of the sailor men, and pulled her head around. We had had nothing to eat since supper on Sunday night, and both Swanson and Hanson were famished and frightened. There was not a drop of fresh water or a scrap of bread in the boat. The thole pins [rowlocks/oarlocks] broke early in the morning, and we had to split up our steering paddle to make new ones.

'When I gave up the second lightship it was daylight, and as near as I could make out from my watch we had been rowing five hours, and all the time losing ground. Later I lost the new paddle that I had fixed to steer with, and then I broke an oar. The wind and sea were still high, and our boat was in danger of swamping.

'About 8 o'clock on Tuesday afternoon,' Bertrand continued, 'when we were 35 miles off Cape Henlopen [near Lewes, Delaware], and still drifting out, we made out a square-rigged vessel running out and bound across our bows. She hove right down on us and we hailed her. The Captain and crew were on deck and looking at us. I stood up in the bow as she passed us and shouted, "Captain, in the name of God throw us some bread or give me a line." I held the painter in my hand ready to throw it and jump when it was made fast to the bark, but the Captain just waved his hand and took no further notice of us.

'I said: "By---, I hope you'll sink before sunset ...",
and if there's anything in cursing he will have had bad
luck. I'd have shot him if I had had a gun. When the bark
passed us we had been 36 hours without food or water.
Swanson went crazy.'

Here Bertrand went back in his narrative to recall an
important incident. 'Swanson and Hansen,' said he, 'were
scared nearly to death all the time, and before Swanson
drank some sea water I found him sharpening his knife on
an oar. I asked him what he was doing that for. He said he
meant to kill me and drink my blood. When it was dark,
both men got out their knives to kill. After a while, when
Swanson was quiet, I went forward pretending to look at
the painter, and slipped his knife away from him. I also
took Hansen's knife from his pocket.

'Late that night we sighted the ship *Kingsfork*, which
I recognised out of the Capes, and we tried to row for
her, but when we got within two miles of her, the night
shut down dark. Swanson was raving of his mother and
sisters in Sweden and still drinking sea water. I drank no
sea water, but only moistened my lips with it, and now
and then chewed the sticks of some matches I had in my
pocket. I had a toothbrush with me and I dipped this in
the salt water and brushed my teeth, taking care to spit
out the water. In this way I kept my mouth moist, so that
my tongue did not swell or my lips crack. I would think of
pure, fresh water and have an awful longing for it, and then
I would drive it from my mind, but it always came back.'

Cannibalisation of the Dead
'About 2:30 o'clock on Tuesday morning Swanson, who
was lying in the bottom of the boat, said he was frozen. He
spoke once more of his people in Sweden, then groaned

several times and died. Hansen woke up soon afterward and cut him open to drink the blood and liquids from his body, but there was nothing to drink and then he cut off about three pounds of flesh from Swanson's thigh. He ate a part of it and offered me a piece, but my stomach revolted against it, and my piece was lying in the bottom of the boat when we were picked up.'

At this point Bertrand's memory again failed. At first he said Swanson died on Monday morning, while Hansen, who seems to recollect the facts better, says that the death occurred on Tuesday, and that the body was not cut open until Wednesday morning. 'After Hansen had eaten the flesh,' Bertrand resumed, 'it seemed to ease him and he went to sleep. I took his head between my legs and beat his face to keep it from freezing as it was blue with cold. We drove before the wind and sea, I don't know how long, God only knows. I had lost count of the days.

'Hansen went to sleep again and I beat him to keep him from freezing. I didn't lose hope, for I thought we would come out all right. I let the boat go all night. It rained that night and I caught half a cupful of rainwater by holding up the ends of my oilskin. I gave it to Hansen and he drank it greedily.'

Rescue

'Wednesday morning dawned clear, but it was still blowing hard. An hour later I made out a three-masted schooner coming by the wind. We were then 100 miles from the Cape, and about 35 miles from Absecom. I took my mast down, tied my oilskin to it by the sleeves, and waved it with all my might. The schooner came half a mile to windward, but didn't see us until it got past. The wind had then moderated. I wet my hand with the sea water, rubbed my lips, and gave the hardest yell I ever gave in my life. They heard me and the Captain put his helm hard up. He ran to leeward, and when he got within hailing distance, I heaved the corpse of Swanson overboard.'

At this moment Bertrand hesitated for the first time and did not speak freely. 'Why did you throw the body overboard?' he was asked. 'I didn't want the Captain to see it,' he replied. 'The boat was all bloody. I had kept Swanson's body up to that time because I meant to eat it that night if it was necessary, and I saw it was fast coming to that.'

On this point Hansen says much the same thing. 'The body was so badly cut up,' he said, 'that we didn't want any one to see it.'

'The schooner bore down on us,' Bertrand continued, 'and threw us a rope. Hansen was too weak to take it, so I did, and as the schooner's ladder was down I got aboard without help. Hansen was hauled in over the side. The schooner was the *Emma F. Angell*, Capt. George Tripp, and a guardian angel she proved to us. They treated us as kindly as could be. Hansen went mad for water that night, but I only moistened my lips when they offered me a glassful. At night Hansen broke into the washroom and drank from the washbasin.'

Hansen, who is a Dane, is not yet 17 years of age. He is a shambling, round-shouldered fellow, with a good, dull face, and evidently just such a mind as it indicates. His story agrees in the main with Bertrand's, save that he rather weakly asserts that Bertrand ate some of the dead man's flesh – in fact, asked for it. Whether this reticence hides a tale of thirst and hunger, crazed men in a desperate fight for life, each against the other, probably no one will ever know, and how far the cannibalism of the survivors extended will perhaps continue as great a mystery. Bertrand's honest face and sincere manner precludes the idea of any serious wrongdoing on his part, and Hansen evidently bowed to him as the master mind. (*The New York Times*, 29 November 1884)

The *Sallie M. Steelman*: A Blighted Voyage

The American schooner *Sallie M. Steelman*, 394 tons, was on a short voyage from Charleston, South Carolina, to Baltimore, Maryland, when she was assailed by a winter storm off Cape Hatteras, North Carolina. The vessel was rendered a floating wreck. The virtual derelict and her crew drifted for more than a month on the wild and frigid winter seas of the North Atlantic.

All the provisions were long since finished, the sufferings of the crew 'terrible beyond description', when one of the crew, George Seaman, 'driven mad by starvation' attacked another man, Walter Sampson, who shot and killed Seaman, apparently in self-defence. The rest of the crew proceeded to eat parts of the dead man, in order to survive. The morning after their cannibalisation of sailor Seaman, the castaways were rescued by the schooner *Speedwell*, just east of the island of Bermuda, and brought to New York:

Cannibalism at Sea – How the Crew of the Schooner Sallie M. Steelman *Kept from Starvation – Butchering, Cooking, and Eating a Negro Sailor Who Was Shot While Insane*

There are few tales of hardship and suffering at sea more terrible in their details than the story of the almost incredible experiences of the crew of the *Sallie M. Steelman*, whose rescue was briefly described in yesterday's *Times*. The story of the exhaustion of provisions, of the shooting of the maniac colored sailor and his subsequent butchery to furnish food for the famished crew, is fully corroborated by several of the seamen, who were brought to this City late yesterday afternoon by the *Speedwell*, which anchored at Pier No. 28 East River.

The entire crew of the wrecked vessel were the Captain, S.G. Higby; the mate, James L. Somers; the steward, Sylvester R. Herbert; David Barrett, a white seaman, and three colored seamen – George Hicks, Walter Sampson, and the butcher George Seaman. Sampson, Barrett, Hicks, and Herbert only were found on board the *Speedwell* upon her arrival at this pier, the Captain and the mate having left early in the morning for their homes in New Jersey. The seamen, while they answered inquiries put to them, seemed to do so unwillingly, and continually inquired if any punishment was liable to be inflicted upon them for their act of cannibalism.

After their provisions gave out, their sufferings were terrible beyond description, but it seems that the butchered sailor, Seaman, who was reported to have been driven mad by starvation, was subject to fits of insanity, and according to the story of his fellow seaman, Hicks, who had shipped with him on other vessels, had acted violently on other occasions than that narrated below.

Deprivation brought on a renewed attack of insanity during the week in which the vessel was tossed about unprovisioned, after being over a month at sea, and as day after day passed without the famished men being able to obtain anything but coffee to appease their pangs of hunger, he became at times raving, and would jump from his bunk at night and tramp through the vessel, talking incoherently, and acting so strangely that his fellows feared to go near him.

The Assault

On Jan. 30, after being out for 43 days, Seaman sprang from his bunk early in the morning, and ran up on deck where he again talked wildly, and threatened to shoot the Captain. The latter having gradually got out of his way, Seaman returned to the forecastle, where he yelled to Sampson, who was asleep in his bunk, to come up on deck.

While Sampson was hastily dressing himself, the maniac sailor called to him again, threatening to shoot him if he did not instantly obey. Sampson began to retreat slowly toward the door, keeping his eye upon the insane man to guard against being attacked unexpectedly. When he reached the deck he saw Seaman, so he says, place his hand in his pistol pocket, and then, fearing for his life, he drew a pistol – which he had previously borrowed from the steward – and fired at Seaman, striking him on the head behind the ear.

The shot was heard through the vessel, but only one man, George Hicks, says that he saw the shot fired or heard anything of the conversation that preceded it. After being shot Seaman rushed wildly to the deck, but fell dead in his tracks when he had gone but a few steps.

Cannibalisation

The crew, it seems, let the body lie where it fell for some four hours, during which time the proposition that the dead man's flesh be eaten was discussed. After the body had lain in a pool of blood for about four hours, Sampson, who had fired the fatal shot, was given an axe by the mate, and, approaching the corpse, severed the head from the dead man's body. After the completion of this fearful task, the head was wrapped in canvas by Herbert and Barrett and thrown overboard.

Barrett then by means of a knife stripped off as much of the flesh from the legs and trunk as he could, and when he finally ceased the butchery, the flesh he had removed was placed in a barrel and salted down, and the mutilated carcase was wrapped, like the head, in canvas and thrown overboard. Some of the flesh was immediately afterward removed to the galley, where it was thrown into a pot and parboiled, and then fried in a pan. Most of the crew turned sick at the thought of such unnatural food, but their hunger at length prevailed over all qualms of conscience and revulsions of taste, and they partook of two meals.

Their experience of the cannibalistic repast was varied. Barrett, who butchered the corpse, and who ate about a pound and a half of the flesh, declared that it tasted as 'good as any beef-steak he ever ate'. The necessity for partaking of such food, however, ended on the following day, when, after 45 days of almost unexampled suffering, the crew of the partially dismantled and fast sinking vessel sighted the *Speedwell* on New Year's Eve, and soon they were safe on board the vessel and bound for New York.

Although nothing was broached upon the subject yesterday, there can be no doubt that the conduct of the crew in eating the colored seaman will be a subject of investigation by the United States Shipping Commission of this port. Capt. Higby was on Monday recommended to personally call the attention of the Government officials to the matter, but whether he had done so or not could not be ascertained yesterday. (*The New York Times*, 13 February 1878)

Although the crew of the *Steelman* were questioned about the incident, no further action was taken against them. Sampson's story that he killed Seaman in self-defence, and the subsequent consumption of Seaman's flesh, for the survival of the other crew, did not, apparently, constitute criminal acts.

The *Maria*: Appalling Tale of Shipwreck, Hunger and Death

In November and December of 1876 a British barque, the *Maria*, leaking and battered by bad weather, was rendered a derelict of horror on the high seas of the North Atlantic. The vessel's fourteen crew succumbed one by one to starvation and death. Surviving shipmates drank the blood and ate the flesh from the corpses. But never, even in the utmost depths of their deprivation, did they actually kill any of their comrades to survive on their flesh and blood.

After a month of horror, only two men remained alive to be rescued. One of them died a few hours afterwards. An Irish seaman, the sole remnant of that floating charnel-house, was left to tell their story:

An Appalling Tale of Shipwreck, Hunger, and Death

Boston, February 21st – One of the most appalling tales of shipwreck and starvation that has ever startled and horrified the civilized world reached this city yesterday in a letter from Captain Kane, of the American schooner *F.B. Macdonald*, dated from Gorce, on the West Coast of Africa, on January 24th.

The British barque *Maria*, Captain Grayson, sailed from Darien, Ga. [Georgia], on the 21st of November last, with a cargo of timber for Belfast, Ireland. She was 590 tons burden, and was built at Yarmouth, Nova Scotia, in 1863, and was classed A2½ at Lloyds. Her crew numbered fourteen, including the captain and officers.

Shortly after leaving port, the carpenter reported a serious leak. The weather had been rough, and it is supposed that some of her cargo shifted with the rolling of the ship and damaged her frame and sheathing. Notwithstanding the efforts of the crew, the leak gained steadily on them, and the ship began to settle lower and lower in the sea. The cargo being timber, the ship did not sink, but the weight of her masts caused her to fall over on her broadside with her spars in the water.

The unfortunate crew managed to scramble over the bulwarks and gain the side of the ship that was out of water, and clung with desperate grip to the channels and rigging in the hope of being seen and rescued from their dreadful position. While thus hanging on for their lives, the sea frequently made a clean breach over them, threatening them with death and exhausting their rapidly-failing strength in their efforts to retain their hold on the ship's side.

The labouring of the wreck in the heavy sea threw such an immense strain on the masts, which were alternately buried in the waves and lifted above the surface, that they broke off one after another, thus relieving the ship of her weight. The result was that she righted again, but lay buried in the sea, waterlogged and unmanageable. Everything moveable on her decks had been swept away. Her boats were destroyed, and the crew, after another desperate effort, dragged themselves to her decks, which were under water.

Starvation and Cannibalisation

All this time the unfortunate crew had been famishing with hunger and thirst. The ship's stores were beyond their reach, being stowed below, and the consequence was that all the horrors of starvation stared them in the face. The dreadful gnawing of hunger rendered them utterly savage. One by one the poor wretches died of sheer starvation, while their surviving messmates crouched watching for the last breath to depart.

No sooner did one die than the famishing survivors cut his throat and drank the still warm but almost putrid blood. The wasting effects of hunger, thirst, and exposure reduced the frames of the miserable creatures to mere skeletons, and caused their blood to decompose almost in their veins. Yet the living tried to live by these dreadful draughts, and watched with eager eyes for signs of a comrade's approaching death in order to enjoy another horrible meal.

Not content with draining the veins of the dead, the hungry survivors cut up the bodies, and divided them between the hearts and the brains. The other parts were found to be too offensive even for cannibals, and the odour from the bodies could only be endured while the ready knife ripped them open and cut from them the hearts, or while the ship's hatchet broke in the skulls in order that the brains might be extracted.

Notwithstanding the horrors of their situation, and the awful lengths to which they were forced to go to preserve life, no violence was offered to any of the living. The cannibals from necessity did not murder their companions, but waited with patience until they died.

For thirty-two days after the date of the first disaster, this fearful tragedy was progressing in the mid-Atlantic, and the number of the crew of the *Maria* grew smaller

Our Seamen – a waterlogged timber ship. (*The Graphic*, 1 March 1873)

and smaller, until only two remained out of the fourteen. These were rescued on the 17th of December, 1876, in latitude 37° 23' and longitude 32° 30' by the schooner *F.E. Macdonald*, Captain Kane, bound from Boston to the West Coast of Africa. By mere accident Captain Kane fell in with the wreck, and took the two survivors on board his vessel. One of them, however, died in four hours after he was taken from the wreck.

The solitary survivor of that awful voyage is James M. Linden, seaman, of Belfast, Ireland. He alone was left to tell the terrible story of his dead shipmates. (*Otago Witness* [New Zealand], 26 May 1877)

Adrift on the Grand Banks: Cannibalism by Scotchmen

In March 1886 four fishermen in two dories from the Gloucester, Massachusetts, fishing schooner *Cicely H. Low* found themselves separated by fog and adrift from their mother ship on the Western Banks off Newfoundland. One of the men, Colin Chisholm, upon reaching the safety of land, recounted the horrors that left only himself and one other companion alive from their ordeal:

Horrible Tale of the Sea – Cannibalism by Scotchmen

A despatch dated Louisburg, Cape Breton, 7th April, in the *New York Herald*, contains the following heart-rending revelation:

A tale of the sea that makes the blood run cold is that of the agonising experience of four fishermen cast adrift in a dory on the Western Fishing Banks. Early this afternoon this little village was thrown into a wild state of excitement by the news that a fishing dory with two lifeless bodies and two half dead men had reached one of the wharves. A ghastly sight met the gaze of the crowd that assembled about the boat when from beneath the piece of canvas covering them in the stern were brought to light the remains of James McDonald and Angus McDonald.

The former was in a frightfully mutilated condition. The right arm was missing from the elbow, the throat was cut and hacked in a sickening manner, and two great pieces of flesh had been chopped, as by a knife, from each thigh. In the bottom of the boat, washed to and fro by the motion of the waves, lay three large pieces of human flesh that had been bitten, partially masticated, and then spat out. The spectacle was of a nature witnessed but once in a lifetime, and the feelings of those looking on were so wrought with horror that the strongest in the crowd turned away, unable to stand it any longer. An old American soldier who had passed through the civil war said the scene was the most harrowing he had ever experienced.

Chisholm's Narrative

The two half-perished survivors of the terrible voyage are Chisholm, of Harbour au Bouche, N.S., and Angus McEachern, of Long Point, Strait of Canso, N.S. When found at the boarding-house to which the pair had been removed, Colin Chisholm was stretched on a sofa, pale and emaciated, and apparently suffering much agony from the awful ordeal. His feet, greatly swollen, were enveloped in bandages, and slowly he gave the following account of the distressing affair:

'I will do my best,' he said, 'to give you the story of our trial, but I don't care to go back over all my experience. It has been the most awful time in my life. We belonged to the American fishing schooner, *Cicely H. Low*, Captain McKenzie. The vessel had fourteen hands altogether, and sailed from Gloucester [Massachusetts] on Wednesday 14th March. After a fair passage we arrived on the Western Banks on the succeeding Tuesday.

'On the Monday following, about eight o'clock in the morning, McEachern and myself left the vessel to attend to our trawls, in company with another dory containing the two McDonalds. While at our work fog suddenly shut down, hiding the vessel from our view. As soon as the trawls were all set we started [off] to find the schooner, and in trying to do so fell in with the other boat. The four of us hunted and shouted, but could hear no sound of horn or anything else, and after hours of weary searching we came to the conclusion that we had been lost.

'We kept in company all day and night and until noon of the following day, when the McDonalds got into our dory, and we set the other adrift after securing the oars. Several hours later we observed a sail about two miles distant, and going, as we supposed, east. We made all manner of signals to attract her attention, and rowed as rapidly as possible toward the vessel, but it was of no use. Those on board had not seen us, and we were soon again left with nothing but the dreary waste of water. We had no provisions of any kind, nor a drop of water, and by this time the gnawing pangs of hunger were beginning to tell on us.

'On Thursday evening James McDonald, who was more thinly clad than the rest, and had been gradually growing weaker and weaker from hunger and exposure, felt that he was dying, and looking at the three of us from the stern, where he was lying, said in a voice I shall never forget, "Good-bye; good-bye, mates. I am dying." These were his last words. We kept his body, thinking the rest of us might yet be rescued. We kept on rowing in the direction we thought land lay, though every stroke was weaker than the last, and none knew at what moment one of us would give up in despair.

'On Friday, after James McDonald died, Angus McDonald said he was starving and thirsty and that as he must have something to eat and drink he was going to drink Jim's blood. He had no sooner uttered the words than he seized his knife, and cut off Jim's arm, sucking some of the blood and eating some of the flesh. Then looking at me with his mouth smeared, and with a piece of flesh in his hand, he asked me if I would have some, remarking at the time that the blood tasted like cream. I tasted it, and at once spat it out saying if I was to die within an hour I would neither eat the flesh nor drink the blood.

'In the afternoon Angus turned to me and said: "I am going to cut Jim's throat to get some more blood." I begged him not to do so, saying: "For God's sake, whatever else you do, don't cut his throat. Do what you like, but don't do that." In the morning we found he had cut the dead man's throat, and not finding any blood there, had also cut pieces of flesh out of his left thigh. His hunger and thirst not being then appeased, Angus cut another piece out of Jim's right thigh, and during Saturday ate several pieces. McEachern attempted to eat some, but could not. The taste made him sick.

'On Saturday night, having kept rowing, we met a quantity of drift ice, and were then, I should judge, 60 miles south-east of Guyon Island. By this time Angus McDonald, I noticed, was becoming crazy, and, going aft to try and get him to lay down, he picked up an oar and struck me twice, but not hurting me much. Some time afterwards McEachern and myself lay down to sleep. At daylight we awoke to find that Angus McDonald had thrown all the oars overboard. We took the thwarts [seats] and paddled through the ice searching for the oars, and at last found five of them. All day Sunday we rowed through the ice as best our weakness would permit us.

'About noon Angus died, never having spoken after striking me the previous day.

'As evening drew near we made out what afterwards proved to be Guyon Island, but darkness coming on and snow squalls setting in we were then unable to find it. We lay down to sleep, but cold and anxiety to reach land made sleep impossible. All night long the waves beat over us, and when dawn broke at last we were covered with ice and hardly able to move, but land was now close by, and by strenuous efforts we managed to make gradual headway.

'About ten o'clock on Monday morning our dory grounded on the beach of the island, and the lighthouse-keeper, who had observed us through the ice, came down with his two boys and carried us up to the house. Neither of us were able to walk when we were assisted to land.

The Newfoundland fisheries – hardships and perils of the fisherman's life – scenes on the banks and at Gloucester. (*Frank Leslie's Illustrated Newspaper*, 8 March 1884)

The feet of both of us had turned purple and raw, and were horribly swollen. After we got into the ice we used to suck it to allay our thirst, and that was the only thing we had in the shape of water for over eight days.' (*The Evening Post* [Wellington, New Zealand], 7 August 1886)

The *Drot* Affair: 'A Gruesome Story'

In mid-August 1899 the Norwegian barque *Drot* was sailing through the Florida Straits, on passage from Pascagoula, Mississippi, to Buenos Aires, when she was overcome and sunk by a hurricane. Eight crewmen survived the wreck and scrambled on to a raft. Two of the men became separated from the six others when the raft split in two. A few weeks later, in mid-Atlantic, a British steamship rescued the only two survivors from the six man raft. Their story of survival by cannibalisation of the bodies of their shipmates who died included the killing of a German sailor, whose fate was determined by drawing lots:

Cannibalism at Sea – A Gruesome Story

A despatch from Charleston [South Carolina] dated September 2, says: The British steamer *Woodruff*, from Hamburg, Captain Milburn, arrived here this morning, having on board Morris Anderson and Goodman Thomas, two Swedes, who had been seamen on the shipwrecked Norwegian barque *Drott* [*Drot*].

The *Drott* was caught in the recent hurricane off Florida Straits and went down in the storm. Of her crew of seventeen men, eight clung to a raft consisting of part of the vessel's deck, while the others went down with the ship. After tossing about day and night at the mercy of the waves, the raft split in two pieces. Six of the men clung to the larger portion and two remaining on the other part. One of these latter was lost while the other one was picked up some days ago by the German steamer *Colonia* [*sic – Catania*] and taken to Baltimore.

When the *Woodruff* sighted the larger part of the raft just before nightfall on Thursday only two of the six men who had originally clung to it were still alive. These were Anderson and Thomas, and they were in a half-crazed, half-famished condition. While being brought here in the *Woodruff* they told a terrible story of what happened on their raft before it was sighted by the British steamer.

The *Drott*, they said, went down on August 11th and it was next day that the raft split in halves. They had no water and no food and their only hope of sustenance came from a fishing line and hook that one man had. He caught many small fish and these kept life in the six seamen, but as day followed day and they had no water, the men were crazed with thirst. The owner of the fishing line lost his mind and jumped into the ocean crying out that he was saved.

The five men left began to fight against hunger as well as thirst. One sickened and died and before the breath was well out of his body his comrades drank his blood and devoured his flesh. A second man of the company met a similar fate. Thomas and Anderson declare that these men died natural deaths, but a worse fate remained for the third comrade, a big German. When they could no longer eat the two bodies, the three survivors decided that one of their number must die so that the others might live. They agreed to cast lots and abide by the decision of chance.

Un nouveau radeau de 'la Méduse' (A new raft of 'La Medusa'). (*Le Petit Journal*, 17 September 1899)

Quelques marins du navire norvégien Drot, échappés au naufrage sur un radeau, sont sauvés au moment où ils cherchaient à se dévorer les uns les autres. (Some sailors from the Norwegian ship *Drot*, having escaped from the wreck on a raft, are saved just as they try to devour each other.) (*Le Petit Journal*, 17 September 1899)

The Short Straw

Luck was against the big German and it is asserted that he met his death without a murmur. He even tore the clothing away from his chest, that the blow from the knife might reach a vital spot more readily. He was stabbed to the heart and his blood was drank by Anderson and Thomas as it gushed from the wound. They also cut strips of flesh from his body and devoured them.

When discovered by the *Woodruff*, the raft presented a terrible spectacle. Two crazed men sat beside the three bodies and Thomas was throwing bits of human flesh to the sharks. Two of the dead bodies were half stripped of flesh and were decaying. The men were emaciated and were covered with sores and stains of blood. They were nearly mad.

They told the men of the *Woodruff* that they had agreed between them to cast lots to see which should kill the other, and if the steamer had arrived a few hours later, there would have been but one living man on the raft. Anderson is suffering from the effects of a blow which injured his chest. Captain Milburn, of the *Woodruff*, asked about the story told by the men of his ship, said that he did not wish to discuss the matter but admitted the truth of all the facts that had been given out. He said that the raft presented a spectacle too horrible for words when he found it. (*Northern Territory Times and Gazette* [Darwin, N.T., Australia], 3 November 1899)

The fate of the chief mate and a seaman on the other piece of raft was reported by the steamship *Catania* and published in *Shipping Gazette and Lloyd's List*, on 1 September 1899:

Aug. 20, lat. 30 43 N, long. 75 38 W, rescued from a raft one of the seamen of the Norwegian barque *Drot*, from

Pascagoula for Buenos Ayres, which, on Aug. 11, off the
Florida Straits, got into the centre of a hurricane, which
wrecked the vessel. The crew consisted of 15 men, eight
of whom got on a raft, part of the *Drot*'s deck. In a short
time the raft parted, six of the crew on one part and one
seaman and the first mate on the other part. They were
five days on the raft without food or water. The mate
jumped overboard and was drowned. Nothing is known
of what became of the others of the crew [i.e. those rescued by the *Woodruff*].

The *Angola*: 'Madness and Murder
– Forty-Two Days on a Raft'

On 12 October 1900 the Nova Scotian barque *Angola* sailed
from Cavite, a port near Manila in the Philippines, bound
for Singapore for orders. She was manned by a crew of
nineteen, including officers. Six days later she struck on a
reef. Two sailors were killed outright. After four days the
remaining seventeen crew abandoned the wreck on two
rafts: fifteen on one and two on the other. The two-man
raft eventually became separated from the larger one and
was never heard about again. The men on the other raft
drifted around the South China Sea, surviving on whatever
they could scavenge. After three weeks:

A Frenchman went mad and attacked the captain with an
ax, and when the mate went to the captain's assistance,
he killed him with the ax and drank his blood and ate his
brains. The others killed the Frenchman and ate part of
his body. Then one of the survivors died, until but two
were left, who subsisted on small fish taken with hooked

nails and lines made of pieces of canvas. (*Los Angeles Herald*, 15 May 1901)

That description was colourfully embellished by the lurid imagination of the writer. It nevertheless suggested the carnivorous character of the *Angola* mariners' grisly fate, which was eventually more fully described by her two survivors.

A Sea Tragedy – Shocking Story of Shipwreck – Madness and Murder – Forty-Two Days on a Raft – Seventeen Men Perish

Early last year the ship *Angola*, a Nova Scotia owned vessel, sailed from Newcastle [New South Wales] bound for Manila. She carried a cargo of coal for foreign warships at the Philippines. Taking the outer Torres Straits route she reached Manila safely, and duly delivered her cargo. On October 11 last, having taken in ballast, the vessel set out for Singapore, the captain being under instructions to call there for orders, though it was generally understood that the ship was returning to Newcastle for another coal cargo.

Weeks, even months, passed without bringing tidings of the ship, and her disappearance remained a mystery until to-day, when news reached the Sydney underwriters that the vessel had crashed on a reef somewhere in the vicinity of the Philippine Islands. It was a sensational affair, as may be imagined when it is stated that of the crew only two survived [the] disaster.

Their story forms one of the most appalling tales of suffering resulting from shipwreck on record, bristling as it does with tragic incidents.

The Survivors' Narrative

The account of the disaster reached the underwriters from Singapore, where the two survivors, H. Jatmar Johannsen and Miguel Marticorna, landed last month from a Chinese junk, which had brought them across from Soubi Island. Their story as told to the marine police at Singapore is as follows:

'We left Cavite, near Manila, on October 12, 1900, in the barque *Angola*, 1,550 tons, belonging to the port of Nova Scotia, New Brunswick [*sic* – in fact, Windsor, Nova Scotia]. Our captain's name was Croker. We, the survivors, were able seamen. There was a crew of 19 on board, including the officers. Six days after leaving Cavite, the *Angola* struck on a barren reef. Two sailors were drowned when she struck. We all remained on the vessel for four days, she being hard and fast on the reef. Then, fearing the food supply giving out, and there being nothing obtainable to eat on the reef, we decided to leave the vessel, so we made two rafts, one large and one small. On the large one were 12 men and the remaining five were on the small one.

'After floating together for one day we (Johannsen and Marticorna were on the big raft) lost sight of the small raft and never saw it again. We drifted on and on with wind and tide day after day, and provisions were getting shorter and shorter. By the 25th day things had become absolutely desperate. We had had no proper food for some time. We had been eating our boots, barnacles from the sides and bottom of the raft, chewing seaweed which came floating by, and the salt flavour of everything had made all of us well nigh mad. Two, indeed, became crazy, and jumped into the sea.

'Suddenly one of us, a French sailor, jumped up, seized an axe, and cleft open the skull of the first mate, killing him instantly. He then tried to eat the body, but we got it away from him and threw it overboard. He seized the axe a second time, wet with the mate's blood, and rushed at the captain to strike him. Before the Frenchman could do so the second mate felled him to the ground with an axe, despatching him on the spot.'

Here the narrator, Johannsen, became very reticent as to what happened. He said he could not remember much, but he admitted that they ate a part of the Frenchman's body. He, however, continued his gruesome story, said that after this they drifted on in a most awful plight for seventeen days longer, their suffering being too horrible to describe. Barnacles and seaweed they sucked and chewed, and one after another – there were only eight left now – they became mad and died. The captain succumbed 28 days after they started, or three days after the murderous attack on him by the Frenchman, and finally but two were left – the present survivors, who floated on the raft to Soubi, a small island between Borneo and the Philippines.

It is more than probable that the bodies of those who died, or at least parts of them, were eaten by the two survivors, but of this they are naturally reluctant to tell. Doubtless their awful sufferings impaired their reason at the time, so that now they cannot properly recall what did take place.

When they arrived at Soubi they were in a terrible condition, their bodies being covered with sores, and both being unable to lift themselves from the raft. Some Malayans found them, and to their credit be it said, tenderly took them ashore, tended them carefully, and when they recovered procured a passage for them to Singapore in a Chinese junk.

Johannsen is a Swede, but speaks good English, whilst Marticorna, his comrade, is a Spaniard, and had no knowledge of the English tongue. According to 'Lloyd's', the *Angola*, which was built of wood, was owned by W.H. Mosher, of Windsor, Nova Scotia. She was commanded by Captain H. Croker. (*The Advertiser* [Adelaide, South Australia], 10 May 1901)

The Marine Court of Inquiry into the wreck of the *Angola*, held at Singapore on 13 April 1901, included the statement, 'The Court did not consider that it would serve any good purpose to inquire too closely into what happened on the raft during the thirty-eight days it was drifting about.'

The last survivors. (*The Illustrated London News*, 3 March 1888)

AMONGST SAVAGES

The prospect of seamen being speared to death by 'savages', then pot-boiled or roasted and served up at cannibal banquets, hardly seemed to deter the captains of trading schooners in the South Seas of the Pacific Ocean from pursuing their commercial intercourse with the indigenous tribes of the Fiji Islands, New Guinea, the New Hebrides and elsewhere. Missionaries in those islands, and in Patagonia, at the southern tip of South America, sometimes suffered the same fate in their crusade to Christianise the heathen. The trade in coconuts and copra, and the Godly civilising of men's souls, was regularly paid for in the cannibal currency of human butchery.

The Wulaia Bay Massacre

The Fuegian people of Tierra del Fuego were feared by the white man for an aversion to and predilection for picking off missionary crews that dared to proselytise amongst

Massacre of a mission party of the *Allen Gardiner* by the natives at Woolya [Wulaia], Tierra del Fuego.

them. Not all their victims were eaten, though many were, especially considering the scarcity of fresh meat in that bitter Patagonian wilderness. The massacre of the crew of the Anglican missionary vessel the *Allen Gardiner* in 1860 – The Wulaia Bay Massacre – was notorious for the multitude of its casualties.

Massacre of a Missionary Party in Tierra del Fuego

We have received from Mr. Thomas Havers, of Port Stanley, Falkland Islands, a minutely-detailed narrative of the circumstances attendant on the massacre of a mission party, on board the *Alan* [*sic – Allen*] *Gardiner*, by the natives of Tierra del Fuego; and we extract from it a few passages for the better understanding of the accompanying Engraving of the massacre, for the Sketch of which we are also indebted to Mr. Havers:

Port Stanley, Falkland Islands, Tuesday, March 27, 1860

'In the third week of October, 1859, the schooner *Alan Gardiner*, belonging to the Patagonian Missionary Society, left the port of Stanley (a diminutive British settlement on East Falkland Island), bound to the Beagle Channel, in Tierra del Fuego. The European party on board of her consisted of Captain Fell, the master, his brother, Mr. Fell, the mate, Johnston, carpenter, Alfred Coles, cook, Hugh McDowell, (known as "Hewey," an old man-of-war's-man), three Swedish sailors, named Jahnsen, Braun, and Petersen, and Mr. Garland Phillips, missionary catechist – making in all nine individuals. She also carried a party of native Fuegians, and the object of her voyage was to return these people to their native country and bring back a further supply to be Christianised at the station upon Keppel Island (West Falkland), under the superintendence of the Rev. George P. Despard, resident missionary there.

'The native party consisted of Mucklerwenchey, alias Billy Button (a brother of the notorious Jemmy Button mentioned in Captain Fitzroy's *Voyages of the Adventure and Beagle*), and his wife; Mackooallan, alias Tom Button, another brother, and his wife Winnieeennagowenkeeper; Laccaenges and Oocockowenshey, lads of sixteen and nineteen years of age – all of the tribe of Jemmy Button, resident at Woollya, on Navarin Island; and Schwymuggins, with his wife Ohditlowhylekeeper and little girl, three years old, named Kiattagattamattamowleykeeper, who are of a tribe called Oens-men, living chiefly on Lennox Island and about Good Success Bay, and possessing bows and arrows, which the Woollya men have not. In all there were nine natives.

'It appears that the *Alan Gardiner* came to anchor in Woollya Cove on the 1st of November, and on the 2nd landed some of the natives, who were searched before going over the ship's side, a proceeding that had on a former occasion given grave offence at Keppel, where the injured party vowed vengeance, made signs that they would cut the throats of some persons, and threatened to "put 'em in the ground" some day. Mackooallan submitted quietly to the search, and was taken ashore in the ship's boat that evening, apparently satisfied; but Mucklerwenchey and Schwymuggins were highly indignant; the latter violently so, and threw away and destroyed their presents. Schwymuggins in his rage seized Capt. Fell by the collar, but was knocked off by him. The two then bundled their wives into a canoe alongside, refusing to go in the ship's boat, and paddled ashore in high dudgeon, Laccaenges accompanying them, and none being left on board but Oocockowenshey, who did not feel disposed to leave the schooner, and had expressed a wish to return in her.

'Next day the whole of the crew went ashore to cut wood, and a quarrel arose on the part of Jemmy Button, who considered his presents were not good enough, and charged Captain Fell with having kept some back. The storm with Jemmy appeared to blow over.

'The large hut formerly built by the mission party on the flat near the beach was repaired, and the shipment of wood was proceeded with. Many canoes were arriving daily (a very unusual circumstance), and by Sunday, November 6, the assemblage of natives – men, women and children – amounted to near 300. Several of the crew of the *Alan Gardiner* became uneasy and apprehensive at the threatening aspect and increasing numbers of the natives; but the leaders of the party seem to have disregarded all the obvious signs that should naturally have suggested extreme caution.

'Oocockowenshey still remained on board, and did not go ashore until the Sunday morning, when he accompanied the European party, who all (with the sole exception of the man Coles, who remained on board to cook the dinner) went ashore to hold a prayer-meeting in the large hut near the beach, into which they were accompanied by many natives. Coles, full of anxiety and alarm, closely watched from the vessel's deck every movement. There were a few native huts on the beach and many canoes, and many of the women and children retired to these shelters, or got aboard the craft, whilst others went back in the boats.

'No sooner had the schooner's party entered the hut than Coles saw two natives come and take the oars out of the boat, carry them off, and conceal them in a wigwam. The certainty of treachery was at once apparent to him, and the action immediately commenced, for seven of the Europeans were seen rushing out of the hut followed by natives, and the groups of natives outside joined in an attack commenced with stones, and quickly terminated by clubs and other weapons. One man ran back to the hut, was caught, pulled forward, stoned, and killed in front of it. Two others – the carpenter and a sailor – were speedily butchered in like manner; whilst another party was attacking the two Fells, who were conspicuous by standing back to back in front, and were savagely beaten to death.

'Mr. Phillips and one of the Swedes distanced all the others and rushed into the water, attempting to get on board the craft. Both were there overtaken, the Swede was knocked down by stones and drowned, and Coles distinctly saw Mucklerwenchey (Billy Button) knock Mr. Phillips down by a blow of a stone on the head, after which he was speedily dispatched. There remained of all the party but one unaccounted for – the old man Hewey,

Falkland Islands and Patagonia (incl. Cape Horn). (J. Tallis/J. Rapkin, 1851)

who never came out of the hut, and was afterwards ascertained to have been killed within it.

'Alfred Coles, after suffering great hardships, was ultimately picked up by Captain Smyley, who had started from Port Stanley in the *Nancy*, in quest of tidings of the *Alan Gardiner*.' (*The Illustrated London News*, 4 August 1860)

Fiji: The Killing of Rev. Thomas Baker

The Christianisation of the Pacific Islands by Protestant and Catholic missionaries started in the late eighteenth century. The London Missionary Society established an outpost at Tahiti in 1797. By the 1820s and '30s there were Methodists in Tonga and Samoa, and a Wesleyan Missionary Society presence in Tahiti and the Marquesas. The first Catholic priests arrived in Polynesia in the 1830s and later expanded the tentacles of their reach further west into Melanesia. By the mid-nineteenth century Christian missionaries of all evangelical stripes and colours abounded throughout the central and western Pacific Island groups, most notably Fiji, Samoa, Tonga, the Solomon Islands and the New Hebrides.

The local name for Christianity in the central Pacific came to be known as 'lotu' (or variations of it, such as 'lota'; it could also be a verb: to Christianise). The term was thought to have originated from Tonga and then extended around the region by Tongans converted to Christianity.

From accounts of the notorious killings in Fiji of a young Wesleyan minister, the Rev. Thomas Baker, and the massacre of his party of Fijian converts in 1867, it was clear that not all 'heathens' welcomed the call to convert to *lotu*. This was particularly true of the mountain tribes in the interior of Fiji. The *lotu* converts were mainly from the coastal regions where the first contact with missionaries took root most deeply.

The English-born Rev. Baker, described as 'a passionate and ambitious evangelist',* had emigrated with his family to New South Wales, Australia, in 1839. From there, in 1859, he was sent to the Methodist mission in Fiji. In 1865 he was stationed at a new mission, at Davuilevu, on the Rewa River on Viti Levu, the main island of the Fiji group. His specific mission was to proselytise amongst the interior tribes most resistant to *lotu*. During one of those evangelising treks – his last – in July 1867, with an ordained Fijian minister and eight young Fijian acolytes, he and his party were ambushed by cannibalistic tribespeople in the Navosa district. Most were killed and later eaten. Only two escaped: a young catechist (assistant religious instructor) named Aisea Nasekai, and Josifata Ngata, a student of Rev. Baker.

Thakombau/Cakobau

The king of Fiji, Thakombau (or Thakobau, also Cakobau), who, with his wife, had adopted Wesleyanism in 1857 and were baptised in 1858, was 'the leading Wesleyan patron'** amongst Fijian chiefs in the north and east coastal lands and Rewa River areas of Viti Levu. He was 'enraged at this frightful massacre' of the Baker party and promised H.M. Government representative 'Acting Consul J. [John] B. Thurston, Esq.' that he would organise a revenge assault on the 'murderers' tribe'.

---

*/**/*** From Andrew Thornley's *Exodus of the iTaukei: The Wesleyan Church in Fiji, 1848–74*, published by The Institute of Pacific Studies, University of the South Pacific, Auckland, in 2002. The term 'iTaukei' was legislated by the Fijian government in 2010 to replace the terms 'indigenous Fijian', 'Fijian', or 'indigenous'.

King Thakombau/Cakobau was a central character in trying to suppress the continuation of barbaric acts by the mountain tribes of the interior of Viti Levu. Originally a warlord chief from Bau (Ba) on the north-west coast of the island, he renounced cannibalism in 1854. His later conversion to *lotu* 'made his inland enemies even more determined to defend their gods. Rumours abounded of a determination to drive the lotu out of the land':***

Murder of the Rev. Thomas Baker, Wesleyan Minister, and Seven Native Teachers at Fiji

We are indebted for the following account of the murder of the Rev. Thomas Baker, Wesleyan Missionary, and seven teachers, at Fiji, to C.S. Hare, Esq., of Adelaide, who has an establishment at Fiji, and who is now in Sydney. The following letter was received by him on Tuesday, from his agent at Rewa, Fiji:

Vuna, Vesi-Vesi, Rewa River, Fiji August 18, 1867

'Dear Sir, You know the Rev. Mr. Baker very well. You will be sorry to hear that he was killed just a few miles above this place on the 21st July, with seven of his assistant native teachers.

'He intended, as you had also intended, to cross the mountains above us, but had only got one town from the "Lota," or Christian people. He went into the town and asked the chief to be good enough to show him the road to the next place on the proposed way, and if he would become a Christian. The heathen's reply was, "The road is all right, but for the Lotu (or Christianity); there is the axe and the salt for the first Christian that comes here."

'It appears from the sole survivor's account that Mr. Baker and his Christian teachers, on the Saturday night or on the Sunday morning, started for the next town, and two chiefs accompanied them, one heading the party, and the other following in the rear behind the last teacher, all walking Fijian fashion, single file. When they had just got outside the town, the chief that was behind Mr. Baker's men struck at the last man. This last man was carrying Mr. Baker's box of clothing; and owing to this fact, as it will appear in the sequel, this one man's life was saved.

'On the tailing chief striking this man, the box partook of the blow, causing a great noise, which made Mr. Baker turn round to see what was the matter; when the leading chief, who was in front of Mr. Baker, struck him with an axe, and nearly severed his head from his body. The two chiefs then gave a loud scream, so loud that the people in the town rushed out and killed the remainder of the party, except the teacher who was first struck. This man rushed into the bush before his assailant could strike another blow. He saw from his hiding-place in the bush the whole of the massacre, and expected every moment to share their fate, which he would have done if he had been discovered.

'After they had killed them all, they dragged the bodies into town, and piled them up one on another, placing the Rev. Mr. Baker's body on the top of the pile, while they made ovens hot in which to roast them. You knew Mr. Baker and some of the native teachers; one of them accompanied you to Bau.

'Thakombau, the King of Fiji, is enraged at this frightful massacre, and has determined to proceed up there in a month. He declares he will bring them all down to Bau, and that they and their children shall be slaves for ever, and that the tribe shall be called for the future the "Murderers' tribe".

'Mr. Thurston, the acting consul, at once waited on Thakombau, to know what he intended to do. He has promised as soon as he can muster his men – which will be in two months, as it is now the season for planting the yams – that he will proceed into the interior with his army from four different points, and surround the whole of the cannibal districts and bring all he can get alive to Bau; that those who had a hand in the murder he will hang; and the rest shall be slaves for life. He does not want the whites to take part in the fight, but said that as he was very poor, he hoped the settlers would supply him with ammunition, &c.

'We attended a meeting of the settlers at Viti, and sub-scribed for your interests. There were about thirty white settlers present who all did what they could in money and munitions – 150 dollars, 50lbs of gunpowder, 100lbs lead for bullets, &c.

'I wish you were down again. I am sure you would go heart and soul into the war; for the sooner it is over the better; we can get no Fijian labor to work our cotton plantations until it is terminated.' (*Hawke's Bay Weekly Times* [Napier, New Zealand], 21 October 1867)

Another report on the massacre from 'the *Herald*'s [*Sydney Morning Herald*'s] correspondent at Fiji' offered more details about the massacre. Legend had it that the attack on Rev. Baker and his group was caused by the Reverend touching a tribal chief's head, a grave insult in Fijian cul-ture. The *Herald* surmised it was more likely to be either a challenge to the authority of Thakobau/Cakobau, or a defence against the incursion of *lotu* missionaries into their territory. Whichever, it was a none too subtle warning to 'Keep Out!'

After hard and rough walking, Mr. Baker's party arrived at Gagadelavatu, at about three p.m. and, almost immediately after, sent a message to ask for an interview with Makatakataimosi, the chief of the place. He, with several of his people, came out, and sat himself down upon a stone in the village courtyard. Mr. Baker at once went up to him with the native minister and shook hands with him, and when all were seated, the native minister, according to the Fijian custom, presented a whale's tooth, and asked the chief to embrace Christianity and to grant them permission to pass on to the next tribe. The old man took the tooth and said, 'As for the lotu [Christianity] I hate it. The path is yours in the morning!'

Mr. Baker was then informed that H.M. Consul had stopped at this village, and that a pig had been killed for his entertainment. Upon hearing this, Mr. Baker at once made up his mind to sleep there. After the meeting in the courtyard, the whole party went into the chief's house, and waited for any food that might be presented, according to Fijian custom. Nothing, however, was given; Mr. Baker, therefore, sent a few yams out to be cooked, but the chief would not allow it.

The Lotu Message
The chiefs and people of the place crowded about them, and pressed them to talk; the native minister therefore urged them to lotu, and explained its requirements and advantages: they, however, replied by asking how many guns, and how much powder – how many pieces of print [cloth] and axes would be given to them if they complied? They were asked to conduct their lotu so that the townsfolk might see them – the native minister, therefore, led Mr. Baker's party's evening devotion. After which they

were left to themselves, and although footsore, weary, and hungry, they were all soon fast asleep.

It is said that the native minister's suspicions were aroused when he looked out of the door in the middle of the night and saw a number of men coming to the town from surrounding villages, for their torches could be seen all round. No one, however, thought of making their escape from the town in the night.

Early in the morning Mr. Baker was astir, and looked over the country with his telescope, when it is supposed that he saw the natives excitedly moving about and engaged in other business than planting, for he said, 'Boys, dress yourselves, and let us be off, for we shall be killed to-day!'

When Mr. Baker had conducted their morning devotions singing, reading, and praying – he stepped out again, whereupon the chief Makatakataimosi came up and said, 'Come, let us show you the path to Vuda!' Mr. Baker called his party out and when all were ready they took their departure, the chief leading the way with a small battle-axe in his hand, being closely followed by Mr. Baker, Shadrack Seileka, the native minister; Nemani Rapio, and Aisea Nasekai, catechists; and Sisa Tuilekutu, Taniela Ratuvesi, Josifata Ngata, Nafilalai Toran, Setereki Madu, and Jasitifa Nakarawa, who were students in the Circuit Training Institution under Mr. Baker's superintendence; these all followed in single file.

After proceeding thus for about 100 yards, Josifata Nagata saw a small bag belonging to the party in the hands of one of the heathen; he went to him and asked for it, when the man replied, 'No, go on; I will carry it.' Whilst Josifata was thus turned round he saw the heathen coming rapidly out of the different houses with their guns and clubs, and hurrying likewise very suspiciously after them. He turned and ran, and with a companion from the institution, who too was a few yards behind the main party, rushed past Aisea, the catechist, into the middle of the line, saying at the same time, 'We are to be clubbed!'

Aisea, who was carrying a small tin box on his shoulder, replied, 'If we are, that won't save you!' which he had no sooner uttered than he was struck by a club from behind. The box, however, received the full force of the blow and merely glanced against the left side of his head. He dropped the box and rushed from the path. Mr. Baker turned round at once on hearing the stir behind occasioned by the two boys running into the line from behind, and also the noise occasioned by the blow upon the box, and with his right hand upraised he said, 'Don't run away;' or 'Don't;' when the chief, who was immediately before him, turned sharply round at the same time, and struck him on the lower part of the back of the neck with his axe, and he fell dead upon the spot.

The native minister, who was only a few yards or feet behind, stooped down over the body to kiss it, saying as he did so, 'We will die together with our missionary,' in which he too was chopped down. The catechist Nemani was shot, and all the others, with the exception of Aisea and Josifata, were instantly despatched.

The men only ran a few yards and then threw themselves down and crept under the long and decayed reeds, not daring to move lest the least rustle should betray their whereabout to those who were diligently seeking them.

Aisea lay close until the murder was finished and the bodies were dragged off to town, when all being quiet, he endeavoured to get away from the place, but had not gone many yards before he was seen by two women, who instantly gave the alarm to the men of the town, who rushed out at once and in the direction pointed to by the woman; but he doubled upon his pursuers and crept back to the town, and there lay concealed under the long grass and reeds not a great many yards from where the bodies were piled.

Distribution of the Corpses

The two guides from Dawarau prepared to leave with Mr. Baker's party, but were stopped by the people of the town, and detained in the house, but in such a position as to be able to see all that transpired. They confirmed all the particulars given me by the two men who escaped. The bodies after being dragged to town, were then stripped and thrown one on top of the other – the late Rev. T. Baker being placed on the top. They were then formally presented to the god, and afterwards divided out to different towns – three being kept for the chiefs and people of No Gagadelavatu – two to the next town of importance, the remaining three to three separate towns. The guides were then sent off to report what they had seen.

Aisea's Escape

Aisea, meanwhile, lay still close at hand, not daring to move throughout that long Sabbath day. From eight a.m. until eight p.m. he was compelled to listen to that awful death drum, and to the noise of their singing and dancing as they fiendishly rejoiced round and insulted the bodies of the slain. He heard the clapping of hands as the bodies were presented to the god, and again when they were given to those who received them on behalf of the chief, of neighbouring towns.

He heard too the chopping up of the firewood with which the bodies were to be cooked, and he dared scarce breathe lest it should be used to roast himself.

When all was dark and still he crept forth and made a circuit round the town until he came to the path over which he had passed with the murdered party only the day before. He says:

'I did not then run fast, as I thought my strength might fail me, as I had not eaten all day, and I knew it would be a long time before I could again eat. The morning rose, and I turned away from the path and sought a place of hiding. I found a cave and entered and slept.

'When it was again night I hurried off, I came to Namara, the town of Darawan, and there met a little boy. I seized his hand and said, "Tell me, now, are the teachers here or not?" He said, "No." I, therefore, thought perhaps Waquahquali and the people here knew of the plot, that was tried to kill the missionary, and if so, it would not be good for me to stay there. I went into the house of the teacher, I felt about for his mats and pots, and they were gone. The teachers are gone, I said, so I must go too. I went into the house of pots (kitchen) and there found two yams, these I grasped and ran.

'When the morning was nigh, I went again from the path, and rubbed the sticks; they smoked and I blew the spark and lit the fire and roasted my yams, and ate but one. I then went on until I came to a town where the teachers are, and then I said, I live.'

Josifata's Escape

Josifata Nagata, who sprang out of the path at the commencement of the mischief, also hid himself under the dry reeds, and did not stir until all was over, and darkness had set in. He heard them several times say, 'Some go for a firestick, and let us burn the reeds,' but no one went for the light. He therefore escaped. One of the enemy, whilst

Massacre of missionaries in the Fiji Islands. 'Our artist has portrayed a terrible occurrence, of which the intelligence has recently been received. The vigorous attempts which for some years past have been made by missionaries from the Australian colonies to Christianise the savage aborigines of the Fiji group of islands have been temporarily checked by the massacre of a party of eight, comprised of the Rev. Mr Baker, of the Wesleyan church; Shadrach Seleika, native assistant missionary; one catechist, and five students. These unfortunate persons, while on a missionary tour through the island, were attacked and slaughtered by the savages of the Navosa tribe, and – horrible to relate – there is strong evidence to support the belief that cannibalism was subsequently resorted to by the savage murderers. (*The Illustrated Melbourne Post*, 25 October 1867)

thrusting his club amongst the reeds to raise them, stood for a short time upon his leg; but so well had Josifata buried himself, that he was not even then noticed. This young man was wandering in the bush from Sunday until Thursday before he arrived at a Christian town; and when being brought home in a canoe, he was wrecked, and again narrowly escaped with his life.

As yet it is uncertain as to the cause of the murder, and it is likewise uncertain how far the plot was known. Reliable information has been obtained that a chief of an influential tribe sent some months ago a club to the various tribes, which Mr. Baker visited, and asked them to murder any who might attempt to cross over the land. Whether it has been done to stop the further advance into the interior of white settlers, or is an attack upon Christianity by the heathen, or is a challenge to Thakobau, cannot yet be satisfactorily ascertained.

The two latter reasons appear the most probable. For all those tribes look upon the advance of Christianity into their territories as political confiscation of their power, land, and persons by the influential tribes on the coast.

For these reasons the lotu is opposed by the heathen, and not, as in many other heathen countries, because it is an attack upon the gods and worship of the people. The heathen Fijian is almost without a religion, for they have no faith in those whom they call gods. So that, when the old chief replied to Mr. Baker that he hated the lotu, he meant that he hated the authority and power of the people of Bau and Rewa. In fact he is reported to have said that he 'had the fork with which he was going to eat Thakobau's tongue'. (*Hawke's Bay Weekly Times*, 21 October 1867)

The *Meva* Massacre

In November 1871 a brutal attack of multiple killings occurred at sea on a small cutter, the *Meva*, in Fijian waters. The cutter was transporting forty Solomon Islands labourers from Levuka, at that time the capital of Fiji, to a plantation on the Fijian island of Tavinui (Taveuni) 100 miles to the north-east. The vessel also carried: the two co-owners of the Tavinui plantation, Messrs Whittaker and Williams; Mr Warburton, the agent who was being paid for the labourers; two other plantation owners, Messrs Kington and Robson; and the vessel's captain, William Owen, and two Fijian boys to assist him, one of whose name was Mariki.

At some point during the short voyage, the Solomon men slaughtered all the white men, including Capt. Owen, plus one of the Fijian boys. The only survivor, Mariki, swam to an island where he communicated news of the atrocity to his countrymen. White plantation owners there soon heard about 'the abominable outrage' and organised an expedition to pursue, capture and punish the perpetrators on the *Meva*:

Fiji – More Brutal Murders by Natives – The 'Meva' Massacre

The brigantine *Lismore*, owned by M. Da Costa, a Frenchman, returned from a four months' labour cruise, superintended by him, on Sunday, October 22nd, having on board 59 natives from the Solomon Islands. After the *Lismore* had been in the port of Levuka a few days, her agents on shore, Messrs. Warburton and Co., negotiated the hiring of 40 of the natives from on board, at the price of £12 per man. This would produce a net sum of £480. Mr. Whittaker was the purchaser on behalf of himself and co-partner Mr. Williams, for their plantation at Tavinui, about 100 miles distant by sea to the north-east of Levuka.

The Meva

A cutter of 10 tons named the *Meva*, owned by W.R. Scott, Esq., was chartered to convey the natives to the plantation. The *Meva* is well known to nautical men in Auckland, for she was a favourite in that port, and purchased there by Mr. Scott about 18 months ago. In addition to 40 natives, the number of human beings on board a vessel of 10 tons was augmented to 47 persons. The commander was William Owen, who navigated the boat with the aid of two Fijians.

Mr. Warburton was a passenger on board, who purposed receiving payment for the natives upon their arrival at Tavinui. Mr. Whittaker had the natives in [his] charge, and Messrs Kington and Robson were passengers to their own plantations. Four out of the five white persons were married. Mr. Warburton leaves a wife and family in Melbourne to deplore his loss. Mr. Owen has a wife in Auckland, and is expected in Levuka by the next trip of the *Sea Gull*; and Messrs. Kington's and Robson's wives are in this kingdom [i.e. Fiji]. The two last-named are from Ballarat, and subsequently purchased, in conjunction, a promising plantation.

The Voyage ...
This 10-ton cutter, with a living freight of 47 persons, left the port of Levuka on Tuesday morning, October 31, in a light breeze and beautiful weather, such as can only be witnessed in tropical climes, no one seriously thinking that several good citizens were so speedily to meet a violent and bloody death at the hands of untutored savages. Such, however, was the lamentable sequel; for at sundown on the evening in question the sanguinary struggle for life was enacted upon the deck of this small craft, and only one escaped to relate the particulars of this horrible instance of savagery. He was an intelligent native of Fiji, named Mariki, a powerful youth of 18, whose breadth

of chest and general excellence of physical development testifies to his manual prowess.

... and the Massacre

When the affray took place the cutter was lying, almost becalmed, off Angua [Gau], about 27 miles south-east of Ovalu – the island on the shores of which Levuka is built, and the whites were on deck (aft) at tea. Mariki, the Fijian native who escaped, was at the tiller; his other countryman was lying down forward, surrounded by a group of Solomon Islanders. It began by the Fijian native who was forward receiving a severe blow on the head with a club, nearly stunning him; he, however, arose in affright, and jumped into the sea.

The mutineers, headed by one of their number who understood English and the mode of sailing a boat – from having been some years on board a whaleship and visited Sydney – now rushed aft, maddened by the demon of mischief. Mr. Warburton turned round in order to grasp his revolver, when a blow from an axe nearly severed his head from the body. Death was instantaneous. Robson and Kington were next despatched, their deaths being the work of a few moments; and Whittaker, in attempting to go below into the cabin, with one hand leaning on each side of the companion, was struck first on the back, which knocked him powerless on the floor; he was at once jumped upon by several Solomon Islanders, and killed immediately.

Mariki, who was steering, was not a quiet spectator of this foul scene of bloodshed. He first brought the boat up to the wind, and then attempted to unloose the tiller in order to secure a weapon of defence against the blood-thirsty savages. The tiller, however, was firmly fastened. He then grasped an oar, and in bringing it down upon the heads of the foremost murderers, with the strength of a giant, it became entangled in a rope, and therefore the blow so well aimed was utterly futile. Resistance to the overpowering numbers being thus frustrated, any further delay on board would have been sheer madness; he jumped overboard, the captain of the cutter [Owen] having preceded him by a few seconds.

This Fijian, being an excellent swimmer, once in the water afforded him an opportunity for reflection, and he speedily joined [Capt.] Owen, and subsequently they found the Fijian who had jumped overboard at the commencement of the affray. Speedy council was held in the water, but the first step was the removal of Owen's shirt, boots, and trousers from his person, which was expeditiously accomplished by his Fijian companions in distress.

They were now in the channel between the islands of Batiki and Angua, nearest to the former, but the wind and tidal current were in favour of the north-west point of Angua, distant upwards of five miles. The Fijian who was the first to leave the cutter was in favour of swimming to the nearest land – Batiki – which he struck out for, but he has not been heard of since, and unquestionably he met with a watery grave. The powerful Fijian, however – the native Mariki – who was steersman, resolved to make for Angua, in which resolution he was followed by Owen.

They had accomplished about a mile of the distance, when Owen showed signs of distress. Mariki again and again rendered assistance, and in his native tongue made cries of encouragement, but alas! all of no avail, for suddenly Owen sank, to rise no more.

Lone Survivor
The Fijian then pursued his watery path alone, and after much exertion he finally reached the shore in an exhausted

condition about nine p.m. With much difficulty he crawled a short distance into the scrub, and became insensible. In this condition he remained for the night, and when consciousness returned in the morning he hastened to a native village a mile and a half distant, and furnished the alarming news to an assembled crowd of his own countrymen, who gave vent to their acute feelings of indignation by discordant wailings of grief peculiar to them.

Messengers were immediately despatched to the several plantations, conveying the sad news to the white residents, and Mr. John Manton manned his whaleboat with alacrity in order to reach Levuka with all haste. He, however, did not reach the metropolis of the kingdom until midnight of Thursday, November 2nd, and upon landing gave information to Mr. Warburton's employees – Messrs Klinesmith and Fullerton.

Pursuit of the Meva *and Murderers*

In a strange and inexplicable manner, many hours were now allowed to pass without any steps being taken to arouse the Government to action. Information of the abominable outrage was not taken to them until six a.m. of Friday, November 3rd, and as soon as it was brought under the notice of the Premier – the Hon. G.A. Woods – the most active measures were initiated to pursue the missing cutter *Meva*.

A powerful expedition was immediately organised under the command of that distinguished officer of the British navy, Captain Armstrong, consisting of three sail – namely, the Viceroy Maafui's yacht, *Zariffa*; the Hon. G.F. Sagan's yacht *Pomona*; and the missionary schooner, *Jubilee*; the last-named being sailed by the experienced worthy commander, Captain Robert Cocks. In addition to the above the schooner *Kate Grant* was sent to sea under the orders of the late Mr. Warburton's employees. All those vessels were manned by volunteers, who had assembled in great numbers at the station house in response to the bugle-call which had sounded the alarm throughout Levuka. In the course of a few hours provisions and arms were sent on board, and the foregoing fleet set all sail and were out of the harbour and hull down before noon.

Every one on shore wished her God-speed in their well-directed efforts to discover the missing *Meva* with her piratical crew; and no expedition ever set out which commanded to a greater extent the good wishes, hearty support, and sympathy – both the native Fijians, and white residents – than did this united and unusual one from Levuka. (*The Daily Southern Cross* [Auckland], 4 December 1871)

A few weeks after the massacre, a certain Mr Murray arrived at Nadi, on the west coast of Viti Levu, from the small island of Biva (or Viwa), to the north-west. He said that he was looking for handcuffs to secure what he thought were the renegade Solomon islanders from the *Meva* on Biva, 'so that they might be brought over to Levuka'.

The Fiji Times reported on how the *Meva* murderers came to be on Biva:

On the 8th inst., Mr. Murray was on his way to Vaviti [Naviti, to the east of Biva/Viwa], when he observed a cutter with her sheet close-hauled, and behaving in a very strange manner, and he accordingly made for her. When the men saw that they were pursued, they let off the sheet, and ran the cutter upon Biva reef, and then jumped overboard and swam ashore. The first question they asked on reaching land was, 'Is this Tanna?'

[a notorious cannibal island in the New Hebrides] and the answer was 'No'. They then asked, 'Are you going to club us?' and were again told 'No'.

They then promised to share the trade they had on board the vessel with the Fijians, saying that they (the Solomon men) had been working on Ovalau [Fiji] for eighteen months, that their time was out, and had given eighty pigs for the vessel to take them home. They also stated afterwards that they had eaten the white men, and got hungry again, and had killed three of their comrades and eaten them, so that now there are only thirty-seven men left.

The *Peri*

On 5 January 1872 the naval steamship HMS *Basilisk* left Sydney to cruise up the north-east coast of Australia 'to proceed to Cape York with [supplies of] horses and stores for that settlement'. A month later, in early February, the *Basilisk* was off the mouth of Rockingham Bay, near the settlement of Cardwell on the north Queensland coast, when she sighted a small schooner out at sea – the *Peri*. It was suspected for some time that the natives the *Basilisk*'s crew found on board the *Peri* were remnants of a crew sent in search of the *Meva* murderers, as well as some of the murderers themselves taken as captives by the *Peri*.

Later, however, the truth about the *Peri* emerged: that there had occurred on her an altogether different atrocity, around the same time as that on board the *Meva* and with stark similarities of a white crew being murdered and deepsixed by a gang of blackbirded (kidnapped) island labourers:

The Schooner Peri

With reference to the vessel, picked up at sea by H.M.S. *Basilisk,* with a number of Solomon Islanders on board [the *Peri*], the *Fiji Times* observes:

'The mystery in connection with the above vessel, is cleared up by the receipt of intelligence from the colonies, per [the schooner] *Dancing Wave*, and there is every reason to believe that a bloody tragedy, similar to the *Meva* murders, has been perpetrated.

'It will be remembered that the Peri, schooner, left Rewa for Levuka, on the 28th December last year. There were on board Mr. Bergin (late master of the Lulu, which was wrecked on a labor cruise), master, Mr. Woodside, and another white man, three Rotumah men, three Tanna natives, besides between fifty and sixty Solomon Islanders, who had arrived by the schooner Nukulau, and been landed at Rewa. The vessel had a large whaleboat belonging to the Nukulau, besides a good boat of her own. Not any tidings of the unfortunate vessel were received in Levuka, until the arrival of the *Dancing Wave*, from Sydney, on Monday.' (*West Coast Times* [Canterbury, New Zealand], 18 June 1872)

The Sydney Mail of 24 April 1935 recalled the *Basilisk*'s encounter with the vessel and the fate of many of the *Peri*'s crew:

H.M.S. Basilisk's *Voyage*

There was something unusual about the vessel [*Peri*]. No life was discernible on her decks. Her torn sails were flapping against broken masts and rigging, and her uncontrolled rudder swung loose. An armed crew from the *Basilisk,* under the control of the Lieutenant [Mourilyan], set out to investigate, and on boarding the schooner an amazing sight met their eyes. On the blood-stained disordered deck were sprawled thirteen gaunt, emaciated black men, gibbering and frothing as they endeavoured in vain to raise their weakened bodies and attack the visitors with knives.

They were immediately disarmed and transferred to the *Basilisk,* where, after their starvation and thirst had been assuaged, they told a terrible story. The schooner was the *Peri*, which had been engaged in the native labour trade. Her white officers and Fijian native crew had kidnapped 80 natives from Bougainville Island [in the Solomon Islands], south of New Guinea, and set sail with them for Fiji. But a few days later the captive natives mutinied, took possession of the schooner, and threw the white men and Fijian overboard. Then, ignorant of seamanship and navigation, they drifted helplessly for the next seven weeks, travelling more than 2,000 miles until the schooner was sighted by the *Basilisk,*

The voyage had been a terrible one, as after the food and water had run out the natives resorted to cannibalism, and 67 of the natives met their end in this way. The thirteen [14?] survivors were later returned to their home island.

In 1871 the *Nukulau* (or *Nukulu*), out of Fiji, recruited (kidnapped) around eighty men from the Solomons and brought them back to Fiji. Sixty of them were there transshipped on to the *Peri* to take them to work on a plantation at Taveuni Island. Just like the blackbirded men on the *Meva* around the same time, the starving islanders attacked and killed the *Peri*'s crew. They then drifted for months around 2,000 miles across the Pacific to just off the Queensland coast where the *Basilisk* came across them. By that time their number was down to just thirteen or fourteen who had survived by eating their shipmates. In August 1873 HMS *Dido* returned the survivors to their Solomon Islands home:

> H.M.S. *Dido* ... returned, last August, to their homes in the Solomon Islands the 14 natives found by H.M.S. *Basilisk* on the water-logged *Peri*, off Cardwell. These were the remnant of 80, who, having been starved on their way from the Rewa to Taviuni [Taveuni Island], captured the vessel they were in, and drifted about for months, *living on each other*, until the schooner was found by the *Basilisk*. (*Australasian Sketcher*, 29 November 1873)

Fiji Cannibal Feasts, by an Eyewitness

A 'cannibal bowl from the South Sea Islands' on exhibition in San Francisco in 1898 reminded an old South Seas seafarer of the cannibal feasts he had witnessed around the islands, and in Fiji in particular. He recounted to *The San Francisco Call* newspaper his memories of what he said was the last cannibal banquet in Fiji:

Last Feast of the Fiji Island Cannibals, by an Eye-Witness

There has lately been placed on exhibition in the Academy of Sciences a genuine cannibal bowl from the South Sea Islands. It is an ugly, blood-soaked relic that it took days to scrub clean and rid of a sickening odor of human flesh. The bowl is about five feet across at the top, is hewn out of a single block of wood, and in days gone by was used for holding the cooked bodies of human beings after they were taken from the oven to be carved and served to the cannibal feasters.

The Schooner *Peri* Picked Up By H.M.S. *Basilisk.* (*The Illustrated Australian News,* 29 February 1872)

Captain George E. Jackson, who spent years cruising among the South Sea Islands, on hearing of the arrival of this bowl a few days ago, at once hastened to examine it. He scrutinized it from all sides to assure himself that it was genuine.

Capt. Jackson's Reminiscences

'I've seen bowls of that kind used many a time,' he said. 'In fact, I think I was present at the last cannibal feast in the Fiji Islands, when several of them were in use. I never want to see such sights again. It is generally thought that cannibalism in the South Seas is at an end. But it was not stamped out in a day. The conversion of the Fijians was accomplished from the coast inland by missionaries. And so it was that the interior mountain people for many years captured victims for their feasts from the inhabitants along the coast. Several attempts were made by white men to reach and punish these mountain cannibals, but it always resulted in loss of life followed by a feast of human flesh in the camp of the cannibals.

'The principal town and stronghold of the mountain people was Nivotheene, situated at the head of the Reeva River. The case of the last white man they captured and ate was very sad. The Rev. Thomas Baker, a Wesleyan missionary, with seven of his native teachers, attempted to reach Nivotheene, but when within a short distance from the place they were set upon by the Na-Vosa tribe, killed and eaten [on 21 July 1867]. Baker had been strongly urged by the coast natives against making the attempt, as it was well known the Na-Vosa tribe had long been eager to eat a white man.

'I was with an expedition that was bent on stamping out cannibalism when the report of this crime came to hand. Of course, it roused every white man in the party, and we redoubled our energies to round up the man-eaters and give them a lesson that should forever end their appetites for that kind of food. Old Chief Thakambau [Cakobau] of the coast tribe had loaned us a lot of his best natives as guides and soldiers. It was on this trip that I was forced to witness one of their horrible feasts.

'Well, we tracked the man-eaters to their villages after a deal of hardship, but invariably found the huts empty. The rascals, by some native wiles, were always warned of our approach in time to decamp. As if to taunt us they always left behind a pile of human bones and other signs to show that they were still man hunting and defied us.

'On our last advance, when we were quite deep in the mountains, one of our scouts came to us with the news that a missionary and his entire party of native followers had been killed by the inhabitants of a small village near by. "Did anybody escape?" asked our captain. "Three white men," answered the scout. "They had firearms and the cannibals were afraid to approach near them, so the white men backed away and escaped."

'After ascertaining the exact location of the village our captain decided to raid it and if possible prevent the forthcoming feast. To prevent any chance of its coming off he ordered another man and myself with several natives to go ahead with him and reconnoiter, while the rest of our party of seventy-five men should follow as fast as the rough character of the country would permit.

'It happened, however, that our guide was entirely mistaken in regard to the locality of the village. It was much nearer than we had figured, and before we expected it we heard distant shouting. "Those are the cannibals," we all cried at once and ran for the nearest defense thicket. But this plan brought us closer to the village. Then we found it advisable to climb into a cleft in the cliff to see and to prevent being seen. From this point we could look across into the village and see the women piling wood into the ovens and making other preparations for the coming feast.'

Cannibal Feast
'The distant shouting drew nearer each moment, and soon the most ferocious-looking crowd I ever saw came dashing into the village dragging the bodies of several dead men. Then the feast commenced and we could do absolutely

nothing but stand and watch it, hoping against hope that our main party would hear the shouting and close up.

'The first thing the natives did was to prepare the bodies. This process was much as a housewife does in preparing a chicken for roasting. Then they were trussed and tied into position, and after being placed on a long hardwood board, were shoved into the heated ovens. There they remained about eight hours. All the while the people of the village shouted, danced and yelled and drank large gulps of the island liquor. The scene at this time beggars description. It was one wild whirl of licentious debauchery.

'At a signal from the chief the dancing suddenly ceased and the ovens, made of bricks and stones, very much like a baker's oven, were opened and the bodies were dragged out and placed in the immense wooden bowls waiting for them. "The same kind of a bowl as this," indicating the one on exhibition. Then an official of some sort came before each bowl and with spear and knife cut the bodies into portions. These portions were quickly seized and greedily devoured.

'From our hiding places in the cliff we could catch the voices of the feasters, and our natives translated the Fijians' opinion of roast white man. It seems that this white man had been roasted in a special oven and special care had been bestowed on his preparation. There was, however, some disappointment among the feasters. They decided that white man was "too salt" and not as good as they had expected. Some of them thought it would have been better to have kept him awhile and fattened him for the feast. It was decided that this should be done with the next white man they captured. But the chance never came to them.

'The question has been raised about women being allowed to eat with the men on the occasion of these cannibal feasts, but old Fijians told me it was not customary, although not absolutely forbidden, and it was usual for the men to eat their fill first; then women came in and took what was left. One old chief replied that he would like to see the woman "who did not contrive to get her fill". Another old chief, when asked about pork and man, said there was no comparison between them, human flesh being so much the best. A man was called "long pork", while a hog was called "short pork".

'One custom of revenge and insult among warring cannibals was to collect the bones of the bodies thus eaten and reduce them to a powder. Then when peace was restored and the tribes feasted together this nice ingredient was added to some favourite pudding. Afterward, should war again break out, it was the height of triumph to taunt the late guests with having eaten the dishonored bones of their kindred. In the mad quest to satisfy their craving for human flesh, these cannibals would often dig up the bodies of those who had died natural deaths.

'On a hill at the head of the valley, near Nivotheene, stands another town named Balavu (the long town), which in 1871 was surprised by neighboring tribes, who slew and ate 260 victims. This was the last great feast on the island, and it continued several days.' (*San Francisco Call*, 13 March 1898)

New Guinea: The *Franz* Massacre and Cannibal Feast

For many years in the nineteenth century, Prussian German interests (and from 1871 the unified states of Germany) held

Defeat of the cannibal tribes of Fiji. (*The Illustrated Australian News*, 1 November 1876)

sway over the north-eastern part of New Guinea, named Kaiser Wilhelms-Land, and nearby archipelagos off the east coast, as well as Samoa and other island groups in the central and western Pacific. Between 1884 and 1914 the islands near New Guinea were part of the German protectorate of Kaiser Wilhelms-Land. The Bismarck Archipelago, to the north, included the Admiralty Islands. To the south of them were the two largest off-lying islands of Neu-Pommern (later New Britain) and Neu-Mecklenburg (New Ireland). Off the south-east tip of New Guinea lay the D'Entrecasteaux Islands; further south, the Louisiade Archipelago.

All these were fertile grounds for pearl fishing (for the nacreous shell and the gem itself), but dangerous, too, for the tribes that killed men for trading in human flesh, and who lopped off heads for trophies.

In 1872 a pearl-fishing schooner, the *Franz*, was working around the islands just off the mainland of New Guinea. On 12 November the master, Capt. Redlich, sent out two well-provisioned boats for a three-week expedition 'to prospect for pearl-shell'. After almost a month the boats, with eighteen men, had not returned. Capt. Redlich sent out a whaleboat to search for the two overdue boats. He was anxious that they 'had been seen steering towards a place on the mainland of New Guinea, where the natives are very treacherous, and known to be very dangerous'. The whaleboat returned to the *Franz* with no news of the missing men. Enlisting the aid of the local rajah, Capt. Redlich eventually discovered how his men had been ambushed, killed and eaten by cannibals:

Shocking Massacre and Cannibal Feast at New Guinea

By the barque *Prince Alfred* we have particulars of the massacre of two boats' crews belonging to the brigantine

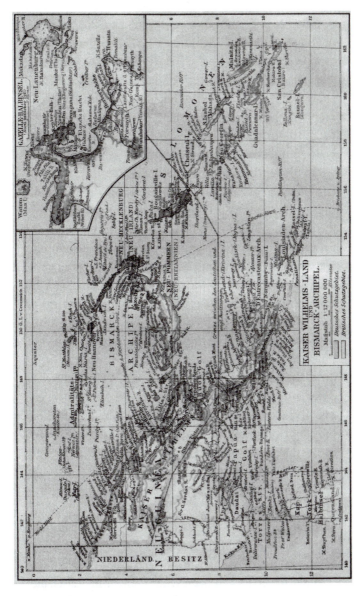

Kaiser Wilhelmens-Land und Bismarck-Archipel. (German New Guinea & Islands, Solomon Islands, etc. *c.* 1890)

Franz, at New Guinea, as furnished to the Chief Secretary of Queensland. The brigantine was pearl-fishing, and the captain [Mr. Edwin Redlich] states that on November 12 [1872] he started the two large boats away, well armed, in charge of the mate (Henry Schelouter), with seventeen men and three weeks' water and provisions, to prospect for pearl-shell. More men would have been sent with the boats, but eleven were laid up with fever.

On December 6, the boats being overdue, the captain became anxious, and sent another boat to search for the missing men. This boat returned unsuccessful, and the captain of the *Franz* then appealed to the Rajah [of Salwatti, nearby island] for assistance; and he instituted a search. He discovered up the Crarbera River seven guns, a revolver, the mate's watch, a boat compass, and the Hamburg colors, but had seen nothing of the boats.

On December 30 the Rajah came on board the *Franz* with three armed proas [canoes] and forty-five men. The captain, steward, and two men accompanied him in his proa; the second mate, with two men, went in another proa; and one man in the third proa. On January 5 [1873] two of the proas returned with three bush natives whom they had caught; one of them, according to his own confession, had been one of the crowd that had actually murdered the poor men.

Murder and Cannibalism

The captain relates the way the boat's crew had been murdered and eaten, as ascertained from the captured natives in the following words:

'The two boats had been lying under Efmatal Island, three canoes from the mainland (New Guinea) and in each canoe fifteen men, had come off with bananas and pineapples, which they gave to my men in the boats, and then went away, pulling towards the land. They had behaved quite friendly, and my poor men had not the remotest idea that these horrible men were cannibals, who contemplated coming back in the night to kill them all. My men in the boats had divided into two parties, some had lain down in the boats to sleep, and some had gone on shore to light a fire and sleep there.

'Meanwhile the savages had returned, and landed at the back of the island and walked across; here they had lurked in the dark bush close to my poor men, and watched them for some hours until all were asleep, when they rushed upon them, killing them in the twinkling of an eye, without a cry being raised, and the whole party on shore was dead, without those in the boat having any foreboding of it, and that they would themselves be corpses a few minutes after.

'When the horrible cannibals had killed the men on shore they went noiselessly into their canoes, rushed upon the men in the boat, and killed all of them without a shot having been fired or a cry had been raised. They returned with all the bodies to the village of Crarbera. There they cut off the heads, and kept them as trophies, and sold the bodies to a neighbouring tribe, which has cooked and eaten them.

'The three prisoners were horrible looking fellows, especially the fellow that had helped to murder my poor men; they are a different race to that of the more civilised Papuans; they have a dirty brown skin, short poodle hair, flat African noses, projecting lips, and are of a horrible appearance.'

Revenge and Retribution

'If my poor men had fired at them as soon as they caught sight of them, and kept good watch, they would never have been killed in such a manner by those miserable wretches. As soon as the abominable wretch saw us two white men he knew at once what was the matter, and made an effort to jump out of the canoe, which only caused him to get his feet tied up. After the prisoners were well secured all the proas went further up the river, and I hoped that we would go slap up to Crarbera village, which is about twelve miles distant. We saw two canoes with eight men in them; a shower of arrows and bullets were fired after them, but without avail – they were in the bush in an instant, and there they are as quick as wild pigs.

'The Rajah could not be persuaded to go above Crarbera, as there are some thousands of savages living there and he considered his party was not strong enough for such a number. To my regret we had to go back. At noon we started on the homeward voyage, and anchored at Efmatal towards morning. Here I ordered the terrible cannibal to be brought on shore, exactly to the spot where my poor men had been killed, and right in front of where the two boats had been lying at anchor, tied him fast to a tree, and shot him.

'I fired the first shot, which went right to his breast; the second mate the second shot; then the natives cut off his head and strung him up to a tree, where we left him as a warning example to the other cannibals who visit here now and then. My men had witnessed the execution, and the Rajah had given his sanction to it. The two other savages remained in the Rajah's hands, and both died a most horrible death. I witnessed the execution of one of them. He was in the true sense of the word cut to pieces by women and children, the widows and orphans of those who were killed in the first expedition when the Rajah went out and recovered my guns, etc.' (*Wellington Independent* [Wellington, New Zealand], 30 May 1873)

The New Hebrides: The Big Nambas Tribe of North Malekula – 'A Ferocious Race'

To the south-east of the Solomons, the New Hebrides group included a number of 'cannibal islands', the tribes of which presented a very real menace to the labour recruitment vessels and trading captains who called there: Tanna and Erromango in the south, Sandwich Island (Efate, or Vate) in the middle of the group, and Mallicolo (or Malekula) to the north.

Cannibal 'outrages' occurred in the New Hebrides (the Republic of Vanuatu, since 1980) well into the twentieth century (the last was reported to be in 1969 on Mallicolo/Malekula Island). The killings were perpetrated particularly against the missionaries there, and included indigenous Hebrideans proselytising for the white man's *lotu*, but also against any outsiders (such as labour recruiters) who ventured thereabouts.

In December 1913 a Presbyterian missionary at Uripuv, on Malekula, noted that 'about 1,500 Malekula natives were Christians, but there were still 10,000, the majority of whom were still cannibals'. One of the most notorious tribes on Malekula was the Big Nambas of North Malekula (so called because of the bulging penis sheath (the *namba*) which is almost their only garment; the penis sheath of the Small Nambas is much less protuberant). Early in 1914 the crew of a labour recruiting vessel, the ketch *Guadeloupe*, and, a little later, native teachers from a local mission station suffered the fatal consequences of the tribe's 'chief enjoyment' of warfare and cannibal feasting:

Murders at Malekula: Native Missionaries' Fate
– A Terrible Outrage

The Big Nambus [or Nambas] tribe of natives in [North] Malekula, New Hebrides, which recently killed and ate three of the crew of the ketch *Guadeloupe*, are credited with another terrible outrage, details of which were brought to Sydney by the island steamer *Makambo* last week. The victims were six native teachers attached to the Presbyterian mission, who were killed and eaten. There were eight teachers altogether in the party attacked, but two of them escaped with their lives, one, however, being wounded.

It appears that the party were invited by the Nambus chiefs to hold a service at North Malekula. Dr. Sandilands, of the Presbyterian Mission, at Walla, thereupon arranged for a service to take place in the bush settlement on Sunday, March 8. The teachers on arrival were attacked by armed natives. Six were shot dead. The remaining two made off to the beach, with the natives in hot pursuit, and firing at them as they ran. One of the fugitives was shot through the hand, but eventually the terror-stricken men managed to reach their boat, cast off, and row away to Walla, the little island which lies off the mainland of Malekula, where Dr. Sandilands has his place of residence. All the teachers are reported to be married men with families.

The second tragedy, following so soon on that of the Guadeloupe, has created an absolute panic amongst the native populations near North Malekula, and they are now living in terror of their lives.

The Guadeloupe *Tragedy*

The *Guadeloupe* tragedy, according to Captain Weatherall, of the *Makambo*, has been added to by the death of the skipper of the ketch, Captain Comboy. It will be recollected that the *Guadeloupe*, a French vessel, was engaged on a recruiting trip through the islands some time ago. She called at Malekula to ascertain if some of the natives could be induced to take service on the plantations.

A Man-Eater of the Big Nambas. This Big Nambas warrior is very probably a cannibal! In Malekula a feud between villages nearly always results in a man-hunt, and the victim must be eaten to prevent his spirit taking vengeance! (1938)

In former years North Malekula was always considered to be a good recruiting ground, and many thousands of natives have worked on the plantations. They have always had a bad reputation – in fact, right from the time Dr. Selwyn nearly lost his life in 1851, when the bishop and his boat's crew were attacked without warning – and in consequence traders and others have rarely landed except with a strong and well-armed force.

The three men of the *Guadeloupe* who were killed, landed by themselves. They were immediately attacked and killed, and preparations were then made for a cannibal feast. Captain Comboy went in search of his men, but upon reaching the beach he was fired at by the natives, and as he scrambled back to the boat, the murderers chased him, firing as they ran. Although it was not reported at the time, the captain was shot through the chest, and the wound ended fatally.

The Big Nambas tribe live in villages in the mountains. They are the biggest race in the New Hebrides, and are well armed. So far nothing has been done to exact reparation for the recent atrocities, and, in consequence, the greatest uncertainty prevails in the region of North Malekula.

This cannibalistic tribe is credited with practising unspeakable tortures, tying their victims to stakes or trees, and subjecting them at times to a living death. Often they are dismembered, limb by limb. In the eating of human flesh the head chiefs have the selection of sections of the bodies of their victims. The men are armed with bows and arrows, in addition to guns, and their chief enjoyment is tribal warfare and cannibalistic banquets. They have a special liking for white flesh. (*Otago Daily Times* [New Zealand], 3 April 1914)

A *rongavai*, or cannibal club-house, New Hebrides. The house is used by the natives for feasting, many of the repasts partaking of a cannibal character. It is decorated with human skulls, which are at once trophies of battle and reminders of past scenes of cannibal carouse. These hang from the roof, together with bundles of the bones of birds, fish, etc., and the gable support on the right is decorated with human jawbones. The further end of the interior is railed off, and live pigs are kept there, to serve at feasts in the absence of nobler game. The sketch was taken when the *Pearl* visited Montague Island to rescue the natives of Pentecost Island who had been conveyed there for cannibal purposes. (*The Australasian Sketcher* [Melbourne], 2 October 1875)

Part II

CARNAGE

'CARNIVAL OF MURDER ON THE HIGH SEAS'

The *Herbert Fuller* Axe Murders

On Tuesday, 14 July 1896, the American barquentine *Herbert Fuller* was in the North Atlantic on passage from Boston, Massachusetts, to Rosario, Argentina. In the early morning hours, someone on board hacked to death with an axe the master of that vessel, Capt. Charles Nash, his wife Laura, and second mate August W. Blandberg. After four days decomposing on deck and becoming increasingly noisome to the vessel's crew members, the three corpses were placed in a small dinghy and towed behind the *Fuller* as she put back to the port of Halifax, Nova Scotia. They arrived there about a week after the triple-axe-murder at sea.

The *Fuller* murders achieved notoriety for the mystery of the killer and his motive, and the personal stories of those variously accused of the atrocity. Chief amongst the *dramatis personae* was the first mate, a mixed-race West Indian, Thomas Bram, originally from the Caribbean island of St Kitts but who latterly claimed to be of Halifax, Nova

Scotia. Charles Brown, the seaman at the helm of the *Fuller* around the time the murders were committed, also came in for scrutiny, not least for the suspect nature of his past life.

The third intriguing character in the *Fuller* drama was Lester Monks, a passenger on the ship. Monks, from a cultivated Boston family, had been a student at Harvard and was voyaging to Argentina for the adventure. As it turned out, he got more than he bargained for.

The Killings

A Carnival of Murder on the High Seas – Captain Nash, Mrs. Nash and Mate Blandberg Hacked to Death in the Early Morning of July 14th in their Berths on the United States Barquentine Herbert Fuller, *Seven Hundred Miles Off Halifax, by First Mate Brain* [sic – Bram] – *An Ocean Tragedy That Rivals the Famous* Saladin *Murder and Piracy Story*

The Harrington, Me. [Maine], barquentine *Herbert Fuller*, came into port yesterday morning with her flag at half-mast. In a boat, towing at her stern were the bodies of the captain, his wife and the second mate, mysteriously murdered by one of the crew. The dead were:
Captain Charles J. Nash, 42, of Harrington, Me.
Mrs. Laura Nash, 37
August W. Blandberg, Finland

One of the most thrilling tales of murder on the high seas ever related in the new world, startles the people of this continent to-day. It was a story only rivalled once before in North Atlantic annals and that was the famous case of the *Saladin*, the story of which, though it occurred half a century ago, will never be obliterated from the annals of ocean tragedies.

This latest horror took place in the United States barquentine *Herbert Fuller*. Three deaths resulted from the *Herbert Fuller* tragedy, and eight on board the *Saladin*. The *Saladin* was from a South American port and had a cargo of gold, silver and guano and robbery was largely the motive of the murders on that ill-fated ship.

The *Herbert Fuller* was bound to a South American port with a cargo of lumber; and added to the motive of the robbery of the comparatively small amount of money in the captain's possession, and perhaps the hope of finally disposing of the vessel and cargo, was, it is believed, the more diabolical motive of outraging the captain's wife in order to accomplish which two lives had to be previously sacrificed.

A fortnight ago to-day the barquentine *Herbert Fuller*, 670 tons, of Harrington, Maine, sailed out of Boston harbor with a full cargo of lumber, also deckload, for Rosario, Argentine Republic. The ship was principally owned by the captain, Charles J. Nash, a native of Harrington, who was accompanied by his wife, a brunette of about 35 years; by Lester Hawthorne Monks, a young Harvard graduate, son of Frank Monks, of Boston (an intimate friend of Henry M. Whitney), as a passenger, and the following crew:

Thomas Brane, mate, a native of St. Kitts, West Indies, but who signed articles as hailing from Nova Scotia.
August W. Blandberg, of Finland, second mate.
Jonathan Spencer, steward (colored).
H.J. Steer, of New Jersey.
Charles Brown, of Holland. [Real name Justus Leopold Westerberg.]
Oscar Andersen, of Sweden.
Luke Weelaner, of Sweden, and
Frank Loheece, of France, as seamen. [This seaman's name, which, as with other crew members' names, would

be spelled in a variety of different ways in reports of the *Herbert Fuller* case, was Francis M. Loheac.]

Before leaving Boston First Officer Brane (or Brown, as he was sometimes called [*sic* – Thomas Bram]) obtained a couple jars of whiskey. The cabin of the *Herbert Fuller* was well arranged and furnished in a cosy manner. The berths were occupied by the captain, his wife, the passenger and the first and second mates. After they had been out a day or two,

The Two Mates Got Drinking in the Evening
and next morning, First Mate Brane told the steward (Spencer), that he and Second Mate had been drinking and that Blandberg had vomited over the lumber on the deck.

'Strange that he should be so affected by whiskey; perhaps he was poisoned,' remarked the steward to First Mate Brane; 'what did you give him the whiskey in?'

'In a cup,' replied Brane.

'Where's the cup?' asked the steward.

'Threw it overboard', was the reply.

'What did you do that for? I'd like to have seen if there was anything in the bottom of it. But as I can't get the cup, I'll save the vomit and have it analysed when we get to port, just to see if there was any poison in it,' continued the steward.

Thereupon Mate Brane took a piece of clothing and removed all trace of the vomit from the lumber. This significant incident may have considerable bearing upon the motive of the tragedy that was subsequently enacted – viz., to get out of the way one of the occupants of the cabin.

On another occasion the mate had made suggestive remarks to the steward. He had been telling how anxious Americans were to make money; and how they were not particular about how they made it as long as they did make it. Then dropped some remarks about how much the vessel and cargo would be worth to the Cuban insurgents [in the 1895–98 Cuban War of Independence]. The steward says he paid no particular attention to these conversations at the time.

Nothing of particular moment occurred until the night of Monday the 13th, or the early morning of Tuesday, just one week ago. From midnight until 4 a.m., it was Mate Brane's watch on deck. Seaman Brown was at the wheel. Captain Nash had retired to the little room in the corner of the cabin used as a chart room and thrown himself down to rest on a couch. Between this chart room and the captain's cabin was the spare stateroom, in which passenger Monks slept. Mrs. Nash occupied her own room – the captain's cabin. On the other side of the saloon, near the companionway, Second Mate Blandberg was asleep, and the sailors were all asleep in the forecastle.

The vessel was then seven hundred miles off Halifax, on her voyage to the Argentine Republic. It was a calm, warm night, and everyone on board appears to have slept soundly. All of a sudden:

Monks Was Awakened by a Woman's Shrill Cry

He jumped up out of his berth, put on a few clothes and groped his way in the darkness to the chart room, where he knew the captain was sleeping, put his hand in the berth, and quickly drew it back all smeared with blood. The terrible reality that an awful tragedy had taken place now dawned on young Monks, and he made his way in the darkness up on deck. There he ran against Mate Brane. The latter armed with a piece of lumber, made a vicious lunge at him whereupon Monk exclaimed, 'For

God's sake don't kill me; I'm Monks.' Meanwhile the young student whipped his revolver out of his hip pocket, and pointed it at Brane's head, which cowed the ferocious mate and doubtless saved his own life.

Full Extent of the Tragedy Revealed

Lester Monks and Brane might be imagined by an onlooker each to have supposed that the other was the murderer. This was doubtless the role adopted for the time by the mate. His excuse for assaulting the passenger was that he believed him to be the author of the tragedy and that he must defend himself. With this plausible understanding they went back together to investigate, when a new horror was revealed to Monks. He had before found the blood in the captain's room; now a dead body was found there; the captain's wife was dead in her bed, her body horribly mangled, and Second Mate Blandberg had shared the same awful fate. Charles Brown, the seaman, was still at the wheel.

Mate Brane, if it was he who committed the fiendish murders, and the circumstances point to him with fearful ominousness, and the helmsman were the only ones on active duty at that time were the man at the wheel and the mate on deck. The sailors were under cover, ready to be called at a moment's notice, and the captain was in the chart room, sleeping lightly on a lounge, prepared for any summons that might come to him except the dread beckoning of the angel of death.

No man could obtain access to the cabin except the wheelman, and he could not do so without his absence being instantly seen by the mate. Ten seconds away from the wheel, if there was anything at all of a breeze, and the vessel would have to come up in the wind, be caught aback and either dismasted or capsized. Even if there was but a breath of air she would have worked up in the wind and no mate who ever stepped on a plank could help instantly noticing that the wheel was unmanned. Seaman Brown could not, therefore, have entered that fatal cabin and been unseen, unless he was in collusion with the mate.

How He Entered the Death Chamber

The murderer, it was discovered, had entered the cabin from the forward companion-way. There, at his left, was the second mate's room, and at the other end, the captain's chart-room. Whether it was the captain who first endured the murderous blow of that fatal axe, or the second mate, is not known. But the murderer made sure, quick and silent work of it. The dented mark of the axe over the door of the second mate's room in two places, shows how he had once missed a blow and another time took the edge of the moulding with the weapon as it swung high in the air. It would seem from these marks as if the second mate had risen from his bed half-dazed and been struck down as he was attempting to come forward. The axe crashed through his neck and severed the artery so that the blood spurted to the walls behind the bed.

The captain met his death as he lay on the lounge. The light burned in front of him in a hanging lamp, casting its rays full on the prostrate form. At the end of the room in line between the wheelman's eye and the form of the captain is a small window commanding a good view of the chart-room. The axeman entered and a well directed blow was all that was needed to instantly kill. But more than one blow was dealt, for besides the gashed and mangled head, the captain's hands were almost severed from the arms, as though he had put them up for protection.

Here is a new mystery. Helmsman Brown, two whole days after the awful murder, tells that he saw the mate kill the captain. Why did he not raise an alarm at the time? And why did he delay in telling what he knew? If he was not in league with the murderer, or if he were not himself the murderer, the reason may be that he was a coward; that he feared the consequences to himself, both at the time and subsequently.

Attempted Outrage Then Murder

The axe-armed demon's way was then cleared to the room where lay Mrs. Nash, wife of the captain, except that Lester Monks was asleep in the cabin which separates the captain's chart-room from the wife's room. It was 2 o'clock in the morning, and the ill-fated woman had been asleep. What could prompt an attack on her but one motive. The mate if it was he, was bent on committing the foulest of crimes. The woman's night clothing was disturbed, showing the fiendish purpose of the murderer. The woman startled out of slumber, and seeing the swarthy visage and the ferocious eyes of the mate near her face screamed. That was her death signal for an alarm meant the certain conviction of the murderer. He swung the axe for his third killing in that brief minute or two.

The bed is two feet from the floor, leaving comparatively little space between the ceiling above, and the dread work of the weapon is shown above, as it passed along before its descent upon the devoted head of the victim. The head and body were mangled beyond all recognition. One hand was completely severed as it was feebly raised to ward off the blows and the other hung to the arm almost cut off.

Then came the murderer's turn to be alarmed. Monks had heard sounds in the captain's chart-room and calmed himself by thinking that it was the captain talking in his sleep, or suffering from nightmare. But when his ear caught the scream of Mrs. Nash he was thoroughly aroused. He rose from bed and hastily clothed himself, grasping a revolver. Carefully he felt his way along to the companion-way, but the mate was ahead of him. They met and the encounter between them, already alluded to, took place.

Helmsman Brown in Irons

All hands were summoned and a consultation held. Charles Spencer, a colored man, was steward, and he proved himself a natural-born teacher. It was on his advice that helmsman Brown was placed under arrest, though the sequel showed that this was done with many misgivings. It was hard to believe that the mate was the murderer and Brown might have been. Besides, if Mate Brane was placed in irons the barquentine would be without a navigator. So Brown was ironed. Spencer and Monks kept a good watch on the mate, however. They doubted him, and in two days they showed what they thought.

The murder had been committed on Tuesday, July 14, when the ship was 700 miles from Halifax. It was decided to abandon the voyage to Rosario, which they believed to be the nearest port. The mate's conduct was so strange that the conclusion come to was that he was not directing the vessel in the way he professed to be. Then Brown told his story of seeing the mate's axe strike the captain, and nothing could withstand that testimony, late though it was in coming. The fatal axe the mate had thrown overboard.

Last Sunday Spencer and others watched their chance and coming up behind Brane threw him down and handcuffed him. He was the prisoner of the steward and the crew. He was dragged aft with his irons and made fast by a stout chain to the bitts near the wheel hard alongside the entrance to the companionway.

Passenger Monks and Steward Spencer in Command

Passenger Monks and Steward Spencer were now the two navigating officers. They took none of the advice given them by the mate. It was found that he was misleading them, and evidently attempting to send the vessel adrift, or at least to keep her from reaching Halifax. He may have seen that it was all up with him, and it might be an advantage to have the vessel go ashore, with the chance for him to escape. On Sunday the vessel was in the neighborhood of Sable Island, but Brane told the steward and Monks that they were near Cape Sable.

Monks, with his knowledge of the theory of navigation, obtained at Harvard, was of much assistance in taking observations, and the ship, with good weather, was independent of the manacled and chained mate. There he lay on a mattress which had been placed beneath him, but firmly made fast to the ship, with the ship's boat night and day towing behind within a few yards of him and containing the bodies of the three victims of his or of someone's axe.

Dead for Eight Days

The killing took place on July 14, so that the three bodies have been exposed for eight days. For four days they remained on board, till the process of decomposition made it impossible to longer endure it. Accordingly the ship's boat was draped with canvas and prepared to receive the bodies. These were carefully wrapped in canvas and placed in the boat, and a tarpaulin closely fastened over to keep out the water and dry as far as possible. A line was passed around the boat in thorough shipshape fashion, and to make it perfectly secure. Then the boat was allowed to drop about twenty feet behind, and for four days more the ghastly load was drawn behind the slowly moving barquentine.

What a pathetic spectacle it was for the crew and how horrible it must have been to the mate, manacled as he was, and tightly secured to the vessel with his feet at the end of the line that kept the death-laden boat in position.

The Mate's Peculiar Advice

Every circumstance as it comes to light places the mate in a more damaging position. One incident that is told is that when he learned at Boston that Monks intended going by the *Herbert Fuller*, he asked him why he proposed doing so, and advised him to change his mind and go south by steamer instead. Mate Brane evidently did not wish the Boston man as a passenger, whatever the reason was.

Brane blames Helmsman Brown for the murder, and his blaming of him is another suspicious circumstance which is almost equivalent to a confession of guilt. As the Herald has already pointed out, the man could not leave the wheel for a half minute without his absence being noticed, nor without disastrous consequences to the vessel.

The captain's log book was found in the chart-room where he had been killed, and in it was an entry made two days after the murder. It was dated Wednesday, July 15. A reporter started to take it down, but before he had finished Detective Power took the book and refused further perusal of it. As far as the reporter got the entry it was as follows:

'On this day at 9 30 p.m., the steward of the said H. Fuller came to me and told me that the sailors all came and made an open statement to him in reference to one of the sailors whose name is Charles Brown. The statement was to his conduct of guilt in regard to the murder which took place on board said vessel. At once got each man's statement. Then on the strength of these statements we concluded to put him in irons at daybreak. At 7 a.m. all hands were mustered aft and thoroughly searched, and no other weapons were given them but their knives. Each man was then placed a certain distance apart from each other until after hours. Myself, the steward and passenger were stationed amidship, and kept a good lookout until daybreak. At 5 a.m. Charles Brown ... '

The names written underneath in different handwritings were:

Thomas Brane, mate; Jonathan Spencer, steward; Lester Hawthorne Monk, passenger; Frank Loheece; Felke Ivassener; Oscar Anderssen; Henry Fitak (?)

By this it is understood that Brown alone was suspected of the murders, as the mate made this entry. The mate was also placed in irons a day or two afterwards, and from then the entries were made by Lester Monks.

Visited by the Medical Examiner and Police
Medical Examiner Finn went aboard about 10 o'clock. With him were Detective Power, Deputy Chief Nickerson, Sergeant Lathan and Policeman Goulding, Harbor Master Butler, Pilot Baker and W.B. McCoy. U.S. Consul General Ingraham gave instructions to have the police requested to bring the crew ashore in irons.

When the police went on deck they were met first by the steward, who said: 'The bodies of the murdered people are in the boat,' at the same time pointing to Brane, who was handcuffed, and stating that he was the murderer.

Below it was an awful sight that met the eye. At the foot of the forward companion-way, the first door opening on the starboard side was into the room that had been occupied by the ill-fated second mate. The bed clothing, which had been of light colored material, was dyed a dark red, and everything about the place was in disorder.

Passing from there to the next room the sight, if anything, was more horrible than in the second mate's room. The bed was sticking to the side of the cabin with gore, which had soaked through on to the floor. On the bed were numerous locks of dark brown hair which had been chopped from the head of the victim by the murderer, as he must have repeatedly struck the poor woman on the head with the axe.

The place where the captain met death was the after cabin or chart house. Here he had slept, on a small stretcher, so as to be ready at any moment to go on deck when called. This room was strewn with books, papers and other articles, and looked as though a struggle had taken place between the murderer and his intended victim. The stretcher was overturned, but the bed was not stained in blood as in the other two cases, there being more blood on the carpet and pillow than on the bed, showing that in his struggles the captain must have overturned the bed and was then cut to death while on the floor. The ceiling of this room is splattered with blood.

All hands were brought ashore. At the station the men were all placed in the sergeants' room, searched, and all articles removed from them. The steward and Monks both had loaded revolvers. Some of the crew had sheath knives. The men gave their names as follows:

Thos. Brane, mate, West Indies; Chas. Spencer, colored, steward; Oscar Anderson, seaman, Sweden;

Chas. Brown, seaman, Holland; Luke Wiessner, seaman, Sweden; H.J. Steer, New Jersey; Frank Loheece, seaman, France; Lester Monks, passenger, Boston.

The men were kept under surveillance of the police, no communication being allowed with them, and they were locked in the cells, with the exception of the passenger, who was taken to the chief's office, and Chief O'Sullivan, Detective Power, and United States Consul Ingraham interviewed him about the crime. Chas. Spencer, the steward, was afterwards taken to their office and also questioned.

Second Visit to the Fateful Vessel
At 2 o'clock yesterday afternoon Medical Examiner Finn, Chief O'Sullivan, Detective Power and Recorder McCoy again visited the vessel, for the purpose of making a more careful investigation of the scene of the tragedy.

On Mrs. Nash's blood-drenched bed they found one stocking, and a pair of garters, while on the floor was a dainty pair of slippers and neat wearing apparel was scattered about. On a table was her wedding ring. All the rooms in the cabin were carefully examined, but nothing was found which would throw additional light on the awful crime. The man at the wheel had at one time given it to be understood that his shirt was thrown overboard. It was found with other underclothing, wet with rain, on the top of the house, and Detective Power took it away.

Medical Examiner Finn decided, on coming ashore, to make his report to Magistrate Fielding, in accordance with the statute. Mr. Fielding will begin his inquiry at 11 o'clock this morning. (*The Halifax Herald* [Nova Scotia], Wednesday, 22 July 1896)

[Finn's subsequent report noted that:] 'all three bodies were horribly mutilated. The wounds found on the bodies were all produced by a sharp instrument, such as an axe. The captain's body was terribly mutilated, the skull crushed in and face torn. The skull of the second mate was smashed in the right part of the head and looked as though he had been in a standing position when he received the blow. The axe entered the head on the top of the forehead. There were other wounds on the body, particularly about the chest.'

The result of the post mortem as regards the wife disclosed the worst features of the case. The head was badly mutilated. There were bad wounds on the chest, on the head and on the face. The skull was horribly injured. One hand was almost completely severed at the wrist and the other hand badly chopped and mutilated. The appearance of the woman is such as to show that she must have struggled desperately with her assailant. The whole condition of the ship, says the examiner, showed that a terrible struggle had taken place. (*The Halifax Herald*, 23 July 1896)

The Murderer's Swiftness and Stealth
One of the most mysterious elements in the terrible crime is how Brane, or whoever did the murder, could kill two men and almost finish a third without wakening Monks, the Boston passenger, who slept in the room situated between those occupied as a chart-room by the captain and a sleeping apartment by Mrs. Nash.

Who Is Lester Monks?
Lester Monks, who took passage by the *Herbert Fuller*, for Rosario, is a good looking, intelligent man of perhaps 25 years of age. He had been a Harvard student and preferred the trip south in a sailing vessel to going by steamer. He had plenty of money, a letter of credit, and a large amount of baggage. He is a son of F.H. Monks,

of No. 10 Federal street, Boston. Soon after the arrest of himself and the crew a telegram was received from H.M. Whitney, president of the Dominion coal company, by the manager of the company in Halifax, for information. This was replied to by William Lithgow, in the absence of Mr. Morrow, and another telegram came from Mr. Whitney asking Mr. Lithgow to inform Lester that his father would start in the evening for Halifax. He will arrive here this evening. While the crew were locked up in the prison, Mr. Monks was kept under guard in the chief's office. He was thoroughly tired and was glad of a chance to sleep.

Navigating the Vessel

It was on July 14th, early in the morning, that the murders were committed. From then till Sunday the 20th, Mate Brane remained in charge. On that date he was arrested by the steward and Monks, who thereafter took charge of the navigation of the vessel. They came to the conclusion beyond a doubt, that he was taking her in one direction and pretending to be going in another, and in addition they became convinced that if he was not the murderer he knew too much of it to be allowed to remain in charge or at large.

The weather was good and the difficulty of two novices thereby lessened. Observations were taken, and the false information the mate gave from time to time, was ignored. On Monday the *Herbert Fuller*, having avoided the dangers of Sable Island found herself not far from Canso [north-eastern Nova Scotia]. A fisherman was hailed and gave them their course for this port.

Pilot William White stated that he boarded the vessel six miles south-south-east of Devil's Island early yesterday morning. At that time she was heading this way, but before he got to her, her helm was put down and the vessel headed off shore. He immediately surmised there was something wrong, as, had the vessel been in charge of a proper navigator she would have acted differently.

As White neared the ship and rowed around the stern those on board hailed him and told him to 'be careful of that boat astern, as it contained corpses'. He then asked what was the matter, and the steward, who was apparently in charge, said, 'There has been murder aboard,' and that the boat contained the bodies of the captain, his wife and that of the second mate.

Pilot White went aboard and took charge and brought the vessel up to the city.

No more gruesome sight can be imagined than that presented by the ship's boat as it came slowly along, in tow of the undertaker's men. The city slip and the Market wharf were crowded with people. The boat was speedily discerned after it had left the ill-fated craft. It was seen to be a jolly-boat, covered over. Slowly it forged into the slip, and was moored alongside. Then one of Snow's men cut the fastenings and ripped the canvas coverings, and the bodies were seen, or rather the packages in which they were rolled. It was a terrible sight – or rather, more horrible from what was not seen, but felt, than from what was discerned. The bodies were lifted out, and into coffins that were brought down to the water's edge, from Snow's undertakers wagon.

It was awful to reflect, as the death-laden boat was coming in, that underneath the canvas were the bodies of two men and a woman, brutally murdered more than a week ago – that they had met a cruel death on the high seas. There they were – lying beside each other, undistinguishable from bags of merchandise, in their horrible companionship of days!

The bodies were first taken to John Snow & Son's undertaking establishment. Later they were removed to the morgue. Last night crowds visited the place drawn thitherward by a morbid curiosity, which was the more shocking from the fact that a majority of these sightseers were women. Many of them fainted and it was no more than they deserved.

Instructions were received by Consul-General Ingraham to have the bodies of Captain Nash and his wife embalmed and forwarded to Harrington, Maine. But the undertaker found this would be impossible, and all three will probably be interred in Halifax. (*The Halifax Herald*, Wednesday, 22 July 1896)

Motives

One of the enduring mysteries of the *Herbert Fuller* murders was the motive for them. That was regularly speculated upon but never determined. Robbery, piracy, lunacy and an attempted 'outrage' upon the captain's wife, Laura Nash, as well as the character of Capt. Nash himself (for alleged cruelty to his crews), were all amongst the theories, supported only by circumstantial evidence and journalists' natural inclination to stir the pot of hearsay and speculation.

Mate Thomas Bram

Thomas Bram, 'a half-breed St. Kitts negro', as one former employer described him, had a 'checkered' life and seagoing history. He professed to be a religious man and insisted that helmsman Brown, and not he, was the murderer of Capt. Nash, his wife and the second mate on the *Fuller*. Though Bram had a complex psychological profile, whether he had the capacity to hack to death three people was for a court of law, ultimately, to decide.

The Great Tragedy on the Ocean

Thomas Bram, the alleged murderer, ate a hearty breakfast yesterday. He was taken from his cell to the sergeants room. He ate with a relish and did not seem the least concerned. He has made a statement that will tend to further complicate matters. He says he is not the murderer and intimates that Charles Brown, when he stated that he saw him kill the captain, lied. 'It was not I who committed the murder, it was Brown,' exclaimed the 1st mate.

'How do you know it was Brown?' was asked.

'He and I were the only ones aft, and it must have been Brown.'

'Did you see him commit the murders?'

'No, but he was the only one that could have done the work under the circumstances.'

'Brown was at the wheel at the time, was he not?'

'He was and I was on watch.'

'Then how could he leave the wheel and kill these people without your knowledge?'

'He could do that all right.'

'If he left the wheel wouldn't the ship sheer off from her course, and would not her sails flap?'

'Possibly.'

'Don't you know it for a fact, and that the noise made by the flapping of the sails would attract your attention?'

'All I have to say is that I did not notice any such change.'

'What have you to say to the story of the passenger Monks, who immediately after he had heard the cries of the woman rushed on deck and was faced by you with a billet of wood in your hand; why had you the piece of wood, and why did you assume such a threatening attitude?'

'I heard a hubbub, and when I saw the passenger with the revolver I thought he was going to shoot me.'

'What have you to say regarding the fact that when the passenger rushed on deck Brown was still at the wheel and the ship sailing on her course with all sails in proper position? How could Brown commit the murder, the ship sheer off, sails become disarranged, and then be at his post when the passenger came on deck with the ship running right?'

The mate could not answer this question. He took refuge in the statement: 'It must have been Brown who committed the murder. It was not I.' (*The Halifax Herald*, 23 July 1896)

Mate Bram's Story: Interview with Alleged Murderer
Halifax, July 23

For half an hour this afternoon the [Boston] *Globe* correspondent stood in the gloomy, barred quadrangle at the local police station, conversing with and mentally analyzing the most remarkable American criminal of the recent generation – Thomas Bram, the now notorious mate of the ill-fated barque *Herbert Fuller*. From Guiteau to Sawtelle, and from Sawtelle to Gilbert [notorious nineteenth-century murderers], the continent has certainly not produced a more notable example of criminal study than this swarthy suspected butcher seemingly presents.

Despite the rigid discipline enforced by the U.S. consul general at the station house, where he has reigned unquestioned for the past three days, several furtive interviews with the chief actor in the bloody drama have been secured by local newspapermen and others, but the *Globe* man's talk with him to-day was the first opportunity presented of receiving a satisfactory impression of the man, both through his words and his actions. The result of it was to thoroughly convince the writer that,

Whatever May Have Been the Underlying Motive
that led the fellow to redden his hands in the blood of his
associates – assuming that he be really the guilty man – the
murders were committed during a period when reason had
temporarily left him. Various things that came to notice
during the interview confirmed this impression, and it is
undoubtedly true not only that Bram is a man of quick
and uncontrollable impulse, but that he is imbued with
a fanatical slant of mind on certain subjects, any one of
which would be a sufficiently strong motive for the commission of the crime under the stated mental conditions.
The psychological and insanity experts of Boston will find
in the man and his mysterious crime a rich mine of research.

An afternoon paper here had published a long and
interesting account of Bram's New York and Boston
career, furnished by a man who had known the mate inti-
mately there. This, with the additional facts telegraphed
from New York and Boston to-day, make up a pretty
complete account of the first mate's life and
Threw a Flood of Light on His Characteristics
It was this printed story that the writer read to Bram line
by line, as each stood in the barred recess of kind-hearted
Chief of Police O'Sullivan's bastille, the man meanwhile
following with eager eyes and ears every word that was
uttered. From time to time he made verbal revisions of the
story, which seemed to please him very much on the whole.

The sketch of his career in substance was that about
12 years ago Bram first came to notice as a habitual frequenter
of Jerry McAuley's, 100 Water street mission in New York.
He made many friends there, and gave out the impression that
He Was Tired of Following the Sea
and wanted to settle down and make a livelihood on
shore. He gave out that he was a native of St. Kitts. Later

he joined the salvation army, and after a while attracted the attention of Rev. Stephen Merritt, who conducted a small mission church, and A.W. Dennet, who was then just starting his famous restaurants. Mr. Dennett appears to have had enough confidence in Bram to send him out to Chicago a year or two later, to supervise his establishments there. Returning to New York, Bram remained there in Dennett's employ a while, and then came to Boston, where he ran a small restaurant on Washington street, nearly opposite the Globe building.

Once more returning to the metropolis, Bram took charge of Dennett's Bowery restaurant, where he appears to have developed a marked religious enthusiasm, becoming a regular adherent at Rev. Dr. Merritt's Franklin street Methodist church in that city. The restaurant on the Bowery was a good aged one, employing four or five waiters, and was well fitted. After it was in operation about a year Dennett met with business reverses and sold out his Bowery establishment to Bram for $1,500. This was not looked upon as the full value, but the owner's friendship for Bram was thought to be responsible for the low price.

Business prospered with Bram and a little later he was married to a young woman of German descent. The ceremonies were solemnized at the Franklin street church, being performed by Rev. Mr. Merritt in the presence of a large number of people, the groom, who was at this time natty and well-dressed, having made many friends in New York. The girl and her relatives were attendants of the same church.

Bram and his wife resided over the Bowery restaurant, where the proprietor was apparently making money 'hand over fist'. Up to the time of his marriage Bram was a teetotaller, both as to drinking and smoking. A short time after taking a wife he introduced a cigar stand in his restaurant and this was viewed by some of his friends as a slight fall from grace and an indication that his religion was gradually leaving him. When the New York despatch stating how the man had

Always Been Noted for His Love of Money

his ambition to become the owner and commander of his ship; his despondency at his failure to have enough money for this purpose, and finally his abandonment of his wife and family for several years, and the subsequent divorce proceedings of Mrs. Bram – were touched upon, his dark eyes took on a new light of interest and his tongue was unloosened in an instant.

'It is not so; I never heard of it before,' he exclaimed when the divorce matter was reached.

Then he calmed down a little and admitted that he had written the letter to his wife in the exact language as published, but denied that he had deserted his wife for two or three years.

'It was only about a year and half,' he said, 'and the statement that I promised her an elegant residence is untrue. I never told my wife that I expected to get into trouble some day, and that I wanted her in that event to notify my Masonic Lodge, and that they would get me out of trouble.'

Just a Brief Reference to Bram's Early Life

was made by the writer, and he was asked to explain why he had called himself a Nova Scotian. He replied that it was because his mother's people, whose family name was Gibbs, and who were born in upper Canada, at one time resided in Bridgewater, Nova Scotia. There followed the most interesting part of the man's reportorial inquisition, and it must be confessed that he stood it pretty well. The man's demeanor during the recital of his 'life' had been one of respectful attention. He had glided forth from his solitary cell with

The Lithe and Active Tread of a Young Panther
possibly as he had done on that fatal night in the dim and peaceful cabin. There was no look of defiance, of dread, of remorse, of anything, in fact, which would connect the patient man in the cell with that bloody happening in the cabin. His appearance, indeed, was one of extreme docility, and even his rough and unkempt appearance failed to conceal the fact that the man was one of at least ordinary intelligence. That he would commit murder, and such murder as that seemed beyond human belief. It was only when the inner spirit was aroused as some topic on which he has a mania was broached, that the lurking devil in the man came out of its hiding place.

The first exhibition of this came when the subject of the man's religious convictions was touched upon, in
The Recital of His Life Story
'You have been a religious man', I said, 'do you still have spiritual sentiments?'

'Indeed I do,' he replied eagerly. 'I do not understand why humanity is all against me in this unfortunate manner. I do not know why this man (Brown) should try to throw the blame for this thing upon me. It looks black for me now, I know, but I know there is an Almighty God who is looking down upon me, and He knows all and will take care of me.'

'Then you have carried your trouble to the Lord,' I said, and Bram meekly bowed assent, quoting the biblical text which expresses the enduring qualities of the tabernacles of the Lord.

'I understand that you still maintain that it was the wheelman Brown, and not yourself that committed the murders?'

'I do, and I cannot understand why the other man wants to make me suffer for it.'

This was said in a tone devoid of bitterness or resentment and

The Absence of Intense Personal Feeling

on Bram's part throughout the interview was as marked as it had been when he was first placed under restraint by the crew.

'But how could Brown get a chance to kill those people without his absence from the wheel being noticed?'

'O, he could have easily fixed that by lashing the wheel in position. Why that has been done often on that very ship. We had beckets all in place for that purpose. He could have left his post for ten minutes without any danger.'

'Assuming that you yourself are the guilty man, don't you think it possible that you might have become temporarily insane, perhaps from liquor, perhaps from some other cause? Such things sometimes happen, you know.'

'O, no, no. I was never crazy in my life. The thing is impossible.'

'Then assuming that it was Brown, what do you suppose was his motive?'

'I don't know. Perhaps he was insane.'

'Ah, then you don't believe that what might apply in his case might also apply in yours?'

'No, sir.'

Going Back to His Own Personal History,

Bram said that it was true that he was ambitious to succeed in life, but that he was not fanatical on the question. He had at one time owned as much as $2,000 and some property in Brooklyn. Now he was penniless. He admitted that he drank and was fond of female society. He had never, he said, been of a quarrelsome nature, and had never been under arrest before for any misdemeanor.

'I see you have a scar on your head,' I remarked. 'How did you get that?'

'I,' he replied rather sheepishly, 'I got that about 15 years ago. I was beating a drum, and it annoyed another young man, and he threw a brick at me.'

Coming down to the voyage of the *Fuller* once more, Brown [*sic* – Bram] was asked if it was a fact, as stated, that he had advised young Monks not to sail in the vessel. He admitted that he had, but said that he had counselled him to go by steamer, as it would save time.

'Now as to the trip itself and the relations of the crew and captain, were they harmonious?'

'Entirely so; there was no trouble of any kind. We all liked the captain and his wife. Mrs. Nash was a pleasant mannered, but sickly woman. I don't believe I exchanged a dozen words with her all the time.'

'You admit that you drank whisky on the night before the murders?'

'Yes, but I only took two glasses. As I said, most of us had been drinking some that night.'

'Could anyone but Brown have killed the people in the cabin?'

'No, sir!' This with great positiveness.

'What do you think of this man Brown, personally?'

The mate shifted his gaze a little, and after some hesitation said, 'Well, I tell you, he is a very peculiar man – very peculiar.'

Not a muscle moved, not an eyelash quivered, as the towering West Indian uttered these deeply insinuating remarks. The mate's control of his emotions, save when the fires of over-cultivated religious feeling course through his mind and body, is simply marvellous. (*The Halifax Herald*, Friday, 24 July 1896)

Seaman Charles Brown

Mate Thomas Bram was accused of having a fit of temporary madness when he was alleged to have axed to death the three people on the *Fuller*. Seaman Charles Brown, who was steering at the ship's helm at the time, actually was, by his own words, hospitalised for being 'deranged' at one point in his past. And his name, Charles Brown, turned out to be an alias. But a triple murderer? If every sailor with a dubious, even duplicitous, character and shadowy past life was a criminal suspect, the courts would be back-logged to hell and back.

In his narration of the events that occurred on the *Fuller* on the night of 14 July 1896, Brown chronicled his own life story, eventually confessing even to his fraudulent identity. His version of the tragedy seemed thoroughly to convince the newspaper interviewer of his innocence:

Seaman Brown's Story

I left my home in Sweden in 1885. My father and mother had died and I started out to make a living for myself. I had a great fondness for the sea. When father was alive he was in fairly good circumstances and none of the family wanted for anything. How [this] changed when father and mother died and my brothers and sisters and I were left to our own resources. I remember well the day I left home. One of my sisters came to the pier to bid me good bye and gave me kind advice. I left two brothers and two sisters home and corresponded with them for two years. For some time after that I did not write, and when I did send a letter, I did not receive an answer. Possibly they have removed from Sweden. I preferred always to ship in Nova Scotia vessels and had a preference for Nova Scotian or New Brunswick seamen.

> The first ship I sailed in was the *Marie Russell*, Captain Nichols … My last ship was the *Herbert Fuller*, on which the tragedy occurred. (*The Halifax Herald*, 25 July 1896)

There then follows Brown's version of events about the *Fuller* murders:

> At the conclusion of the statement the unfortunate fellow poked his hand through the small opening in his cell and said, 'Shake hands.' A talk with Brown would convince anyone that he is not the murderer. He has a great memory, and tells his story freely and in a most straightforward way.

A later report confirmed who 'Charles Brown' actually was:

> *Charles Brown: Under False Colors*
> Charles Brown, who figures so prominently in the case, has confessed that he is sailing under false colors, in other words his name is not Charles Brown, which is one assumed by him. The reporter intimated to Brown that he had heard that the United States government intended to make enquiries in Sweden as to his record and that it had been rumored that he was sailing under a false name.
> 'Are you sailing under the wrong name?' asked the reporter.
> 'Yes, my name is not Charles Brown, that is a name assumed by me.'
> 'Why did you assume such a name? Had you any trouble at home or elsewhere?'
> 'Yes, I had, I am sorry to say.'
> 'What was the nature of the trouble?'
> 'Oh, I had some trouble with a captain. I was given to understand that he was after me and I changed my name to get clear of him.'

'Was the trouble of a serious character?'

'No, not very.'

'What is your right name?'

'Johese Vestbac.' (*The Halifax Herald*, Monday, 27 July 1896)

Trial and Aftermath

The murders on the *Herbert Fuller* were committed on an American vessel upon the high seas. Jurisdiction for the subsequent prosecution of the accused men was therefore in the United States. Mate Bram 'stated ... that he would rather be tried in Halifax than in Boston. Although he did not fear ... a fair trial anywhere, yet in his opinion the citizens of Boston would be prejudiced against him owing to the fact that a Boston man [i.e. Lester Monks] had played so prominent a part in the case.' No matter; the trial was eventually held in Boston.

On Sunday, 26 July 1896 all the men implicated in the *Herbert Fuller* murders, including crew members as witnesses, were transported to Boston in the steamship *Halifax*. Arriving in Boston the next day the accused men were incarcerated at Charles Street Jail and:

Thomas Bram was arraigned on three counts charging him with the murder of Capt. O.J. Nash, his wife Laura Nash and Second Mate August W. Bamburg with an axe on the vessel on the high seas on July 14. He pleaded not guilty to each count. He stated he had no counsel, but desired an attorney before he said any more in the case ... Charles Brown was arraigned on a like complaint, and also pleaded not guilty. His case was continued to to-morrow at the same hour without bail. (*The Halifax Herald*, Tuesday, 28 July 1896)

Eventually, after a United States Grand Jury was convened on 15 October 1896, only Thomas Bram was tried for the *Fuller* murders. The testimony of Charles Brown was critical in the jury's verdict handed down on 2 January 1897:

Guilty of Murder – Verdict of the Jury
in the Case of Mate Bram

Boston, Jan. 2. Thomas Bram, mate of the barkentine [*Herbert*] *Fuller*, was found guilty to-day of the murders committed on that vessel last July ... Bram was convicted on the evidence of seaman Brown, who testified that he saw the murders. Brown was at the wheel that night, and he saw Bram strike Captain Nash with an ax. No motive for the murder was brought out at the trial, and there was a strong feeling in some quarters that Bram was not the guilty person. (*Sacramento Daily Union* [California], 3 January 1897)

Bram's lawyers appealed the guilty verdict and requested a new trial. On 9 March 1897 the appeal was denied; Bram was sentenced to death by hanging, to be carried out on 18 June 1897. Another appeal was lodged directly to the United States Supreme Court, based on sixty-seven contentious legal points that arose out of the trial.

One of the most significant points was the assertion by the Halifax police detective Power to Bram just after the *Herbert Fuller* arrived at Halifax that he, Power, considered Bram guilty of murdering Capt. Nash, and that Bram's response was tantamount to a confession. The appeal was heard in October 1897 and decided a few months later in Bram's favour 'to grant a new trial'.

Second Trial and Aftermath

The second trial of mate Bram started on 16 March 1898, with the same judges, lawyers and witnesses (except Power) as in the first trial. In the time between the two trials, however, the United States Congress had legislated for the possibility that juries in federal murder cases that found a defendant guilty could indicate 'no capital punishment' for the guilty person. On retrial Bram was found guilty a second time, but the jury were now empowered by the new authority it had to indicate 'no capital punishment'.

Two years almost to the day after the *Herbert Fuller* murders, in July 1898, Thomas Bram was sentenced to life imprisonment. He was first incarcerated at the Massachusetts State Prison at Charlestown, Boston, and, from 26 November 1906, in the United States Penitentiary in Atlanta, Georgia (where his prison admission file noted 'Teeth: none'; 'Age: 42'). Thus concluded the final act in the drama of the *Herbert Fuller* tragedy.

On 27 August 1913 President William Taft released Bram on parole, largely on the personal intervention of novelist Mary Rinehart, who had regularly visited Bram in jail and became as convinced of his innocence as she was of Charles Brown's guilt. (She later wrote a novel, *The After House*, based on that belief.) In June 1919 President Woodrow Wilson gave Bram a full pardon.

Thomas Bram eventually resumed his sea-going life as owner and captain of a four-masted schooner, the *Alvena*, amongst others, hauling lumber and other cargoes up and down the Eastern Seaboard.

The *Herbert Fuller* was renamed the *Margaret B. Rouss* and was sunk by a German submarine in the Mediterranean in May 1917.

And who really killed Capt. and Mrs Nash and the *Fuller*'s second mate, Blandberg, in July 1896, by axe attack, on the

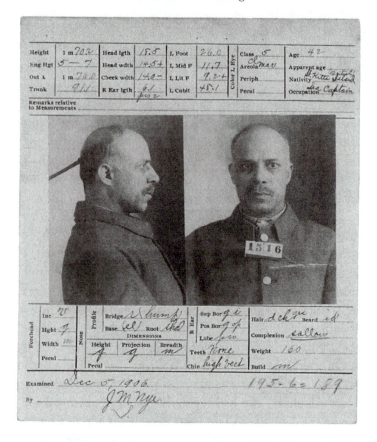

Photos of Thomas Bram (side, front) from Atlanta Penitentiary (1906).

high seas? And for whatever reasons? The certainty is that three decomposing corpses were towed to port in the ship's dinghy. Bram was most certainly convicted of the crime and paid the penalty for that judgment. But the fuller truth of that blood-soaked tragedy was coloured and discoloured and, indeed, highlighted and framed by the human stories involved in that mid-Atlantic 'carnival of murder on the high seas'.

MP3.50.2: Starboard view of SS *Herbert Fuller* in Halifax, July 21st, 1896.

MP3.50.3: Wheel and window of cabin.

MP3.50.5: Main cabin.

Images courtesy of the Maritime Museum of the Atlantic, Halifax, Nova Scotia, a part of the Nova Scotia Museum.

MP3.50.6: Captain Nash's room; passenger's [Lester Monks'] room; Mrs. Nash's room.

MP3.50.8: Mrs. Nash's bed.

MP3.50.10: 2nd Mate's [August Bamburg's] bunk.

The *Saladin*

The *Saladin* affair was a rather curious case of multiple murder and piracy upon the high seas. It concerned two separate but related killing sprees on board the 550-ton barque *Saladin* during her voyage from Valparaiso, Chile, to England, in April 1844, after the vessel had rounded Cape Horn and was somewhere in the Atlantic. Of the fourteen souls aboard at the start of the voyage, just six remained alive when the *Saladin* grounded on an island in a bay of northeast Nova Scotia. All the others, including the murderer of six of the crew, had been despatched to Davy Jones' locker.

At Valparaiso the *Saladin* had taken on a cargo of 70 tons of copper, thirteen bars of silver ('each of about 150lbs weight'), and about $9,000 worth of 'specie' (currency), in addition to her main cargo of guano fertiliser, before sailing for home on 8 February 1844.

The *Saladin*'s master, Capt. Alexander ('Sandy') McKenzie, had allowed another shipmaster, Capt. George Fielding, and his son George, of 'about 13 or 14' years of age, to take free passage on the return voyage to England. Capt. Fielding had been jailed in Peru for trying to smuggle out a cargo of guano on his 460 ton barque *Vitula*. He escaped to Valparaiso where he and his son embarked on the *Saladin*.

The *Saladin* rounded Cape Horn, and, in the early hours of 14 April 1844, Fielding and accomplices amongst the crew whom Fielding had roped into the plot killed Capt. McKenzie and six of the crew. The second event occurred some days later when Capt. Fielding himself, and his son, were bound and thrown overboard by several of the remaining six crew who suspected Fielding of plotting to kill them as well and take the ship and her valuable cargo.

Nova Scotia Landfall

The *Saladin* ran ashore in thick fog on a small island at a place called Country Harbour, near Canso on the north-east coast of Nova Scotia. Suspicions were immediately aroused amongst local authorities by the crew's story that: the captain had died at sea (there was no mention in the ship's log that Capt. McKenzie had been ill, much less deceased); that the mate had been washed overboard and other crew members had fallen to their death from aloft (again, not logged); and by the fact that a tarred piece of canvas and board had been nailed over the name of the *Saladin*, on her stern, to conceal her name. Upon the grounds of those suspicions the remaining crew were taken into custody at Halifax.

Thus began to be unravelled a saga of piracy and murder at sea that rivalled, indeed surpassed in bloodthirsty treachery, any to which even sea-hardened Haligonians (residents of Halifax) had been in thrall, and which the *Herbert Fuller* murders brought back to mind.

The Story of the Saladin Murders – Retributive Justice Overtook Captain Fielding – He Organized the Conspiracy That Resulted in the Murder of Six of the Crew, and Himself and Son Were Then Thrown Overboard – Four of the Survivors Were Hanged in Halifax

The case of the Saladin was similar in so many particulars to the present one [i.e. the *Herbert Fuller*] that a recital of the events connected therewith cannot fail of being read with interest.

In the month of May, 1844, a report reached Halifax that a ship had been cast ashore without officers, with valuable property on board, near Country Harbor. Steps were immediately taken to obtain full particulars. A deputy marshal accompanied by Hon. M. Tobin, proceeded to the vessel, where several seamen, named respectively Galloway, Carr, Hazleton, Jones, Johnson and Anderson, were found to be in custody at Country Harbor.

The vessels were lying at Harbor Island, one commanded by Captain Cunningham, to whom it was reported that a large ship was stranded. Captain Cunningham proceeded to the wreck, boarded her with some difficulty and found the vessel in charge of six seamen without officers. He found she had on board a valuable cargo of silver, copper and guano. He continued by the vessel until a magistrate arrived, to whom he gave the property in charge.

For some time no suspicion was excited in the minds of people there as to the crew. They helped to reload the vessel and secure the property. A few days later when the men had left, suspicions arose, and they were sent after and brought back, and were in custody when Mr. Tobin arrived. The admiral had placed the Fair Rosamond at the disposal of the authorities, and in her the prisoners and part of the property were brought to Halifax.

When taken into custody the men made a plausible statement that the captain had died at sea, leaving the vessel in charge of the mate, who, with another, was thrown overboard off the yardarm. In their statement, however, there were several discrepancies, which it was impossible to account for, if they had spoken the truth, unless they might be attributed to intoxication. Suspicions were too strong to allow of their discharge, and they were ultimately committed until application could be made to Valparaiso.

Captain Fielding

Among other things it had been discovered that there was property on board belonging to a person called Captain Fielding – a chronometer and articles of clothing, which caused suspicion that such a person had been a passenger on board the vessel. The statement of the men gave no explanation of what had occurred to this person. The explanation then given was that Fielding had died at Valparaiso, and the clothing and personal effects had been taken on board to send to his friends in England. But an account, of Captain Fielding, was found, dated the 7th April, and it appeared strange, if their story was true, that he should have been alive on the 7th, when the vessel sailed on the 8th.

While Suspicion Hung Over Them,

those whose duty it was to investigate the case deemed it proper to detain them until everything was satisfactorily cleared. Two of these men sent a note to Mr. Tobin stating that they wished to make disclosures. These were made, and subsequently other confessions were secured. The confessions were altogether voluntary. One said he would divulge nothing there; he might at some future time. The second said it was his intention to tell what he knew. These different confessions constituted the principal evidence upon which four of the prisoners were afterwards convicted.

The trial took place in Halifax, in July, 1844, before Chief Justice Halliburton and Judges Halliburton, Bliss and Hill.

The Prisoners Pleaded Not Guilty

Scott Tremaine read the indictment, which charged the prisoners Johnson, alias Trevaskiss, Hazleton and

Anderson, under four counts, as follows: 1. Piracy; 2. Taking the property on board; 3. Mutiny, and piratically taking possession of the ship and money. James B. Uniacks was counsel for the prisoners, and Hon. James W. Johnston, attorney general prosecuted.

The evidence of Henry O'Brien, seaman, of Ship Harbor, Malcolm Sellers, Country Harbor, and Hon. Michael Tobin adduced the facts that the prisoners had been discovered without officers on the ship Saladin, and that cargo of the Saladin consisted largely of gold and silver specie. The log book of the *Saladin* was produced. The entries from Newcastle to Valparaiso on the homeward voyage were in the same handwriting. The last entry concluded on Saturday, 14th April, 1844, at 12 o'clock noon. It was the handwriting of Byerly, the mate. There was no note of any death during the homeward voyage.

The Confessions of Jones, Hazleton and Anderson
were then produced. They went to show that there were fourteen persons on board the Saladin when she left Valparaiso. Twelve of the crew and 2 passengers, Captain Fielding and his son George. Galloway joined at Cape Horn. [*sic* – In fact, no sailor could possibly join a ship 'at Cape Horn'! Jones's confession included the remark that he 'was working (his) passage as a sailmaker, but acted as steward, by Captain McKenzie's request until after passing Cape Horn, when John Galloway took the situation, and I repaired some of the sails'.]

The captain's name was McKenzie, the mate's Byerly. Besides these and the prisoners, the crew consisted of a second mate and five forward hands. The passenger Captain Fielding and Captain McKenzie, of the Saladin, quarrelled frequently on the voyage, and appeared to be at enmity with each other.

Captain Fielding it was who tampered with the crew. He approached Jones first and suggested that the crew kill the officers, take the ship, scuttle her and divide the freight. Hazleton, Johnson and Anderson were next taken into confidence.

The Mate Thomas Byerly Was the First Killed,

while at his watch on deck. After the mate was killed, Captain Fielding told Hazleton and Anderson to go into the cabin and kill the captain. They were afraid of the captain's dog, and left him for a time, and then decided to throw the carpenter overboard. The captain came on deck just as the carpenter was struggling in the water. He ran to the rail, and while leaning over, the captain was struck from behind, but not killed. Fielding then felled him with an axe, assisted by Jones, who held the murdered man's hands while Fielding struck the blows. The seamen Collins and Moffatt were next killed with a hammer. This happened on Sunday. On the same afternoon

All Swore a Piratical Oath on the Bible.

The suspicions of the crew were then turned towards Fielding, who they discovered had secreted a brace of pistols and carving knife about him, and his plan appeared to be to do away with the remainder of the crew. It was then decided to throw Fielding and his son overboard. This was done by Galloway and the cook. The money on the ship was then divided, and plans projected for concealing their crime. (*The Halifax Herald*, Wednesday, 22 July 1896)

Custody and Trial

The conflicting stories of the *Saladin*'s crew after they were discovered by Capt. Cunningham at Country Harbour led to their being taken into custody at Halifax Gaol where they arrived on 3 June 1844. The men's differing accounts of the disappearance of most of the *Saladin*'s crew soon landed them with charges of piracy and murder on the high seas.

On 13 July 1844 the six men were committed for trial under indictments of piracy and murder: George Jones (aged 27), of Co. Clare, Ireland; John Hazelton (37), claiming to be Irish but suspected of being either American or Nova Scotian; William Trevaskiss or Travascus (*alias* William Johnston) ('about 23'), of London; and Charles Gustavus Anderson (19), of Sweden – for the murder of Capt. McKenzie, and piracy. All pleaded not guilty, as did William Carr ('middle-aged'), of North Shields, England, and John Galloway (19), of Scotland, who were later and separately charged for the murder of Capt. Fielding and his son.

For historical legal reasons, the trial of the six men was conducted not by the usual Vice-Admiral Court, which restricted how it could prosecute criminal cases such as murder and piracy on the high seas, but rather by an extension of that jurisdiction known as Admiralty Sessions, which enabled such cases to be prosecuted more thoroughly.

Confessions

Carr and Galloway, the *Saladin*'s cook and steward respectively, were first to realise that the game was up, with their conflicting narrative of events likely to be exposed by investigation and prosecution. On 8 June, less than a week after being incarcerated in Halifax Gaol, they made full confessions of what had happened on the *Saladin*.

Galloway concluded his signed and witnessed confession, 'I made the declaration because I fear to die without disclosing the truth; no man knows how soon I may die.'

Carr concluded, 'I make this disclosure because I cannot die with such a burthen [*sic*] on my mind, and I am perfectly ready to abide by the laws of my country.'

The four other prisoners similarly confessed their guilt in the *Saladin* crimes in the immediate hours and days after they knew about Carr's and Galloway's confessions. The voluntary confessions of their participation in the *Saladin* crimes eventually undid them, as surely they knew would happen. In his confession, George Jones described how events, animosities and suspicions transpired on the vessel:

I, George Jones, first joiner of the *Saladin*, at Valparaiso, crew 12 in number, and two others (Captain Fielding and his son George), was working my passage as sailmaker, but acted as steward, by Captain McKenzie's request, until after passing Cape Horn, when John Galloway took this situation, and I repaired some of the sails. While in the cabin as steward, frequent differences occurred between Captain McKenzie and Captain Fielding; the latter in consequence would often refuse to come to table at meals; and I have heard Captain McKenzie say to the Mate on these occasions that it served him right for giving Fielding a passage free.

Capt. McKenzie's and Capt. Fielding's Animosity
When Captain McKenzie came on deck Fielding several times cursed him, and used abusive language. Used then to come to me and tell me what he had said about his quarrels with Captain McKenzie, and then talk of the amount of money on board, and what a fine prize a pirate

would make of them. Asked me if I would fight against them if attacked. He would not. Captain McKenzie used to drink a good deal. Fielding on one occasion said to me, 'Now, Jones, if you want to save your life now is the time. I have spoken to the carpenter and I intend to be master of this ship.'

At another time, Fielding, in my presence, made a motion to show how he would cut Captain McKenzie's throat, saying at the same time 'Damn you.' This was when Captain McKenzie was on the ladder going from the cabin to the deck, and had his back to him (Fielding). When I attempted to acquaint Captain McKenzie of it, he stopped me, saying, 'You damned Irishman, I want to hear nothing.'

Fielding's Threats

While I acted as steward I scarcely ever had a civil word from him [i.e. Capt. Fielding]. He was continually cursing and swearing at me. One afternoon Captain Fielding said to me, 'You did not come on deck, as I requested last night; you had best do it. You will lose your own life if you don't. The other watch will do it, and you will be killed.' I understood that he meant by this that we were to take possession of the vessel. I soon after mentioned this to Hazelton, in the galley, by Fielding's directions. Hazelton laughed, and said, with an oath, there could not be a better chance; there was a great deal of money on board. Hazelton went out.

W. Johnston then came in, and I said to him, 'There is a curious work going on; that Fielding is a queer man. He wants to make a haul – Hazelton will probably let you know about it.' Before night it was known to Hazelton, Johnston, and myself. They both told me Fielding had spoken to them about it, and that all was right.

Plan to Mutiny

A day or two passed over, and on Friday we were bending [setting] sails. The Dutchman was getting them out, and I said to him, 'There is going to be curious work on board.' He then asked what was that, and I said that Fielding, Jack and them were going to take the ship and kill Sandy (meaning Captain McKenzie, thus named by the men). Anderson replied to this immediately, 'By God! I'll take a knife and cut his throat (meaning Captain McKenzie); he shall no more strike me away from the helm.'

I then mentioned to Hazelton what Anderson had said, and he replied that he would get him all right – that he would talk to him. He did so when in the foretop, and Anderson willingly consented, and expressed more satisfaction than any one on board. He talked and laughed about it.

Captain Fielding then came to me and said the vessel must be taken that night (Friday). I did not go on deck that night (being sailmaker I had no regular watch to keep), but all the persons engaged in the plot expected me, and afterwards asked me why I did not come. These were Fielding, Johnston, Hazelton, and Anderson. I excused myself to Fielding by saying I did not think he expected me, to which he replied, 'It is of no use making a fool of yourself; if you go back, your life is no more.'

Next day (Saturday) Captain McKenzie and Fielding had a serious quarrel on the poop, which was heard by all the men on deck, about the ship's gig. After this Fielding said, 'This night it must be done; they were all ready, and, if I did not come up, my life would be no more.'

The Plot

I went to bed in the forecastle; Johnston, Hazelton, and Anderson were in the same watch under the Mate

[Byerly], and the deed was to be done in their wa
that night. I went on deck between 12 and 4, while th
were on the watch. I was then told it was arranged that
Fielding should keep up a conversation with the Mate,
during which Johnston should strike him with an axe.

The Mate was lying on the hencoop. Fielding came forward and said to us, Johnston, Anderson, and myself, 'Now
is the time; the Mate is asleep.' He said it was best to send
for Jack to see what he said about it, that there might be
no mistake. Johnston accordingly relieved Hazelton. The
latter agreed to proceed, and returned to the helm. It was
then proposed I should take the helm and Johnston kill the
Mate, and that Fielding, Hazelton, and Anderson should
go down and attack the Captain in the cabin.

The Killings

I accordingly went to the helm. I saw Johnston then
strike the Mate with an axe. I think Anderson also struck
him. Fielding, Johnston, and Anderson threw the body
overboard. Some time was then spent consulting what to
do, and I afterwards learnt they were in doubt how next
to proceed. Anderson and Hazelton went into the cabin
to attack the Captain, but returned, fearing, as they said,
the dog would bite them.

It was then agreed to make an alarm, and strike the
Captain as he came up from the cabin. Nothing more was
done for a quarter of an hour, when the Captain rang his
bell three or four times, but no answer was given to it.

I was much agitated whilst at the helm; it was several times taken from me by Fielding and Hazelton, in
consequence of getting the ship in the wind. Fielding
and the others went to the main deck, and I heard nothing for some time until I heard the carpenter's voice in

the water. This alarmed me, as I understood the Captain was to be killed before the carpenter was disturbed, and I exclaimed, 'Oh, Lord! there is a man overboard.'

The Murder of Capt. McKenzie

With this Fielding ran immediately on the poop, and shouted, 'A man overboard,' as loud as he could, the Swede following him. The Captain (McKenzie) ran out of the companion, and as he came up Anderson struck him. The blow did not kill him. He ran after Anderson round the companion. Fielding then called to me, 'Damn you, why don't you run after him; if you don't lay hold of him I will give you a clout that will kill you.'

I let go the helm and went round the companion, and the Swede and Captain McKenzie were struggling together. Fielding again said, 'Damn you, why don't you lay hold of him?' I then took hold of his hands, and Fielding struck him two blows with the axe, which killed him.

While in the act of striking, McKenzie exclaimed, 'Oh, Captain Fielding! Oh, Captain Fielding, don't!' Fielding hauled him forward in front of the companion, and struck him again, and then threw him overboard.

Takeover of the Ship

Then Fielding, Hazelton, Anderson, and Johnston, went down to take some liquor, and said, 'The vessel is now our own.' I was relieved from the helm, and went below to get a drink. I came on deck, and Fielding addressed his son, saying, 'I am Captain.' The son said, 'It was a pity that I had not a blow at Sandy.'

They all assembled on the quarter deck, and consulted how they were to dispose of the rest of the crew, who were forward. Fielding proposed calling the watch. They all agreed that Hazelton and Johnston were to go forward and call the watch – that I should lie down in the long-boat – that Anderson was to stand by the mainmast, pretending to be asleep – Fielding in the companion. When the man came to relieve the helm they agreed to take his life. During this time Collins came on deck and went on the head.

Killing of Crew

When the watch was called Jem [seaman James Allen] came up. He went to relieve the helm. Anderson struck him, as I understood, with a hammer, and he was thrown overboard. I heard no noise in the boat. The other two men, Moffatt and Collins, who had gone down again, were then called up. They came up and Moffatt sat down on the spar, fore part of the galley. Hazelton struck him, as I understood, with an axe, and killed him. I heard the blow, and after I came out of the boat I saw the body. I assisted Anderson and Johnson in throwing the body overboard.

Before Moffatt was thrown overboard Anderson went forward, struck Collins on the head, and he fell into the water. I did not see the blow, but I heard Collins' exclamation on receiving it. Some time after this it was proposed by Fielding to do away with the cook, Carr, and the steward, Galloway, but the rest would not consent. Fielding then said he would let them work, and he would find a way to get rid of them.

The cook came aft about 6 o'clock. Was alarmed when Captain Fielding told him the ship was ours; that all the crew remaining were on the poop. The cook asked what it meant; he was told, and appeared quite satisfied. Galloway came aft laughing, and when he was informed of what had occurred did not appear alarmed, and said it was a pity he did not know about it, as he would have liked to have had a cut at Sandy, meaning Captain McKenzie. Some time after, on the same day (Sunday), we all swore on a Bible to be loyal and brotherly to each other.

Concealed Pistols and Carving Knife
The day after a carving-knife, which had been in the cabin, was missed, which gave us all some uneasiness. A pair of pistols were discovered under a table by Johnston, and when he was going on deck he beckoned to me not to go up. I, however, went up. Fielding was then on deck, and wanted a screen put down the skylight in the after cabin. He said he wished it to air the cabin. Hazelton and Johnston came afterwards on deck, and the latter told the former about the pistols under the table, which caused us all alarm, as we had thrown, as we thought, all the fire-arms overboard, excepting a musket in the after-cabin, which Fielding wished to keep to shoot fowl.

We went below and asked Fielding what he knew about the pistols; he said he knew nothing. After a search we found a large copper vessel with powder, and threw it and the pistols overboard, with which Fielding expressed himself satisfied. Anderson informed us then that Fielding purposed to do away with the cook, Galloway, Johnston, and myself. When we heard this, we accused Fielding, who denied it. After this we discovered a bottle of poison in a locker, of which Fielding had kept the key, and the carving-knife, which had been missing.

Fielding and Son Thrown Overboard
The cook then said he would not rest until Fielding was thrown overboard. Fielding was then secured by Johnston, his hands and feet being tied; he was kept thus for some time, asking us to heave him overboard,

screaming and shouting so, that Johnston gagged him by our request. He was laid upon deck by Harrison and Johnston, and was laid down close to the quarter.

After breakfast, while we were all sitting on the hen-coop, the cook and Galloway requested that he might be thrown overboard. We all then agreed he should go; and the cook and Galloway went immediately forward, without saying to us what they purposed doing. The first we heard were the screams of the boy as they were putting him overboard. While clinging to Galloway, the boy (Fielding's son George) tore some of Galloway's clothes.

William Trevaskiss's confession was more explicit about the fate of Capt. Fielding and son George:

Jones and Carr then took hold of Captain Fielding whose hands were still tied, and threw him over, and Galloway by the direction of the men put his hand on them. Carr then went forward and seized the boy and called Galloway to help him, and they two [*sic*] threw him overboard. I told Carr not to throw the boy overboard but he said if they did not the boy would inform against them when they got ashore.

Galloway Takes Charge

We then agreed that Galloway should take charge of the ship as navigator, by being the best scholar. It was proposed to go to the Cape Breton or Newfoundland, to scuttle the vessel, and take the long-boat up the Gulf of St. Lawrence. The money was divided amongst us all.

On the night before the Mate was killed, when I came on deck, I was going aft with Capt. Fielding and Anderson. We stopped about the mainmast, and I turned back, being frightened, and there seemed a sort of panic, from which I thought they might give up the plan altogether. Fielding then came after me, and asked, 'What is the matter?' My answer was not satisfactory. He then said, 'Damn you, if you don't go back, and not make a fool of yourself, I will kill you right out.' Fielding had a carpenter's adze in his hand at the time. I was quite alarmed at the threat and returned with him.

(Halifax Gaol, June 8, 1844. Geo. Jones. The confession voluntarily made in the presence of: Hon. Mich. Tobin; Hon. J.W. Johnston, Attorney-General; J.J. Sawyer, Esq., High Sheriff)

Verdict and Execution

Within 'about a quarter of an hour' of deliberation, the jury in the 'Trial of Jones, Hazelton, Anderson and Trevaskiss, alias Johnson, for Piracy And Murder on board barque *Saladin*', found all four men guilty of piracy. The following day the four prisoners changed their plea to guilty, which the court accepted. They were sentenced to 'be taken to the place from whence you came, and thence to the place of execution, and there to be hanged by the neck till you are dead; and may that God, whose mercy, if sought aright, all may obtain, have mercy on your souls'.

The four men were hanged together on a Halifax hillside overlooking the harbour on the morning of 30 July 1844.

Carr and Galloway were tried soon after the trial of their four shipmates. They were speedily prosecuted and adjudged not guilty of murdering Capt. Fielding and his son, primarily on the grounds that they acted out of fear of Fielding and thereby to protect themselves from him; indeed, self-preservation from a man who had already been responsible for the vicious killing of their captain and five others of their shipmates (and possibly the captain's dog, too), and seemed just as keen to exterminate all the other crew of the *Saladin*:

The Execution

Jones, Hazleton, Anderson, and Trevaskiss, were executed on the Common [in Halifax] on Tuesday, 30th June [*sic* – July], in the presence of a large concourse of people, the gallows having been erected on a hill in the rear of the Catholic Cemetery. A company of the 52nd regiment, were early on the ground, and formed a circle round the scaffold, keeping the spectators at a proper distance.

At about 10 o'clock, a.m. the prisoners arrived at the spot from whence they were to take their last look upon the world, and end their mortal career in ignominy. They were conveyed in two close carriages, from the Penitentiary, preceeded by the Sheriff in a gig, and strongly guarded by a body of the First Royals, with fixed bayonets. The Rev. Messrs. O'Brien, Connolly, and Quinan, of the Roman Catholic Church, and the Rev. Mr. Cogswell, of the Church of England, accompanied them, the first of these gentlemen being in attendance on Jones and Hazleton, and the latter, on Trevaskiss and the Swede.

The Condemned Men

The prisoners all appeared much more debilitated than when we last saw them; but their countenances wore a more placid expression. They ascended the steps of the scaffold, and took their stand upon the fatal drop, with great firmness. For some time after they ascended the scaffold, and with ropes about their necks, they were engaged in prayer, the different Clergymen appearing unremitting in their attention to these unfortunate beings in the last moments of their existence.

The Swede alone seemed at all indifferent to his awful situation. He stood perfectly erect, and gazed around on the vast assemblage, on the green fields, the blue sky, and the ocean before him – far, far beyond which dwelt those who were dear to him, whom he should never more see, and whose cheeks would mantle with shame at the degradation of their lost son. It is hard to tell what may have been the secret thoughts of that doomed boy, while standing on the verge of his own grave, with his coffin beneath his feet.

His aged parents, with their silvered locks – his brothers and sisters, who but a little while since shared his youthful joys and sorrows, may have risen up before his imagination at the moment and rendered him regardless of his real state, or, it may be, that his apparent indifference was the result of education – of the difficulties under which he laboured to understand the language of consolation addressed to him – of national pride, which prompted him to die as it became a Swede; yet his rigidity of countenance may have been a token of resignation – of reliance on the atoning blood of the Saviour for salvation. We believe he was really penitent.

It was a melancholy sight to see four young fellows, the oldest not over 23 years, close on their mortal career just as they were entering manhood, on the scaffold. Circumstances alone made them pirates and murderers. We have authority for believing that they were not habitually vicious. It is quite possible, had they not embarked on board the *Saladin* – or had never met Fielding – or knew of the existence of the wealth in that vessel, they might have escaped so ignominious an end.

The Farewell

Before the Executioner adjusted the ropes through the rings of the scaffold, and prepared them for the drop, the prisoners shook hands, and bade each other farewell, Jones kissing his comrades affectionately on the cheek. Before the caps were put on them, Jones addressed a few words to the spectators; stating that he was an Irishman, and from Clare. He expressed his deep sorrow for the deed he had committed, and hoped for pardon from God.

Hazelton and Jones handed papers to the Rev. Mr. O'Brien, containing confessions of their guilt – but alleging that they were innocent of the death of George, Fielding's son. The caps were then pulled over the features of the prisoners, and the clergymen on the scaffold took leave of them. The Rev. Messrs. O'Brien, Connolly and Quinan, knelt in prayer, when the bar which supported the drop was removed, and the unfortunate men were launched into eternity. Trevaskiss and the Swede, alone, struggled a moment, – and not violently.

The bodies after having been suspended for three quarters of an hour, were cut down. Those of Hazelton and Jones were conveyed to the Catholic Cemetery, preceded by the Clergy in attendance, and followed by a large number of people, and deposited in the little Chapel, where prayers were offered up. Those of Anderson and Trevaskiss were taken to the Poor House Burial Ground and, we believe interred.

Thus ended this melancholy and horrible tragedy. It is to be hoped that such another sad spectacle may never be presented to the eyes of our citizens again. Public executions are degrading to our nature, and demoralizing to society. Although the vast assemblage of persons who went forth to witness this execution, conducted themselves with great propriety, it was revolting to see so many

The *Saladin*: Loss of the *Saladin* – Suspected Piracy. (*The Illustrated London News*, 29 June 1844)

females present at such an exhibition. It is true, judging from their appearance, that a majority of them were of the poorest class of our population, but the moral effect is just the same, and the example equally pernicious. (*Acadian Recorder* [Halifax], *3 August 1844*)

The *Olive Pecker* Mutiny and Murders

The murder of the captain and mate on board the American three-masted schooner *Olive Pecker* off the coast of Brazil, and the subsequent burning of the vessel, in 1897, also bore marked similarities to the *Herbert Fuller* murders. Both vessels were owned by J.P. Ellicott & Co., of Boston. Capt. Whitman of the *Olive Pecker* 'was a personal friend of Capt. Nash' of the *Herbert Fuller*. Both vessels were carrying cargoes of lumber to South American ports. The *Fuller* sailed from Boston on 8 July 1896, the *Pecker* almost a year later on 27 June 1897.

In both incidents the captain and a mate were murdered (the second mate on the *Fuller*, the first mate on the *Pecker*), though the two bodies from the *Pecker* were thrown overboard while the three corpses from the *Fuller* murders were towed behind the vessel in a dinghy. And the *Pecker* murders were committed at the same time as the life of the *Fuller*'s mate Thomas Bram hung by a thread, awaiting the outcome of an appeal for a new trial.

John Andersen

The self-confessed *Pecker* murderer was the Swedish-born but American-naturalised cook-cum-steward John Andersen (who was misidentified in early reports as a 'Dane' by the name of 'Peter Thompson' or 'Thomsen'). He claimed that Capt. Whitman's severe treatment of and cruelty towards the crew of the *Olive Pecker* forced his hand by provocation to kill Whitman, and, incidentally, the mate, 'to save his own life'.

The other *Pecker* crew members later claimed it was Andersen's idea to burn the schooner in order to destroy the evidence of the crime, and escape by two boats to the north-east coast of Brazil about 120 miles away. Lots were cast to decide who would accompany Andersen in one boat while the other four went in a second boat (the five sailors 'being anxious to have the authorities here [in Bahia] believe that none of them was desirous to be Andersen's shipmate'). The lot fell to another Swede, John Lind.

As soon as the four sailors in one boat landed, near Bahia, they 'immediately went before the authorities and united in a statement regarding the crime, placing all the blame on Andersen and representing that they had no complicity in the affair'. Andersen (who later complained that the other men 'must have peached on us' [i.e. himself and Lind]) – was soon caught, admitted to his crimes, and transported back with the rest of the crew as prisoners to Norfolk, Virginia. He alone was tried and, just before Christmas 1897, convicted for killing the captain and mate, and the burning of the *Olive Pecker*.

As with Thomas Bram in the *Fuller* affair, Andersen appealed his conviction, but to no avail. Bram eventually received a 'get out of jail free' card, was released from imprisonment, and went back to a seafaring life. Andersen, for his part, almost escaped death by the sentence of hanging – and, indeed, re-hanging – but not quite.

Mutiny and Murder at Sea – A Captain and Mate Killed and Their Vessel Burned

Boston, Mass., Aug. 18. A sea tragedy which in all its horrible details will probably equal the famous *Herbert Fuller* butchery has been enacted on board another Boston vessel. What adds to the remarkable coincidence is the fact that this vessel was owned by the same firm, loaded at the same wharf, with a similar cargo, and sailed for the same port, in the same month and almost on the same day of the month a year after the sailing of the barkentine *Herbert Fuller*, and as in the latter case, the captain and mate were murdered.

Olive Pecker

The terrible affair, which resulted in the violent deaths of Captain J.W. Whitman and Mate William Saunders, occurred on the three-masted schooner *Olive Pecker*, owned by J.P. Ellicott & Co. The tragedy occurred in South American waters. On Sunday, June 27, she sailed from this port with a cargo of lumber, for Buenos Ayres, Argentina.

The intelligence of the murders and the destruction of the vessel by fire was cabled to this city this morning by a banking firm in Buenos Ayres. The crew reached Bahia, a port some distance north of the ship's destination. It is presumed from the fact of the murder that the crew mutinied, and after killing Captain Whitman and the first officer they set fire to the vessel and escaped to the shore. The supposition is that the men are under arrest. The *Pecker* must have been very near her destination when the tragedy occurred. When the intelligence reached here it spread rapidly throughout the shipping community and caused intense excitement among the shipbrokers and shipmasters.

The Crew

The crew of the *Olive Pecker* consisted of Captain J.W. Whitman, aged 44, who resided at Rockland, Me., where he leaves a widow and little girl about 12 years of age. The mate, William Saunders, 46 years old, belongs in Nova Scotia. He leaves a widow and four children. The second mate's name is William Harrisburg, 21 years old, a native of Scotland. Steward Peter Thompson [*sic* – John Andersen], a Dane [*sic* – Swedish–American], aged 43, and seaman Andrew March, a native of England, 36; Manuel Barial, a Spaniard, 33; John Lind, a native of Sweden, 27, and William Saunders of Nova Scotia, 46.

The *Olive Pecker* was a fine vessel of 823 tons net, built at Belfast, Me., in 1889 by George A. Gilchrist, and one of her principal owners is J.F. Ellicott of this city, although the captain held a large interest in the vessel. (*San Francisco Call*, 19 August 1897)

Murdered by the Steward – Captain Whitman of the Olive Pecker *Slain by a Swede Who Then Killed the Mate*

A special cable dispatch to the *Boston Globe* [newspaper] from Bahia, Brazil, regarding the *Olive Pecker* tragedy says the facts in connection with the mutiny and murder on the American schooner *Olive Pecker*, as elicited by a preliminary examination conducted by U.S. Consul McDaniel, are as follows:

The ringleader of the mutiny was John Andersen, a Swede, but naturalized American citizen, the steward of the *Olive Pecker*. Andersen claims that he killed Capt. Whitman justifiably, the harsh and overbearing conduct of his superior officer provoking him to commit the deed. Saunders, the mate, attempted to save the life of the captain, and Andersen, to save his own life, was also forced to kill the mate. The remainder of the crew do not appear to have made any attempt, or at best only a feeble one, to protect the lives of their officers.

Andersen is very reticent, and has declined to give the particulars of the captain's harsh treatment, or the particular acts which led up to the killing. After Capt. Whitman and Mate Saunders had been killed, Andersen appears to have taken complete control of the vessel and to have intimidated the five other members of the crew.

Alliance of Deception

According to their stories Andersen suggested the firing [i.e. burning] of the vessel, evidently with the hope that the fire would conceal all traces of the crime, and that it would be believed the vessel had foundered and the captain and mate had been washed overboard. The crew were to represent themselves as survivors, and to pretend they had escaped in the small boats. The vessel was accordingly fired and the crew took to the boats about 120 miles from the Brazilian coast.

They drew lots as to the way they were to divide themselves up in the two boats, the five members of the crew being anxious to have the authorities here believe that none of them was desirous to be Andersen's shipmate. The lot fell to John Lind, seaman, a Swede, the four others William Hasburgh, engineer, Juan Dios, Barriel Gumierrez, Andrew March and Martin Barstad, going to the other boat.

Ashore – The Truth Revealed

When these four men reached the Brazilian coast they immediately went before the authorities and united in a statement regarding the crime, placing all the blame on Andersen and representing that they had no complicity in the affair, but it is not quite clear why they were unable to protect the lives of their captain and mate. Andersen and Lind attempted to ship on two Norwegian vessels in Port Bahia, but a description of the men had been given to the Brazilian authorities and they were promptly arrested. When visited by the American Consul, Andersen freely admitted having killed the captain and mate, but it is believed Lind was his accomplice.

The entire crew are now prisoners in the house of correction and are being held there until the arrival of an American war vessel to convey them to the United States. No merchant steamer is willing to take the prisoners, who will be held in confinement until the government sends after them. Consul McDaniel expresses great satisfaction at the co-operation given him by the Brazilian authorities and the promptness with which they arrested the alleged murderers.

Hasburgh, the engineer, is an Englishman, Gumierrez is a Spaniard, March is an Englishman and Barstad is a Norwegian. Andersen is believed to be the only naturalized American. (*Lewiston Evening News* [Maine], 23 August 1897)

The six *Pecker* prisoners were at Bahia for about a month before being taken away 'in military confinement' by a United States warship, the cruiser *Lancaster*. John Andersen, having already confessed to the crime, was kept 'in the ship's brig, closely ironed'. They were landed at Hampton Roads, Norfolk, Virginia, early in November 1897. About a month later the District Attorney dismissed charges against the five other seamen:

> After conferring with seafaring men and learning the important position which the cook occupies on a merchant vessel, I have determined to accept the statement of these men that they were forced by John Anderson to throw the bodies of the Captain and mate overboard after he had shot them, and then to help burn the vessel, obeying his orders at the pistol's point. In a word, I have reached the conclusion that the United States would not under the circumstances be justified in prosecuting these cases. (*The New York Times*, 15 December 1897)

By this time, John Andersen had nothing to lose; he had confessed to killing the captain and mate, and to burning the *Olive Pecker* before trying to make good his escape. From his confinement at Norfolk he offered his version of events of the '*Olive Pecker* Sea Horror':

> *The U.S. Steamer Lancaster Arrives at Hampton Roads, Having Aboard the Crew Who Murdered the Captain and Mate – The Cook Relates the Story of How He Put to Death His Shipmates and Then Saturated the Vessel With Oil and Set Afire*

Newport News (Va.), Nov. 5. The United States steamer Lancaster dropped anchor in Hampton Roads this morning from Bahia, Brazil. In military confinement on the war-ship are five men of the crew of the schooner *Olive Pecker*, whose captain, J.W. Whitman of Rockland, Me., and first mate, William Saunders of Sandy Cove, N.S., were murdered at sea in August. In the ship's brig, closely ironed, is J. Anderson, the cook, who is the self-confessed perpetrator of the murders, and who afterwards set fire to the vessel.

The *Pecker* sailed from Boston on the 27th of June, and the story of this tragedy of the sea is told best in the words of the murderer, who to-night gave to the Associated Press the following version of his crime:

The Cook's Story
'I was the cook aboard the *Olive Pecker*, and had to serve the captain as his servant. I had good reason to believe that the captain did not take to me, and I was always in fear of my life, whenever he got into his mad fits. He had a dog which was always coming into the cook house and annoying us. On the day of our little difficulty, the animal came inside, and I threw a boiler of hot water on him.

'Well, he howled, and the next thing I knew the captain was calling for me. I went to his cabin and he commenced cursing me, telling me that this sort of thing had to stop. I did not say anything to him, and he ordered me into his cabin to make up his bed. This was in the morning.

'I made up his bed, and he ordered me out with a volley of oaths. I saw he was in a mean humor and determined to arm myself against him. I knew the captain had some pistols in his cabin, and I went back to get one of them. Just as soon as I entered the captain fired a beer bottle at me, and, seeing that I dodged it, he picked up a pistol from the table and sent a ball in my direction. I had got my hands on a weapon which was lying on the corner of his table and of course I opened fire on the --- rascal. My first bullet took effect in his forehead, and the second went into his breast, killing him almost instantly.

'I then went upon the deck and called to the mate, who was in the fore rigging. He shouted down to me, asking what I wanted. I told him to come down; that the captain wanted him in the cabin. He started down and when he reached the deck I went for him. He was an old fellow with whiskers and I felt like smashing him with my fist. He looked at me as if to inquire my authority to order him about, and I levelled the weapon at his old bewhiskered head, saying at the time, "Now, die like the dog you are." With that I pulled the trigger, and the mate dropped to the deck, rolling to the port side of the ship.

'I then went down into the cabin, thinking I would be able to take the ship by myself. I saw that the Captain was a ghost, and I came on deck. The mate was groaning, and I felt it my duty to put him out of misery. One more shot did that.

'I secured the Captain's other pistol, and after giving the mate a second bullet, I started toward the crew who were aft, with a pistol in each hand, and gave them to understand that I was to be master of the *Olive Pecker*, and that the first man who undertook to disobey my orders would have to suffer the consequences. They carried out my commands without a murmur.

'I first ordered them to throw the mate's body overboard, and we went down into the cabin and brought up the Captain's corpse, disposing of it in like manner. Next I ordered the men to get out the oil and saturate the whole vessel fore and aft in such a manner that she would burn up like h-ll. They did that, and then we got our belongings and prepared to take the boats, first setting fire to the ship.

'My chum and I went down in one of the boats, while the other four men took the other. They pulled off in different directions from us, and we never saw them again until we met in prison in Bahia. They must have peached [grassed, informed] on us, for no sooner had we landed from the ship than the officers placed us under arrest and sent us to Bahia.' (*Sacramento Daily Union* [California], 6 November 1897)

John Andersen's trial at Norfolk for the murder of mate Saunders and Capt. Whitman, and for the burning of the *Olive Pecker*, began on 20 December 1897. The testimonies of the *Pecker*'s crew members contradicted Andersen's version of events that he offered to the court on cross-examination on the second day of proceedings:

Schooner Olive Pecker Tragedy – Trial of John Anderson for the Murder of Mate Saunders

Norfolk (Va.), Dec. 20. The trial of John Anderson, cook of the schooner *Olive Pecker*, for the murder of mate William Wallace Saunders on the high seas in August last, was begun in the Federal Court to-day. Anderson is also under indictment for the murder of Captain Whitman and the burning of the schooner. Attorney McIntosh, for the accused, in outlining the defense, stated that he would show that Anderson had been subjected to unheard of cruelties, and that the murders were committed in self-defense.

Barstad's Testimony
Martin Barstad, a Norwegian, a member of the schooner's crew, was called to the stand as the first eye-witness to the

terrible tragedy that will go down as one of the most dramatic and remarkable of modern times. Barstad testified that he was at the wheel during the whole affair. He saw Anderson throw water on the Captain's dog on the morning of August 6th, the day of the crime; then he heard the Captain curse Anderson, after which followed a noise as of some one falling. He had supposed the Captain had struck Anderson, who came up and asked the mate to protect him. The mate said: 'Go to ---, you've got to die anyway.'

Shortly after this Anderson came out of the Captain's cabin and called the mate down out of the rigging, and shot him four times. He summoned all hands, and made them throw the body overboard. Then he made them go down into the cabin and get the body of the Captain and throw that overboard, after which he took the crew down into the Captain's cabin and gave them whisky.

The story of the burning of the vessel under Anderson's orders, and the voyage to land in the small boats, varied little from the published accounts.

Lind's Testimony

John Lind was called to the stand and told essentially the same story as Barstad, except that he did not see Anderson shoot the mate. Anderson came up to him and told him that he had killed the Captain, and that the mate had to go, too. The witness then went and called the watch, and while he was doing this, he heard three or four shots on the other side of the vessel. Witness helped to throw the bodies overboard, and Anderson, he said, cursed the dead body of the mate. He could not state what language he used.

Speaking of the whisky Anderson gave the crew, Lind said it was only half a bottle, and no one was drunk. The Captain and mate were dead when thrown overboard. Anderson fired three shots when the small boat left the burning schooner, though why he did so witness could not say.

Lind told how the crew drew lots to see who should go together, and his lot fell with that of Anderson. He said Anderson shot the dog which came ashore in the boat, and on the way to Belmont sold the Captain's watch. Upon cross-examination Lind said he heard Anderson, prior to the killing, ask the mate to protect him from the Captain, and he heard the mate tell Anderson to 'go to --- ; you will be dead, anyway.' Anderson that morning had thrown water on the Captain's dog; the Captain cursed him in the 'worst language he had ever heard,' and then 'made for him,' after which Lind heard a noise as of some one falling, and presently Anderson came out of the galley and asked the mate to protect him.

Andrew March, another of the schooner's crew, testified that he did not see the killing of the mate, but heard Anderson say he had killed him. Witness was in his bunk at the time, and heard Anderson call the mate down from aloft. He heard the conversation between Anderson and the mate, and heard four shots, after which Anderson said, 'Come out here, boys, and lower a boat and put me ashore. The Captain and mate are dead, and I am in charge of the ship.'

On cross-examination, March's testimony was not shaken.

Juan De Dios Barrial did not see the shooting, but heard the shots. His story varied essentially from those of his mates. Referring to his conversation with Anderson after the tragedy, Barrial said Anderson took him aside and told him that he (Anderson) was a murderer, but that he had killed the Captain and Mate to save their lives, and before they left the vessel they would all be just as guilty as he (Anderson). Barrial said he urged the cook not to burn the schooner.

William Horstborough, another seaman, was the last witness examined. His story did not differ materially from the others and when he had concluded his testimony court adjourned until 10 o'clock to-morrow. (*Sacramento Daily Union* [California], 21 December 1897)

Since Andersen had confessed to the crimes of which he was accused, a verdict of guilty, handed down by the jury two days before Christmas 1897, was hardly surprising. The surprises came at his execution a year later:

Guilty As Charged – John Anderson Will Hang for the Murder of Mate Saunders
Norfolk (Va.), Dec. 23. 'We, the jury, find the prisoner, John Anderson, alias John Andersen, guilty as charged in the indictment.'

This is the verdict returned in the famous *Olive Pecker* case, the specific charge being the murder of Mate Saunders of the schooner *Olive Pecker*, preferred by the cook. As the case stands, Anderson will have to hang. He received the verdict with apparent indifference. His counsel made a motion for a new trial. (*Sacramento Daily Union* [California], 24 December 1897)

After the jury convicted Andersen, for which the sentence was death by hanging, his counsel made several appeals to the Supreme Court to overturn the verdict on the grounds of unconstitutional procedure. In mid-November 1898 the Supreme Court dismissed Andersen's final appeal; it scheduled him to be executed on 9 December 1898. On the day, however, the event did not go quite to plan.

Hangman's Rope Was Weak – Broke When the Trap Was Sprung Under Cook Andersen of the Schooner Olive Pecker Norfolk, Va., Dec. 9. John Andersen, the condemned murderer of Mate Saunders of the schooner *Olive Pecker*, was executed in the city jail this afternoon. At 3:06 the trap was sprung and Andersen shot downward. The rope parted just inside the knot and his body fell to the cobblestones. A thrill of horror ran through the crowd. Officers and witnesses rushed to the body and snatched the cap from his head to find blood oozing from mouth, nose, and eyes. A doctor was called, and soon Andersen opened his eyes, and it was said began to breathe. He was carried, feet foremost, up the stairs to the platform, and laid down until a chair was obtained. He was then placed in this, but never spoke.

Preparations for rehanging him were hurriedly made. The other end of the rope was adjusted around his neck. He was raised to a standing posture and the straps again placed on his limbs. While being supported by the officers, the trap was again sprung. In twenty-three minutes life was pronounced extinct. Nine minutes elapsed between the first and second drops. Andersen's neck was broken, supposedly by the last drop. Marshall Treat refused to turn the body over to the Virginia Anatomical Society, and it was placed in a handsome casket and buried in the Seamen's Lot in Elmwood Cemetery. When the rope broke, there was a cry from some one in the crowd, 'Telegraph to the President!' (*The New York Times*, 10 December 1898)

The *Anna* Murders on the High Seas

Seafaring in the nineteenth century was fraught with perils not only of the sea but of cruelties meted out by seamen on board ships, as well as by local peoples in wild places that vessels touched at or passed or were wrecked upon. Fortune – good, ill or indifferent – determined how sailing ship crews were treated by their officers. A harsh captain or vicious bully mate could wreak havoc, even death, amongst seamen, and often for the slightest of provocations, or, indeed, none at all.

Barbaric cruelty by the two mates Edmund Lane and George Hires on the American barque *Anna* that caused the death of four seamen was described by *The New York Times* as 'a case of brutality and inhumanity seldom equaled in the annals of sea-murders'. The four murdered seamen were all 'coloured'. The atrocities happened in 1859–60, just before the abolition of slavery in the United States:

Alleged Atrocious Murder at Sea

The first and second mates of the American barque *Anne* [*sic* – *Anna*], New York, have been brought this week before the magistrates for the Isle of Wight, on the infor-mation of John Thomas and Abraham Rock, seamen on board the vessel, on a charge of having murdered John Turtle and several other seamen during the voyage from Laguna [probably in British Honduras then, now Belize] to England. The information of the dreadful circumstance was communicated to the police on the vessel arriving at Cowes.

The names of the mates are Edmund Lane and George Hires.

It appears that the vessel first sailed from New York to Mobile [Alabama], in June last, with a crew consisting of eight men, besides captain and officers, and they included John Turtle, a man known on board as Frank, William Johnson, David Pagins, James Armstrong, and William Pomery, who are now dead.

Atrocities

It was alleged that at Mobile, Lane struck Armstrong on the right eye with a mallet, felled him from the forecastle to the main deck, and knocked out his eye. He was then sent by Hires to do something to an 'earring' [small rope] under the bowsprit, but being unable he was dragged along in the water until Abraham Rock went to his assistance, when Lane exclaimed, 'Don't hand that n****r in! Cut the earring and let him go!' In two minutes after Armstrong let go his hold and was lost.

The ship sailed from Mobile to Laguna in South America, and from thence to Cowes. On the voyage Hires accused Turtle of stealing rum from his cabin, and as he was obeying one of the mate's orders, Hires caught him by his head, hauled him down upon the deck, stamped on his head, and kicked him with his heavy sea boots. Turtle's head and eyes were observed to be bleeding, and he went to his berth.

Hires said to a seaman (Thomas), 'Tell him if he don't come out and get on the pump I'll murder him.' The unfortunate man's reply was, 'I can't get up if they kill me.' Hires went up to him, pulled him out of the bunk by his ears, threw him down in the forecastle, and stamped upon him heavily. He was laid by Thomas in the forecastle. In a few minutes Hires said, 'Tom, is that old n****r dead yet?' He was then dying, and expired the same evening. His body was sewn up, and thrown overboard two days afterwards. While the body was being sewn up it was observed that the bone of the forehead was broken in the centre.

The same morning a scuffle was heard in the sail-room; it proved to be Hires holding Johnston down on the tool-chest, with both hands to his throat, choking him. There was blood issuing from his mouth, and he died at six o'clock the same day. He said, previously to his death, 'Jack, I feel very bad, and am dying, the mate has choked me to death.' His tongue was hanging out of his mouth.

The man Frank died about seven days before the arrival of the vessel at Cowes, having been severely beaten by the chief mate, who said, while the man was at the wheel, 'If you steer a quarter of a point [i.e. a few degrees] off your course I'll murder you.' Directly after Lane struck him on the head with a belaying pin. This took place off the Start Point. The man cried, 'Murder!' twice, said, 'Oh, God!' several times, and called once for the captain. The sufferers were men of color. The prisoners have been remanded. (*Wellington Independent* [New Zealand], 24 April 1860)

Lane and Hires were hauled before magistrates at the *Anna*'s destination port, Cowes, on the Isle of Wight. The magistrates' decision to discharge the men, in January 1860, was roundly condemned by the general public:

The Wholesale Murders at Sea

At Newport [Isle of Wight], on Saturday, the 14th inst., Edmund Lane and Gordon Hires, first and second mates of the American barque *Anna*, charged with the murder of four coloured seamen, were discharged on objection being taken to the jurisdiction of the magistrates, the offences not having been committed within the British waters. The Guildhall was crowded, and the decision was received with a storm of hisses, hootings, groans, cries of 'Hang 'em,' and every possible mark of disapprobation.

The United States Consul at Southampton, applied for assistance in detaining the prisoners until he had made an investigation, but the magistrates said they had no power to grant his application. The accused were free, and all the Magistrates could do was to give them the protection of the police back to their ship. They ruled also, that the witnesses who deposed to the murders, two of them men of colour, must return to the ship, but would be protected so long as it lay in British waters; a most inhumane decision, and we cannot think a legal one. (*The Tablet* [British Catholic weekly], 21 January 1860)

Trial and Condemnation

The two men were subsequently handed over to the American Consul at Southampton, which shipped them back to the United States for trial. In mid-March 1860 they arrived in New York where:

> Deputy-Marshal O'Keefe took charge of the prisoners, and brought them to the office of the United States District-Attorney, where complaints were formally laid, and they were committed to await examination. The testimony, which was lengthy, appeared in the London papers, and as recited presents a case of brutality and inhumanity seldom equaled in the annals of sea-murders. (*The New York Times*, 22 March 1860)

First mate Lane and second mate Hires were indicted and tried separately in the United States Circuit Court of New York, in early 1861, for killing the 'coloured' seamen on board the *Anna*. Hires was convicted of the manslaughter killing of one of the crew. The master of the *Anna*, Capt. Edgar M. Tuthill, was additionally indicted for the crime. He and Lane were subsequently acquitted.

2

MASSACRES IN THE SOUTH SEAS

For seafarers in sailing ship times, uncharted reefs, mis-charted islands, erratic currents and hurricane-force storms were routine perils anywhere. But in the central and western Pacific, the islands of the 'South Seas' were often treacher-ous places for seamen, white traders and missionaries who ventured amongst their inhabitants of un-Christian 'hea-then' and 'savages'. And some were cannibals. When the white man – merchant, evangelist or simple sailor – touched upon those shores, their intrusion could often flash with bloodshed, mayhem, mass murder and human butchery – and not always by the 'heathen'.

Islanders in the Western Pacific were to varying degrees feared by white seafarers for their reputation as 'savages'. Some waged war against other tribes, and against the white man who was, to them, just another tribe, as part of their culture, or simply to protect themselves, their territory and their homeland. For whatever reasons, their infamous reputation as 'heathen savages' was tolerated by the white Christians traders and proselytisers who profited from them,

LEVUKA, LOOKING SOUTH.

BUSH NEAR LEVUKA.

MATANITOBUD CANNIBAL.

KING'S DAUGHTER AND LOUISA.

ROKO TONGAU.

A PLANTER'S RESIDENCE.

CAPTAIN SEWELL'S PLANTATION, LOMA LOMA.

The Feejee Islands. (*Harper's Weekly*, 13 February 1875)

or whose mission was to Christianise them. Inevitably, though, contacts could be, and quite regularly were, bloody.

The white man's imperative amongst the South Seas, as elsewhere, was to dominate, for cash or Christianity: exploitation, subjugation, and evangelisation in the clarion call of Civilisation. The often aggressive response of the 'savage' was in the interests of preserving and protecting their territory, culture or tradition and, as often as not, for revenge. Consider the comments of a New Zealand news report after the murder of Bishop Pattern, bishop of Melanesia (and another white minister, plus 'a native teacher'), by New Hebridean islanders in 1871: 'There is no doubt that the murder has been caused by the exasperation of the islanders through the visit of labor vessels which are reported to be engaged in kidnapping at the various islands, and sometimes taking women.' (*The Timaru Herald*, 4 November 1871)

Savagery on both sides, however, was always a possibility, the one triggered by and feeding on the fears of the other.

The New Hebrides

The New Hebrides archipelago was one of the better places to cruise to recruit labour, and trade in barter and the Christianisation of savage souls in the latter half of the nineteenth century. But it was fraught with danger: cannibalism was common on some islands; the possibility of heathen–Christian confrontation, with bloodshed and butchery, was never far from the realms of reality.

Capture of the Schooner Fanny: *Massacre of Her Crew*
The attack upon and massacre of the crew of the schooner *Fanny*, in 1871, was apparently, it was said, a terrible act of vengeance by the Hebrideans for the abduction of some island women by white sailors some time before. A newspaper report concluded, 'As far as can be gathered from the statements made by the natives, this is one of those

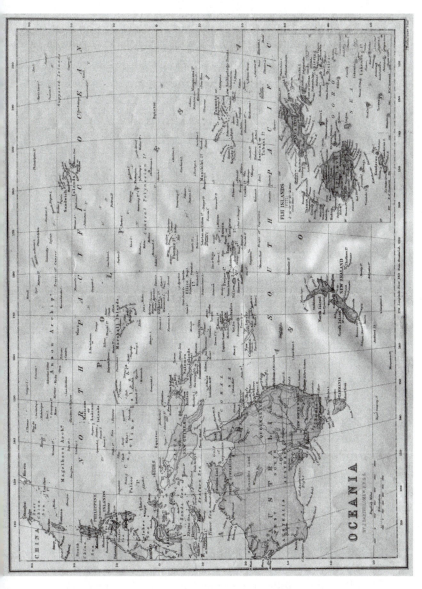

Oceania (1881).

attacks which has arisen from bad conduct on the part of former labor vessels' (*Wellington* [New Zealand] *Independent*, 26 September 1871). Of the *Fanny*'s six crew, only her master, Capt. Bartlett, survived the slaughter:

Capture of the Schooner Fanny, *and Massacre of Her Crew by Natives of the Sandwich Islands [New Hebrides]*

We have been favoured (says the *Fiji Times* of the 5th instant) with the following particulars of a dreadful tragedy, by a gentleman who accompanied the Strathnaver in her recent labour cruise:

July 19 – Went with three boys in boat to Gunu [Nguna] Island, and noticed the masts of a ship, and on approaching saw a small vessel on a reef, heeled over in shore. She appeared deserted, the sails remaining bent [i.e. set], and some of her gear seemed to be cut away. As we approached her the boys observed numbers of natives on shore, who, from their actions, appeared either afraid or else to be playing false.

Presently some teachers appeared; and so, thinking it quite safe, the white men landed. The teachers were Rarotongans [from the Cook Islands], and could not understand English, but, as there were some who understood Fijian, he asked them, 'Where is the ship from?' They replied, 'Fiji.' 'And the crew?' No answer. 'Where are the crew?' he again asked of a Fijian-speaking man. 'Sa moku saka.' ('They are murdered, sir.'). The teachers were anxious for them to go to their house, and, telling the boys to take the boat out into deep water, he went. He gleaned the following particulars respecting the *Fanny*.

The Fanny

She had arrived and anchored at the little island of Ekpeli, ten nights back, and had landed some return labour from Kadavu [the fourth largest island in the Fiji Archipelago]. Her crew consisted of Mr. Bartlett, master; Alick (surname unknown), mate; Jem, a seaman; Levi and Sinaquali, Fijians; and Tommy, either a half-caste or ocean Islander [from Ocean Island, now Banaba, in Kiribati], and a Mau man [Samoan (?)].

Upon the morning after the *Fanny*'s arrival (i.e. the 11th), a number of natives came to the beach and made signals to the vessel for them to come on shore. The master, Mau man, and one Fijian went ashore, and met a body of Niuta people (tribe of the hill land of Gunu), who told them that seven men wanted to go to Fiji as labourers. They were accordingly taken on board, the master being asked to come ashore further down the coast where [there] were more men who wanted to go to Fiji.

Each of the seven men took long-handled tomahawks with him when he went on board. Jem was the only one who noticed this circumstance, and he told the Mau man to tell them to put them away. The man said in reply that 'they had killed a chief of Ekpeli, and were afraid to stay so near the beach of that island.' This did not satisfy Jem, who told the Mau man to listen to their conversation, and 'if you hear them talk bad, tell me.'

The master, instead of returning to the town they had indicated, sent Jem into the boat with two natives who had accompanied him (the master), and went and lay down in his berth, as he had a bad headache, and fell into a doze, Alick and two of the native crew remaining on deck.

Brutal Attack

About noon the captain was aroused by cries on deck, and at the same time the mate rushed into the cabin, crying, 'Oh! oh!' and holding his hand to his jaw, which was nearly severed from his head. Seizing two loaded revolvers, the master tried to rush on deck, but Alick pulled him back, and the Niuta men having killed Tommy, and severely wounded Levi, who fled into the hold, rushed back, and sliding the top of the cabin over, stood upon and around it, waiting to tomahawk the master if he should succeed in getting out. Others, with a heavy American axe, cut the cable [anchor cable], and the vessel drifted towards the shore of Gunu.

The master tried to force the hatch back, to cut through it with an axe, and then twice attempted to blow it up, but without avail. As a last desperate effort, he emptied several pounds of powder upon the cabin table, in hope to raise the whole deck, laid Alick upon the cabin floor out of the way, stooped with a pistol in hand to fire it, when the vessel suddenly heeled over to starboard on the reef.

A yell of triumph arose from the savage fiends, who thronged the beach, as they now thought the prey was in their hands. She could be fired into from the shore at a distance of thirty yards, with security to the natives. The master now bound Alick's jaw, the Niuta men keeping up a brisk fire upon the vessel until night brought a respite.

The position of the two men was indeed pitiable – their vessel stranded, the crew murdered, one of themselves badly wounded, and without a boat, and the shore swarming with wretches who thirsted for their lives.

With morning light came a renewal of hostilities, the natives again keeping up an incessant fire: occasionally the master had an opportunity of replying. Night again brought a cessation of hostilities; and the two men determined to quit the vessel, in hopes of getting to the mission station, where they expected to get some assistance for Alick's wounds.

All the powder and ammunition was thrown into the water; and leaving the trade and Tommy's dead body, they went on shore. They reached the mission station, where the teachers were in a great state of fear and perplexity, as they were without the presence of the white missionary, who was away at the time. They gave Alick water with which to bathe his wounds, and they provided the two white men with food that they might lie hiding in the bush.

Escape

Let us see how the boat fared. After leaving the vessel she pulled down to the town the master had desired to visit, where was a great crowd of Niuta men, who wanted Jem to come ashore. This he declined to do, but threw the kellick [anchor] overboard, so as to keep the boat out of reach of the natives. A chief of Niuta now began to refer to some women who had been stolen from his tribe and never returned; and complained that the men returned yesterday were badly paid. These words were followed by a volley of musketry (at which signal the attack on the ship was made).

Siniquali was shot through the breast and jumped overboard, followed by the Mau man, who from fright, probably, swam ashore. Wata, a young chief, walked out into the water, took him by the wrist, and begged his life. The last this man knew of Jem, he remembered in a confused way was seeing him cut the warp, and endeavoured to pull from shore. The firing on the boat was kept up after the Mau man had been taken into the house. Doubtless Jem was wounded, and the boat was a leaky one and had probably swamped and drifted away with the currents.

Gruesome Aftermath

Our informant then proceeded to the vessel, and found her gutted to the stone ballast, and pitted with bullets. There were blood stains about the vessel, and in the hold a fearful stench. The cause of this was soon manifest, for on looking over the vessel's side, in about eighteen inches of water, was a sail rolled up, with a heap of stones upon it; and the fatty scum which rose from it, as well as the guilty looks of the natives, only told too plainly what lay hidden there.

Going ashore again he found the teachers, who had prepared food, and appeared anxious to communicate something. He told them that a 'white chief did not eat while a lot of people watched him,' and they went out leaving one teacher with him. When they had left, the teacher said 'cap'n no dead, bye and bye night you come take him ship.' Some natives threw ballast out of the ship, and a warp was taken out so as to float her off on high tide. Returned to Strathnaver for more arms, as the natives were mustering on the beach.

Returned after dinner, when a ship's boat from Havannah harbour [on Sandwich Island, also called Vate, now Efate Island, the main island of the Hebrides group] hove in sight, with some settlers on board. They reported seeing the body of a white man lashed to a pole, and standing head downwards on the bench. The Niuta natives had brought the body down for the purpose of throwing it into the sea, but seeing the white men, had run away, leaving it behind them.

5 p.m. – Floated the vessel, and took her to the Strathnaver.

9 p.m. – Went ashore, and found the master in the teacher's house. Alick had been found by the savages three days previously, walking in the bush; they had seized him, and whilst he begged piteously for life had shot him. Every

praise is due to the teachers for their conduct in this affair, and to them Bartlett owes his life and safety.

20th July. Recovered body of white man lashed to pole, and buried it. Got back from natives, rope, sails, compasses, telescopes, and sextant, and returned on board. Bartlett went on board the *Fanny*, and with assistance of people from ship's boat, proceeded to Havannah harbour to get a crew to bring her on to Fiji. At the mouth of the harbour, the Strathnaver parted company, shaping her course for Fiji. (*The Maitland and Mercury & Hunter River General Advertiser* [New South Wales, Australia], 29 August 1871)

The Solomon Islands

Stretching to the south-east of the Bismarck Archipelago of New Britain, New Ireland and other smaller islands off the east coast of New Guinea, the Solomon Islands of San Christoval, what was then called Guadalcanar (now Guadalcanal), Rubiana (New Georgia), Rendova and Malaita were rich hunting grounds for the exchange and sale of trade goods including coconuts, copra, tortoiseshell, bêche-de-mer – and islanders for labour. The Solomons were also notorious for the number of attacks by islanders on trading schooners' crews that often left a blood trail of carnage in their wake. Although attacks *seemed* unprovoked, in many cases they were probably revenge for a previous indiscretion, or worse, by earlier white intruders, especially by labour recruitment vessels' crews.

Horrible Tragedy on the Marion Renny

Towards the end of 1870 the trading schooner *Marion* (or *Marian*) *Renny*, 56 tons, put out from the main Fijian port town of Levuka to sail for the Line Islands on a trading

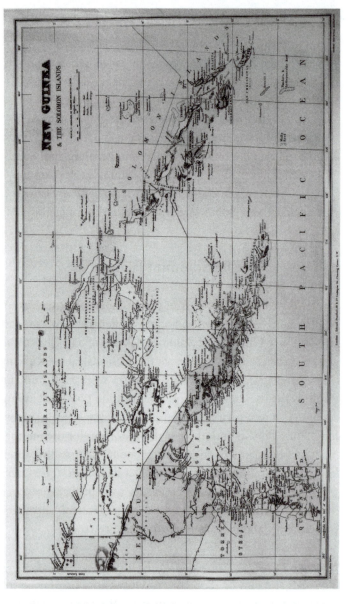

New Guinea & The Solomon Islands. (*Edward Stanford*, London (1896))

voyage. Her master was Mr Rae, a long-time resident of Levuka. The *Renny*'s crew comprised four white men, including a man named Diehl as mate, six Fijian 'boys' from Rotumah, another four Fijians, and a 'Sandwich man' from the New Hebrides island of that name (now Efate, or Vate).

At Anuta Island, at the south-eastern extremity of the Solomons, on 23 December, an attack by islanders apparently killed Capt. Rae, the Rotumah boys and the 'Sandwich man' as they ventured ashore (apparently no one witnessed the actual killing). Diehl, the mate, and Bill, one of the white crew, were despatched by islanders who had got on board the *Renny* herself.

The only two remaining white men on the homeward voyage were a man named Charlie, who had been 'severely wounded' by the Anuta attack, and the steward. The steward was shot and killed by Charlie, who was then bundled overboard by the remaining Fijian crew. In all, nine of the *Renny*'s crew were killed one way or another during the voyage. Four Fijians were the only survivors:

Horrible Tragedy On Board the Marion Renny
– Murder of Nine Persons

It seems reserved for Fiji to furnish the rest of the world with details of tragedies on the sea, exciting and horrible enough for the plot of a sixpenny romance. The America, ketch, arrived here from Loma Loma [Lau Archipelago, Fiji] last Monday, and brought news that the schooner *Marion Renny* had reached that port, brought back by four Fijians, the only survivors of a numerous crew. The following are the particulars of the death of the master, white crew, and Rotumah boys.

The *Marion Renny* (which vessel has twice before lost the whole or portion of her crew by massacre in the South Seas) left Levuka in November last for a trading voyage among the Line islands; she was commanded by Mr. Rae, an old Fijian resident and island trader, and partner in the firm of F.W. Hennings and Rae, of Levuka. Mr. Diehl was mate, and she carried a crew of three white men, six Rotumah boys, one Sandwich man, and four Fijians.

After visiting several ports in Fiji, the vessel left the group and called at Rotumah, where she stayed several days, and then (by the natives' account) steered west for six days and anchored at an island. The 'log' shows this to be Cherry or Anouda Island, 11°35'S, 170°E [Anuta, in the Solomon Islands]. The last entry records bringing up on the 22nd of December. Anouda Island is between Santa Cruz and Banks Group. A message was brought on board that there were plenty of men willing to leave the island.

Attack

On the following morning Mr. Rae, four Rotumah boys, and one Sandwich man went ashore in the longboat. As Mr. Rae was getting over the side the mate asked him if 'he had not better take his revolver'; his reply was, 'Oh, no, I have been here before, they all know me.'

As Rae left the schooner, two canoes, each carrying about a dozen men, put off from the shore, and subsequent events show that the massacre was premeditated and planned only too well – the Fijians state that on reaching the shore (quarter mile distant), Rae and the boat's crew went over the sandy hillocks into a scrub, and a number of natives ran down the bank again and pushed off the boat, some of them even going up to their armpits to send her off shore; at the same time an attack was made on those on board by the natives who had come off in the canoes.

Atrocity and Mayhem

The crew were totally unprepared. The mate was killed in the deckhouse, and a white man named Bill had his head cut off by an axe, and the others were wounded frightfully. The steward got a loaded gun, and a Fijian and the surviving white man fired all together, but killed nobody. It had the effect of frightening the assailants, who jumped overboard. The rest of the crew tried to weigh the anchor, but were not able, so slipped the cable; the longboat was hauled up by the natives on shore.

The mate, Mr. Diehl, and the white man, Bill, were buried at sea the next day. There now remained the steward and Charley (both wounded, the former slightly and the latter severely) and four Fijians.

Now comes the most horrible and mysterious part of the tragedy.

The natives say that the two whites quarrelled about something; the cause of their falling-out they do not know, but it was not liquor; both appear to have drunk nothing but water. The steward took the deckhouse and Charley lived in the cabin. This Charley was from Sydney, and worked with a barber in King-street; he arrived in Levuka about April last, worked at his trade for some time in the Criterion Hotel, went to the New Hebrides in the Zephyr for a trip, and then shipped in the *Marion Renny*. His name was Charles Robey.

More Murder

He stayed in the cabin four or five days, eating nothing, but sipping water from a teaspoon. On the morning of the fifth or sixth day he went on deck, and patted the Fijian at the wheel on the back, saying, 'Sa vinaka ko-iko' ('You're a good man.'). He then walked forward and deliberately shot the steward dead with a revolver, which he fired through the window of the deckhouse. Then he turned and fired at the man at the wheel, and missed him.

The Fijian immediately rushed at and bored him to the deck, calling on his countrymen for assistance; they took the revolver from Robey, who must have gone mad, and held a consultation as to what they should do, and came to the conclusion that as he was beyond hope of recovery, and the wounds on his head and different parts of his body were mortifying [going gangrenous], and their own lives were in danger, their best plan was to ensure their own safety by throwing him overboard. They therefore consigned the unhappy wretch to the water.

As they had steered west from Rotumah, they now went in the opposite direction, and kept the ship's head to the rising sun each morning, and guessed east during the rest of the day and night. The first land they sighted was Vanua Levu (Fiji), which they mistook for Tanna [an island in the New Hebrides], and prepared themselves to resist any attack from natives of that island; they went through Nanuka Passage, and sighted Naitamba [Naitauba], which one of the Fijians recognised being a native of the island, from thence he piloted the vessel to Loma Loma.

During the homeward passage they encountered heavy weather, but the men were well acquainted with a ship, having been with whites some years. Native account agrees with the entry in the log as they said they were thirty days out. Three Cherry Island [near the New Hebrides] natives were killed in the struggle on board. There is a belief in Levuka that Rae still lives, as the natives did not see him actually murdered, but there can scarcely be any probability of his being alive as the two attacks were simultaneous.

Mr. Hennings has made arrangements for the ketch Wild Duck to proceed to the island and ascertain his fate, and it is highly probable that the massacre will be amply avenged. Mr. Rae was not married, and leaves no relatives in Fiji. He has made several trips to the islands and was universally liked. (*The Sydney Morning Herald*, 24 February 1871)

Motive

The question later asked about the Solomon islanders' attack on the *Marion Renny* crew was, what was the reason for such an apparently unprovoked bloodbath? A speculative answer came from a letter to *The Argus* newspaper, of Melbourne, published on 28 February 1871:

Sir, – I have read with painful interest the account of the [*Marion Renny*] massacre, which was copied in your issue of to-day from the Fiji Times. Many of your readers will be inclined to ask what reason there could have been for the outrage. Is it accounted for by the natural 'blood-thirstiness' of the natives? I have seen a good deal of the natives of several groups of islands in the South Pacific, and I answer, no – it is not thus to be accounted for.

The cruelty of South Sea Island natives towards crews of vessels is almost always – always, as far as I have been able to ascertain – in retaliation for cruelty first practiced by white men upon them. They are not careful to execute vengeance upon the individuals who maltreated them. It is enough that white men committed the injury, and that they retaliate on white men. Generally those on board the next vessel which calls suffer for the actions of those who have preceded them.

I feel almost certain that, were the facts known, the massacre of the crew of the *Marion Renny* would be found to be an act of retaliation. The vessel might have been taken, and property stolen, had cupidity incited the natives to the deed. But a desire for vengeance seems to have been their only feeling.

I have recently visited in the [vessel] *John Williams* some islands near the equator, where the people are in a most savage state. On three of these islands we found them armed to take vengeance upon us for cruel treatment which they had received from the crew of a 'labour vessel,' a few months before. We only escaped by having on board our vessel some people belonging to the island who had been on Christian islands, and who explained the difference between 'labour vessels' and the missionary ship. As soon as this difference was known, we were well received. (S.J. Whitmee,* of the London Missionary Society, Castlemaine, Feb. 25)

Massacre at the Florida Islands – The Lavinia

The *Lavinia* was another trading schooner that, like the *Marion Renny*, traded merchandise and transported labour in and around the New Hebrides, Solomons, Fiji Islands and other island groups thereabouts. In May 1872 the *Lavinia*

---

* Samuel James (S.J.) Whitmee (1838–1925) was a missionary who first went to Samoa in 1863. Upon a return sojourn there in later years he became close friends with Robert Louis Stevenson. In 1870 he visited 'Tokelau and the Gilbert & Ellice Islands' – the Line Islands, above – on the mission vessel *John Williams*.

was at one of the Florida Islands (Nggela Islands) between Guadalcanal and Malaita in the Solomons. While her captain was off in the vessel's boat, islanders boarded the schooner and attacked the crew. What met Capt. Brodie's eyes upon his return 'was one of the most horrible sights imaginable'.

Massacre at the Florida Islands – The Lavinia

The schooner *Lavinia* arrived in port on Saturday morning from the Solomon Islands. During her cruise among the group a terrible catastrophe occurred to a number of her crew, instigated no doubt by the outrages that have been committed on the natives by vessels in search of labourers. The following particulars of what may be termed a massacre are taken from the log of the *Lavinia*, and have been furnished to us by Captain Brodie:

'On the 26th of April we anchored in a small bight at the eastern end of the Florida Islands. We fished there for 10 days very successfully – the chief Domo rendering his assistance in keeping order among the natives ashore. It was by his advice that we shifted round to Moboli harbour, about four miles from where we then were.

'On Monday, the 6th of May, we arrived at Moboli, and got our houses up, ready for curing beche de mer. The natives at that place indicated treachery; for not one of them could move without having all his war implements with him, which is a very unusual thing. I told my crew to be very cautious while we were here, and if there was any danger to come on board at once. I also told the people on board, if ever I went away, to allow no natives to come on board.

'On Wednesday, 8th, we loaded the large guns and got other firearms in readiness in case of an attack, as from appearances the natives on shore meant mischief.

'Thursday, 9th. – The shore party went away as usual, and as the mate did not come off to breakfast, about half-past 8 a.m. I sent the boat with one hand to bring him off, and expressly told him to come along with the mate, which he did not do. As soon as I saw that he did not come off, I sent two hands in the whaleboat, and ordered them to fetch him off. As soon as the mate came alongside he began laughing, and asked me what was the matter. I told him that I did not consider that we were safe at this place, but he laughed at the idea of danger; when the natives on shore saw that we were all on board the schooner, and had left everything on shore, they began to disperse. About 11 o'clock we went ashore again and continued our work, everything passing off quietly.

'Friday, 10th. – Everything looking very quiet on shore and not many natives about. After we had our breakfast I told Louis Nixon and five of our natives to get into the whaleboat, as I was going away to look for another harbour; before getting into the boat I particularly told the three men on board the schooner to allow no natives on board.

'We started with a fine breeze right aft. After we got away about four miles, the wind began to freshen into a stiff breeze, and I began to be afraid, if we went away any further, that the natives would not be able to pull back, so I turned round and made for the schooner. When we got about 600 yards from the vessel, we heard a shriek, and, looking towards the shore, we saw a native swimming off to the boat. We pulled towards him, and, to our surprise, found him to be one of our own men, and from what we could make out of him, and seeing no movements on board the schooner, we pulled along shore. The Florida natives were yelling and brandishing their spears at us, and I surmised that there must be something wrong.

'As we pulled up to the schooner we got all ready for boarding, and on getting alongside, we jumped up altogether; seeing no natives on deck we rushed to the hatches to see if they had got possession; there was not a living soul on board, but we saw one of the most horrible sights imaginable.'

Charnel House
'James Shearer was lying alongside the windlass with his head split open, and several wounds in his side; Charles Wolf was lying amidships with his head battered in, and his brains scattered over the hatches; George Sellars was lying aft with his head very nearly severed from his body. I think from the appearance of the bodies that Sellars was the only one that had a struggle with the natives. Shortly after we got possession of the schooner our own natives rushed out of the bush into the water, and I sent the boat and picked them all up. From shore we learned that the mate, Francis Warnham, and Edward Nichols had been murdered on shore along with three of our own natives.

'The Florida natives began to gather along the beach in large numbers, yelling, so we at once buried the bodies and got the schooner under weigh, for we did not consider it safe to wait any longer than we could possibly help. As soon as we got outside in safety, and washed the blood off the decks, we began to look about to see what damage they had done. In the house on deck where I lived, they had taken everything – the chronometer, sextant, ship's papers and charts, and all they could easily carry away; the forecastle was completely gutted; they took nearly all the trade out of the hold, also a large quantity of tortoiseshell – in fact, I believe if we had been away a little longer we should have lost the schooner.'
(*The Argus* [Melbourne], 3 August 1872)

After the massacre Capt. Brodie decided to run for Rubiana, 'as I had two men trading for me there, and I could get their help to work the vessel, also to land the Limbo natives whom we had in the schooner'. At Esau, near Rubiana, Capt. Brodie left the native chief of the place, Tepello, in charge of the *Lavinia* while some of Tepello's men canoed Brodie to Rubiana to find some charts. Upon his return he found all was well, noting, 'Tepello kept watch all day, and never left the deck during the night. He would not allow even one of his own men on board while I was away. In fact, Tepello is the only chief in the Solomon Islands that can be properly trusted.' Trust, however, was in short supply the following year when the *Lavinia* was at New Ireland Island in the Bismarck Archipelago off New Guinea where she suffered another attack:

Piracy and Massacre – Seizure of the Schooner Lavinia, *and Massacre of Four of her Crew by the Natives of New Ireland*

The following particulars of this sad occurrence have been kindly furnished by Captain Neil Brodie, late master of the ill-fated vessel, who with the remnant of his crew arrived in Sydney on Sunday in H.M. schooner *Beagle*:

Capt. Brodie's Narrative
'We left Sydney on Friday, the 21st of March, with a crew of five white men and five natives of Rotumah, making the usual run to Makira (San Cristoval, Solomon Group), calling at the usual places of trading. Then we proceeded to the east side of Isabel to procure bêche-de-mer. While there on the 28th of May, Joseph Nellyer, A.B., died of sunstroke, being only six days off duty. We buried him on an island about eight leagues to the north-west of Port Praslin (Isabel Island).

'From there I went to the station, taking a part of the produce on board, and giving them a fresh supply of trade. Afterwards I went to Eddystone, or Simbo, lying there two days buying copra, and other native produce. From Simbo I proceeded direct to the westward, arriving at Port Praslin (New Ireland) on Wednesday, the 16th of July. We did nothing that day, but next morning we began to water ship, the natives being quite friendly. I have been here several times before, trading with the natives, and as everything was going the same as formerly, I had no suspicion whatever that they intended any mischief, as they had no arms whatever in the shape of tomahawks or spears.'

'Mischief' and Mayhem

'On the morning of the 18th, while we were heaving up the anchor, about twenty of them [natives] came off to sell a turtle; I bought it, and then told them to go into their canoes, but they would not go; I told them a second time, but they did not move; however, as they were always so friendly formerly I thought nothing of it. I went forward to give the men a hand with the anchor, as we were moored in very deep water; when the anchor was a-peak [straight up and down on the anchor chain under the bow of the ship] I sent Francis Martin and Tom (Rotumah native) into the boat so as to tow her out of the calm, as she was under the lee of the land.

'When we had the anchor up, the mate walked aft into the house [deckhouse] and got his revolver. He went on top of the house, so as he could have command over the ship. I went to the wheel. I heard the mate tell the natives twice to get into their canoes. They made a sort of excuse, standing on the rail and singing out to those in the canoes to come alongside and take them ashore. I began to be very uneasy, as they did not go willingly.

'In a moment, a native, who was on the rails singing out to the canoes, jumped on to the top of the house, and pushed the mate (Mr. John Webster) off. Four of them rushed aft, seized me in their arms, and threw me overboard on the port side, taking me quite unawares. They did it all in a moment, not giving us the least chance of protecting ourselves. While in the act of throwing me overboard I managed to get my right hand adrift; I got hold of my revolver and shot one of them while I was going over the rail.

'When I was in the water there was a canoe close to. I swam for it – there were two boys in it. They tried to get away, but I swam too fast for them. When I caught them and was getting into it, one of the boys came towards me with a tomahawk to strike me. I fired at him. When I got into the canoe I could see nothing of either of them. I don't know whether I shot him or not. When I got into the canoe I saw the boat on the starboard bow. I began calling out to Francis Martin to come and pick me up. When he came I got into the boat. I found two of the Rotumah men had jumped overboard and swam for the boat. I smashed the canoe up before we left her.

'While we were doing this we got close to the shore; the natives on shore began throwing stones at us, so we had to go further off. We began to fire on the natives on shore till we expended all our charges but two, which I reserved for fear of any canoes attacking the boat. While we were firing at the natives on board, they were firing at us. I suppose they used the mate's and cook's revolvers. They also threw billets of wood at us. They actually threw the burning wood out of the galley fire.

'When I saw it was hopeless in attempting to recover the schooner again, after waiting about an hour and a half, I thought it best to make for the Duke of York Island (a distance of forty miles), as we had neither food nor water in the boat. Next morning, at daybreak, we arrived at the Duke of York Island, where were received very friendly by Johnny, the chief of Port Hunter.'

One of the Rotumah men, named Billy, states:

'The mate sent me aloft to lose the yard-arm gaskets of the square sails. While I was aloft the New Ireland natives rushed the crew. They killed the cook (Henry Huish) close to the galley, and they killed Mr. Webster in the starboard galley. I saw them seize the master and throw him overboard. They killed a Rotumah man alongside the windlass. When I came down the rigging they tried to reach me with a handspike, but I jumped overboard, and was picked up by the boat. They committed the murder with handspikes.'

Captain Brodie further states:

'There was one of the Rotumah men down below sick, but we cannot tell what they did with him, whether they killed him or not.

'When we were on the Duke of York Island we had a rather precarious way of living. If you have nothing to buy any food with it is very little the natives will give. Johnny, the chief, used to give us a bundle of taro every morning, with the expectation of getting paid some other time.'

Rescue by HMS Beagle

'On Sunday morning, the 27th July, the natives sung out "Sail Oh" which caused us to be very glad. We went off at once, and found her to be HMS *Beagle*, Lieutenant Rendell commanding. When I stated my case to him, he at once proceeded to Port Praslin, arriving there on the 4th August. Having watered, and seeing no natives, we began to look for the schooner, but could find nothing of her nor any wreck about the beach. On the morning of the 5th, he [Lieut. Rendell] got underway, and went inside of the islands – keeping a good look-out for the schooner; but he saw nothing of her.

'We anchored about 5 p.m. in Port Content. Captain Rendell sent the boat away to the village in charge of Mr. Underwood, to see if he could get a native off, or gain any information. As soon as we went down to the village, we went on shore, and had a look in two of their huts, but found nothing belonging to the schooner. They began slinging stones at us, so we got into the boat and went out of their reach. We fired either twice or thrice in the air to frighten them, and seeing no hopes of gaining any information from them, we got underway next morning for the village where the natives lived that took the schooner, arriving there the day following at 5:30 p.m.

'As soon as we came to an anchor the boat was sent away under the charge of Mr. Underwood, with six hands. They fired at us from amongst the bush; there were a great number of natives on the beach. The captain ordered the large gun to be loaded with blank cartridge, and fired. Two or three of the natives came dancing on the beach in defiance, and as they were still firing at us from the bush, the large gun was loaded with cannister, and fired in the direction from whence they fired. Still that did not make them cease firing. Captain Rendell then ordered the men to fire rockets – the rockets seemed to frighten them, as they did not fire any more.

'It was impossible for a vessel like the *Beagle* to attempt to land, as the natives were so numerous, likewise so bold;

the *Beagle* lying so close to the shore, and being open to the prevalent winds – that is, from N. to S.E. – Captain Rendell got underway at 6:30 p.m., and beat out, as he could not do any more with such a vessel as the *Beagle*.'

Need For Retribution

'If the natives of these islands do not get punished for any depredation they may commit, it will not be safe for any vessels to come here at all, as the natives of the other villages and tribes will be envious of their neighbours getting so much trade without receiving any punishment.

'The masters of trading vessels amongst these islands ought to have power to use force towards the natives, if they would not go out of their vessel when they were told. The way we are fixed, if they begin the affray, I believe we are justified in shooting them; if not, if we shoot them without any cause, although we know they are watching every opportunity to kill all hands, we are liable to get severely punished, which is not very pleasant. When the natives of these islands intend to take a vessel they watch their opportunity; they will never give their crew a chance to fight for their lives, but take them unawares.'

Getting Home

'Having a station at Keso, near Rubiana, I asked Captain Rendell if he would take us there (which he kindly consented to do), thinking there might be a chance of getting to Sydney by some of the trading vessels. Arriving there on the 16th August, we found the *Kate Kearney* at anchor. I at once asked Captain Ferguson if it was possible for him to take me and my crew to any port of Australia; but as he had not half concluded his voyage, he at once told me he could not comply with my wishes.

'I then stated my case to Captain Rendell, showing him how I was situated, and asked him whether it was possible for him to take us to Sydney himself, seeing there was no prospect of getting there by any other way – at least for a very indefinite period. Captain Rendell did not give me an answer at once, but said that he would consider the matter over. Next morning he informed me that, after taking everything into consideration, he had decided on taking us either to Moreton Bay or Sydney, according as the winds favoured us.

'Before concluding my account of this unfortunate affair, I would take this opportunity of publicly acknowledging and expressing my gratitude for the very kind treatment received both by myself and crew at the hands of Captain Rendell, and the officers and crew of H.M.S. *Beagle*.' (*The Sydney Mail*, 20 September 1873)

The Sandfly Atrocity

A new 'Imperial Navy' patrol schooner, HMS *Sandfly*, commissioned 'for the suppression of the slave trade' around the islands, left Sydney on 22 June 1873 to cruise amongst the Solomons and other neighbouring island groups. At Duke of York Island, in the New Ireland archipelago, she discovered that the *Lavinia* 'was destroyed the day after being captured' by natives. Off the coast of one of the Solomons, the *Sandfly* reported the following on the cannibalistic (and slaving) practices of local tribes.

Cruise of the Sandfly

At one part of the coast off which the *Sandfly* anchored, the following incident occurred:

The natives of the hill, or as they are designated, bush tribes, are at deadly enmity with the beach or shore natives. The daughter of a bush man had married one of the beach tribe; the father, anxious to see his child, ventured from his hills, and by stratagem an interview was effected with his daughter, but during this interview the husband suddenly came on the scene, and at once tomahawked the parent in the presence of the daughter. The murder took place on the 19th September, on which date the *Sandfly* put in an appearance.

The custom of the natives in this locality is simply to roast and eat the bodies of their enemies, and this was being actually carried out but for the timely advent of the cruiser. Lieutenant Nowell learning the particulars at once took prompt measures, communicating by means of an interpreter his intention of burning the village unless the dead body was given up. His threats had the desired effect, and the chief was compelled not only to bring the corpse alongside, but afterwards to tow it to sea and sink it. This being accomplished, presents were given to the chief.

On October 4, the schooner arrived at Port Praslin, where it was found that some 80 canoes, fully manned, from a neighbouring island, were busily employed in skull-hunting and slave-catching. The practice appears to be that when a strong tribe makes a foray, the older branches of the weaker lot are at once killed and eaten, the skulls being alone retained, while the children are seized and taken into slavery; but the sudden appearance of one of H.M.'s schooners in this instance brought affairs to a very different termination.

Lieutenant Nowell on the following day, manned and armed the boats, himself proceeding in the whaler, and placing Mr. Bourd, the gunner, in charge of the gig, in which was fixed a rocket-tube. The party started at half-past one p.m. The gig was anchored 800 yards from the shore, and the rocket-tube brought to bear on the village. Lieutenant Nowell then pulled in, and by means of the interpreter gave the aggressive tribe to understand that within an hour the slaves must be liberated and the heads given up, or he would fire the village.

The effect is described as electrical. The canoes were at once launched, and all the alive and dead spoil left on the beach, but to teach a lesson, and as a wholesome warning of what might be the result, as soon as the canoes were well clear of the gig a rocket was fired across their sterns, which effected a complete stampede. On Lieutenant Nowell and his party landing, they found fourteen children whose parents had been killed, and a number of skulls, some of them being on the fire for the purpose of removing the flesh.

That night the liberated captives were left in charge of the principal chief, and the next day were sent rejoicing to their homes, with presents of tobacco, pipes, and biscuit. The chief was also compelled to bring all the skulls alongside the schooner, and then take them out to sea and sink them, and on his return was presented with some presents of tobacco, etc. (*Sydney Morning Herald*, 2 December 1873)

In October 1880, at around the same place as the *Lavinia* crew were slaughtered off the Florida Islands in 1872, Lieut. Cddr James St Clair Bower and five crew of HMS *Sandfly* were put to the sword by Solomon islanders. Their grossly mutilated remains were later discovered along the shore. Lieut. Bower had tried to escape the attack by climbing a tree where he stayed during the night. Next morning, however, the attackers shot him. He fell from the tree 'and then a series of nameless horrors ensued'. Only three men of the *Sandfly* survived the massacre: Mr Bradford, acting sub-lieut.; Mr Coughlan, boatswain; and an AB (able seaman) named, appropriately (or inappropriately, certainly ironically), Savage:

Another Massacre in the South Sea Islands

Intense excitement was felt in mercantile and shipping circles yesterday morning when it became known that H.M.S. *Sandfly* had arrived from the Solomon Islands, that the commander and five of her crew had been killed by the natives of a small island of the Solomon Group, and that one man had been wounded. From Mr. Bradford, acting-sub-lieutenant, Mr. Coughlan, the boatswain, and A.B. Savage, the sole survivor of the massacre, we have been enabled to glean full details of a foul outrage, the latest of hundreds which have made British seamen and traders abhor the Solomon Group:

On Wednesday, October 13, the *Sandfly* being anchored at Tesemboko, Lieutenant-commander Bower left in the whaleboat to survey the east coast of Florida Island from Barranaga, intending to be back on the 16th. With him he took a crew of five men: Francis Savage, A.B.; Benjamin Venton, of Bethnal Green, London, A.B.; Alfred Carne, Southwark, London, A.B.; William Paterson, Belfast, Ireland, A.B.; and John O'Neil, Southwark, London, A.B.

The 17th, 18th, and 19th passed without their returning, and on the 20th the schooner weighed anchor, and made for the east coast, Mr. Bradford sending the gig round one side, and going himself round the other, so that a thorough search might be made. The gig was commanded by Mr. Coughlan and manned by four seamen, all being well armed, and the start was made from East Point. When near the south-east coast of Florida Island, a canoe was noticed coming off from the coast, but as the gig neared it, the four men in the island craft rowed for the shore, closely pursued by the gig.

The canoe was beached and Coughlan seeing a number of natives on the beach – he estimates their number at 150 – halted the gig without beaching her, and opened parley with the natives. One of the occupants of the canoe – a chief, whose name was afterwards found to be Billy – spoke a few words in the native tongue, and immediately the peaceful-looking people on the beach appeared armed with spears, and bows and arrows, and English tomahawks. It afterwards transpired that round a little promontory lurked two well-manned war canoes, and that had the gig been beached her crew would have been riddled from front and rear with a shower of spears.

Coughlan, however, was too cautious not to turn his gig's bow seaward, and to have his men ready for a skirmish, and so open hostilities were waived in favour of an attempt to decoy the Englishmen to their death. 'Come in! Come in! Canoe come in, and you come in,' shouted Billy; and then added, 'I speak.' Some native words brought out one Jack, an islander, who could speak pigeon [pidgin] English. 'I Jack, I savee Louis (Mr. Nixon, Master of the schooner Pacific), you savee Louis?' said this worthy. 'Yes,' answered Coughlan. 'Boat gone to island, all same Savo,' rejoined Jack, '5 fellow oar, 6 fellow men' – alluding to the commander and his crew.

Coughlan knew that this was the *Sandfly* boat, and so pulled back to the ship with the news. They then went to East Island, then along the coast, where in the evening they saw many fires burning, and where they flashed lights, and did everything that might possibly attract the wanderers; and they noticed that the beach was literally alive with natives, dancing and yelling like fiends.

They reached Mboli Harbour at 1.30 a.m. on Thursday, and about 8 o'clock Coughlan, with two men – all well armed, and on their guard – went on shore and made coffee, but none of the natives would own that they knew a word of English. The gig then went right round the island, and through Sandfly Passage – traced and named by Lieut. Bower – and so returned to the vessel, to find Savage on board, with the melancholy news of the massacre of which he was sole survivor.

It may be stated that Mr. Coughlan touched at Nogu Island, and searched it thoroughly. He saw the naked headless bodies of the missing crew, but they were baked black by the sun until they looked like natives, and it was only when Savage told his story that the men could manage to examine and identify them.

When the whaleboat left the ship on October 13, her crew rowed to Seserga, where the captain took a sight; and there they stayed that night. Next morning they rowed to East Island, and camped there on Thursday night. On Friday they pulled over to Lavinia Bay on the mainland, the spot where the terrible *Lavinia* massacre took place, and the men, answering the cunning questions of the natives, told them where they had slept the night before, thus letting them see that they were away from the ship.

From this moment their lives were in their hands, and all that savage cunning could devise – in an island group where a man's importance is reckoned by the number of heads of murdered enemies he can show, and where the head of every well-known trader has a price fixed upon it by the chiefs – was set in motion to cut off that boat's crew. The captain was on shore, but his men kept their firearms ready, and he got safely on board; and kept along the coast, surveying, until he got to Nogu Island, on

Friday evening. Here they hauled the boat up and made tea, preparing to camp for the night, in utter ignorance of the fact even then dark forms were flitting through the dense bush; and that opal eyeballs were flashing at the thought of getting the white men's heads as soon as the camp was silenced in sleep.

Ambush

Canoes had followed the boat, and when it landed the trackers stole round to the other side of the island, and crept through the thickets to an ambush where they could be ready for a surprise. The moment came soon enough. Carne and O'Neil got leave to bathe, and splashed into the water. Venton was told off to look after the boat, to spread out the gear, and to dry it and the boat; and Lieutenant Bower, with Savage and Paterson, went along the beach to do a little more surveying. They went a short distance, and then Paterson returned for something. Soon after, Savage heard yells, and, running back, he saw a crowd of about fifty natives whirling round the boat, and more hurrying through the bush.

Returning to the captain, he shouted, 'The boat's attacked'; and the captain, also returning to see the truth, was espied by the natives, six of whom broke off and ran for him. He cried, 'My God, Savage, it is a case!' and darted into the bush. Savage saw no more of him, but subsequently learned that he had eluded pursuit by climbing a tree.

Savage's Flight from Savages' Attack

It was now between 5 and 6 o'clock, just growing dusk, and the sky cloudy; and Savage, as he doubled and zig-zagged through the thickets, which reached to the water's edge, knew that his only chance of life was to get away from Nogu; so, after a brief rest, he plunged into the sea and struck out for a little island near the mainland. The tide was strong, and as he got out he was swept back little by little until he was opposite the site of the massacre.

The savages had piled up the fire pit to make tea, and were dancing and shouting round it, when the clouds broke, and a burst of moonlight showed Savage. With a yell, his foes manned two or three canoes and pursued him. Savage swam for his life, but his pursuers drew up until they were only some fifty yards away, when the moon was once more overcast. When next a gleam of moonlight came the fugitive saw his pursuers far off, making back to their companions. They evidently thought he had gone down.

His next danger was from the sharks, which literally swarm round these reefs. At one time no less than three backfins were sweeping round him in that ominous curve, ever growing closer, which precedes a rush; but he splashed faintly, and so kept them off until, after an eight-hours' swim, he landed on a small uninhabited island. This was tabooed [prohibited, excluded] to the king of the tribe adjoining the murderers, and Savage rested there in safety during a heavy storm which came on.

Next day, on Saturday afternoon, he determined to get over to the mainland, and so made a rough-and-ready raft and paddled across. When he was about 500 yards from the shore two or three canoes put off, and the swimmer was taken on board and conveyed to land. The chief was away, but one of his captors who could speak English said it was 'all right,' and Savage, to his surprise, was taken to a fresh-water spring and bathed. Then he was robbed of his flannel shirt, his sole remaining garment; but in exchange the English-speaking native gave him a pair of trousers, a jacket, and a hat – ordinary trade goods – and taking him to a hut gave him fish and some kind of bread.

On Sunday night the chief returned and tabooed him, and – next best thing – gave him a pipe, tobacco, and matches. But on Monday Savage's life was once more in danger, for he was taken round to Barranago Bay, and all the males in the tribe, about 600 men and boys, assembled for a grand council. Savage was in the centre, and from looks and gestures, he could see that he was being spoken of; but definite information he could not obtain, since to every question the English-speaking native returned only a grunt. Afterwards this old man became more communicative, and confided to him that he was quite safe now, and would be kept until Louis (Captain Nixon, of the *Pacific*) came along.

The party then took to fishing with no less civilized an agent than dynamite, which they knew perfectly how to use [i.e. by detonating it and stunning the fish which they then scooped up]. The captive saw in their possession Snider-rifles and plenty of ammunition. The chief was one Timbacora. The interpreter, who was Captain Nixon's trading agent, gradually told Savage of the fate of his companions.

The Boat Crew's Horrific Fate

The tree into which Bower climbed was a very conspicuous one, situate near the shore, but the captain expected to escape observation there. The murderers sought him in vain that night, but next morning they paddled all round the island, and seeing him in the tree, landed and shot him twice through the body with the rifles they had stolen from the boat. He dropped to the earth, and then a series of nameless horrors ensued.

When found his body was naked, headless, and divested of the right arm, and great pieces of flesh were stripped from the back. The men who were bathing had been clubbed at once; Paterson, taken from behind, had shared the same fate; but Venton, who had time to seize a boat-stretcher, fought hard for his life, as a native afterwards admitted. 'One man very strong,' said the interpreter to Savage 'plenty fight.' The attacking party thought Savage drowned; and as O'Neil's body was not discovered by the *Sandfly*, though the interpreter said five men were killed, it is likely that it was left in the water where the poor wretch was struck down. Savage was told that the arms got in the boat were 'five rifle, one small fellow rifle' (a revolver).

The Sandfly*'s Discovery of Massacre*

Savage remained near Barranago Bay until Thursday afternoon, when his signals were perceived by the *Sandfly*. Mr. Bradford sent the skiff for him.

On Friday morning the *Sandfly* went to Nogu Island, which is shaped like a pear, the thick portion wooded, and the stalk a bare sandspit. On this sandspit, visible a mile away, were two stakes bearing a crossbar, to which the headless body of Venton was bound. The biceps muscle was cut through to the bone, and the wrists were slashed across; he was covered with tomahawk cuts, and the contraction of the fingers told what his death-agony had been. It may have been that he was tortured before he died; he was the only one who was able to strike a blow, and the only one whose body was so treated.

Further on, lay the headless bodies of Carne and Paterson; and a little way in the bush Mr. Coughlan discovered the captain's body, under the tree where he was shot. They buried the remains; read the Service over them, and then returned to Barranago, the only safe anchorage near.

On Saturday, Coughlan returned to Nogu for a rifle, left behind on the preceding day; and on Sunday Mr. Bradford and eight men, well armed, went into Rita Bay to see if there were any signs of the whaleboat. All that they saw was a jumper lying on the beach, and one of the men went for it. It proved to belong to Savage.

They could not get the vessel into Rita Bay; and on Sunday, October 31, Mr. Bradford and his crew again pulled in, in the teeth of a heavy fire from concealed natives. They returned the fire, landed, discovered two water-casks, and a tarpaulin belonging to the whaleboat, burned the village; and were just embarking when fire was opened on them again. Robert Buckle, A.B., was shot through the heart, and a seaman named Whitlock was wounded in the left forearm. On Monday, November 1, the *Sandfly* weighed anchor for Sydney. (*The Sydney Morning Herald*, 30 November 1880)

The Brutal Murder of Capt. Schwartz

In February 1881 a trading schooner, the *Leslie* out of Sydney, commanded by a certain Capt. Schwartz and with a crew of eight, anchored off what used to be called Cape Marsh, since known as the Russell Islands of Pavuvu and Mbanika, just to the north-west of Guadalcanal. Palavering about trade with the local chiefs, King Kook, the 'supreme chief of the tribe,' and King Harry, King Kook's 'big killing man', Capt. Schwartz was suddenly and apparently without provocation brutally hatcheted to death and mutilated by King Harry. The only witness to the dastardly deed was a

SURGEON HENRY GRIER, ARMY MEDICAL DEPARTMENT
Awarded the Albert Medal for Saving Life.

CAPTAIN ALEXANDER LAWRENCE FALLS, 21ST REGIMENT
Killed by the Boers at Potchefstroom, Dec. 27, 1880

COL. BELLAIRS, C.B.
Besieged in the Fort, Potchefstroom, Transvaal

The massacre of Lieut. Bower and five seamen of H.M.S. *Sandfly* in the Solomon Islands. (*The Graphic*, 29 January 1881)

Fijian boy with Capt. Schwartz, named Tolly, who escaped to tell the story of the atrocity:

The Last South Sea Outrage

It is unfortunate that the only source of information with respect to the last terrible outrage by the Solomon Islanders is a black Marabo [island in Fiji] boy. But from the account of the murder which we gave yesterday, it will be seen that he is the only available witness of what took place … The boy alluded to is named Tolly, and is about 14 years of age. He was picked up by Captain Schwartz some three years ago at the island of Marabo, and since that time has been constantly with him in his voyages. He is intelligent and precise as to his facts, and it was therefore from him that our reporter gleaned the following narrative:

Tolly's Tale

It appears that the schooner *Leslie*, of which Capt. Schwartz was the master, left Sydney on 19th January, with a crew of eight, including the boy Tolly. They had a fine passage to the islands, touching for trading purposes at San Christoval, Guadalcanar, and Thousand Ship Bay, and at these places eleven natives were obtained to help in the work of the ship. On the 19th of February Cape Marsh [Russell Islands, north-west of Guadalcanal] was reached, and the schooner dropped her anchor at a distance from the shore of about 100 yards.

This place is well-known as a trading station, and the natives having hitherto been friendly and no disposition to quarrelling or treachery having been shown by them, Captain Schwartz felt perfectly safe. Two canoes soon put off, each of them containing five natives. It appears that Captain Schwartz was not too well pleased with the aspect of affairs at this time. The total absence of women and children from the shore and the limited number of the men who showed themselves, were to his experienced judgement suspicious circumstances. He several times repeated anxiously, 'There is something wrong, or the natives would show up.'

No precaution seems to have been taken, however. The men in the canoes came aboard, and as far as could be seen from their conduct there was nothing to give rise to any apprehensions, certainly nothing which would have led the crew to the belief that so terrible a tragedy was about to be enacted. On the last visits of the Leslie and the Zephyr, which both belong to the same firm, a large quantity of island 'trade' was left at Cape Marsh, and Captain Schwartz asked the head man, King Harry, who is described by the boy, Tolly, as being the 'King's big killing man,' if he had received the trade. He replied, 'Yes, the trade was left.' Schwartz said, 'That's all right, so long as you have got the trade.'

Going Ashore

After some further chat, the Leslie boat was lowered, and the captain went ashore, accompanied by only four natives and the boy Tolly. It seems strange at first sight, that he should not have taken men out of the crew in preference to natives; but the explanation given is that they were engaged in bending on the mainsail and foresail, and that the work was desired to be finished as soon as possible. At any rate, the crew are convinced that, had they accompanied their captain, the murder would never have taken place. The only arms in the boat's party were a revolver, carried by the captain, and a breech loading rifle, which was empty, a supply of cartridges being stowed away in the stern.

The boat was run ashore, and Captain Schwartz landed among the natives, the others remaining in the boat. The boy Tolly afterwards also got ashore and stood by the boat. At this time there was nothing unusual in the conduct of the natives, the number of whom was still very limited. Two chiefs began to talk to the captain, who sat on a log about six yards away from the boat. He began by asking King Kook, the supreme chief of the tribe, and who is a stout, strongly built man, if he had got the trade. The answer was that it had been left, but it had been lost, and it should be explained here that on the last visit of the Zephyr the natives had refused to give the copra, on the plea that they preferred to hand it over to Captain Schwartz when he should arrive.

Murder and Mutilation of Capt. Schwartz

Kook was then asked how he lost the trade, and he stated that he had used it to pay some men for building a great 'tamboo' [taboo] house for him. Schwartz maintained his equanimity, and, according to Tolly, 'never swore,' and did not show any symptoms of anger. While he was thus being held in conversation by the king in front, King Harry and another chief moved behind him, apparently without any particular motive, and for a moment mumbled a few words of 'secret talk that the captain didn't understand.'

King Harry then suddenly drew his hatchet and struck him a fearful blow between the shoulders, the blade of the weapon being almost buried in the body.

The captain, who had been sitting unsuspectingly with his elbows on his knees, looking at the ground, fell on his face without a groan, and the natives immediately fell upon him, hacking and cutting him in a most barbarous manner. King Harry took off his (Schwartz's) hat, and inflicted several additional blows with the hatchet.

At this outbreak of hostility, which, judging by the clever way in which it was manoeuvred, must have been premeditated, Tolly leaped into the boat and pushed off, the natives taking to their oars in the desperation of fear. One of the murderers sprang into the water, hatchet in hand, and tried to catch hold of the steering oar, but failed. A general rush was then made for a canoe, and the natives began paddling after the boat with loud yells and cries. Tolly, however, picked up the empty breechloader, and took aim at them, and the ruse succeeded, for at the sight of the firearm the natives, in the greatest haste and disorder, fled back again to the shore.

The alarm had produced a most surprising effect, for no sooner had the canoes been launched than the surrounding scrub became literally alive with natives, who up to that time had lain in concealment. Several shots were fired at the boat, but without effect. It was noticed that the body of the captain was put into a canoe and taken to the other side of the bay, where it was placed in a hut.

On reaching the ship the anchor was raised, but, the sails being still unbent [i.e. not attached or set], the only means of heaving away was by means of the boat, which was used as a tug. Hundreds of natives lined the beach, yelling, firing and gesticulating, but happily none of their bullets did any damage. Captain Robinson, who was mate of the *Leslie*, ordered the arms to be brought up, but as soon as the crew began to return the firing of the natives the latter again disappeared in the bush. The eleven blacks on board fled into the hold, whence neither threat nor persuasion could drive them. They would not take any active part in this encounter. The ship was fired at until she was out of range, and then, there being no possibility of obtaining the body of the captain, it was decided to sail for Sydney, where the schooner arrived on Sunday morning. (*Wanganui Herald* [New Zealand], 18 April 1881)

The Murder of Capt. Guy on Rubiana

For decades atrocities in the Solomon Islands centred on the Florida Islands, and more so, on the nearby island of Rubiana (now New Georgia) where a number of white traders had outposts ('stations'). A certain Captain Edmunds, writing from Rubiana in a letter to *The Sydney Morning Herald* in 1889, summarised recent outrages, including the ruination of his farmland by 'cheeky' Rubiana natives. Captain Edmunds was keen that 'an example ought to be shown these natives' by the force of punitive retribution by 'H.M. ships': a rollicking good hiding to 'give these Rubiana men a prompt and decisive lesson':

Atrocities At Rubiana

To The Editor Of The Herald

Sir,- The following is a brief account of a double murder, accompanied with robbery, committed by natives at my station, situated at Rubiana, Solomon group. On the 19th of August last [1888] I left here to proceed to Sydney to purchase a vessel to continue my business as trader in and amongst the Solomon Islands. During my absence, or to be more explicit, two months after I had left here, two natives from Simbo or Eddystone Island came to my place, and killed two of my labouring boys, whom I had left, together with two more and my family, to watch and guard the place, they actually succeeded in killing the boys, and afterwards left.

A fortnight afterwards the Banietta [Banyetta] natives called, and broke into my store, and stole therefrom goods to the value of £200; in fact, all they could carry in their canoes. Three weeks after the Rubiana natives called, and broke open the dwelling-house, and took therefrom all the furniture, &c., including partitions, doors, windows, and left nothing standing but the walls. They also went over the cultivated ground and rooted up everything, and left it exposed to rot; in fact, what they could not take, they destroyed.

Rubiana natives are certainly getting more and more forward and cheeky every day. Fifteen years ago they took the *Marian Renny*, schooner, killed and ate the whole of the crew. In January, 1885, Captain Howie and his boat's crew were killed and eaten at Banietta.* Those natives are now living at Rubiana.

About 12 years ago the *Speranza* schooner was taken and the crew killed and eaten. Some Rubiana men were in that also. On the 8th of September, 1885, Mr. Childs was killed and eaten by Simbo natives. Some Rubiana natives were implicated in that also. Lately, again, the Prospect cutter was taken and the crew killed and eaten at Dogbly, Piandova Islands, by Rubiana natives. And in all the above cases her Majesty's ships have been very lenient towards the natives.

Sir, it is the opinion of all the traders right through-out the group that an example ought to be shown these natives, especially around this part of the group, where

---

* On 15 January 1885 Capt. James Howie, master of the trading schooner *Elibank Castle*, able seaman Carl Johann, and 'three kanakas (South Sea islanders)' were just about to get on shore in a boat to trade for copra and tortoiseshell at Point Banyetta, Rendova Island, off the south coast of Rubiana, when they were 'attacked by a multitude of savages, numbering … over sixty'. The schooner's mate, Henry Banks, later reported that 'the natives kept firing at us from the bush, the bullets coming in all directions among us, over our heads and between us'. They had guns, then, as well as 'tomahawks, spears, &c'. Banks observed that: 'The natives were accompanied by a number of dogs, who were licking the blood of the victims.'

the inactivity of H.M. ships is very keenly felt. The cutting of their fruit trees or destroying their canoes, which was done in all the above-mentioned cases, does not seem to affect them in the least. They, on the contrary, are boasting that they will kill the next man-of-war (to use their own phrase).

As no others but English subjects, and no other but English capital is invested in these islands, surely, I say but we are very imperfectly protected. I have calculated my loss at from £400 to £500 sterling. It is hoped here by all traders, and also by some friendly natives, that on this occasion H.M. ships will give these Rubiana men a prompt and decisive lesson, and it is my firm opinion that if this were done nothing need be apprehended from them, if not for ever, at least for some years to come. Trusting that you will permit the above to appear in your most valuable columns,

I am, &c.,

Pratt Edmunds, Master and Owner of Schooner *Magic* at Rubiana, Solomon Islands

Rubiana, February 14 [1889]

Another Rubiana-based trader, Capt. Donald Guy, was assaulted and killed on the south coast of Rubiana in March 1894 'while trading with the natives of a village called Soy'. Four islanders accompanying him, including a woman and her child, were also killed. Two of the islanders, a boy and a man, escaped. The apparent reason for the massacre was that the Soy men wanted 'to get heads for the two canoes they had just built in Soy'. A 'punitive expedition' by HMS *Royalist* subsequently went in search of the 'tribe of head-hunters' who had perpetrated the deed, apparently to 'propitiate the devil of two large new war canoes':

How Captain Guy Lost His Life –
Murdered in the Solomon Islands

Full particulars have been received in Sydney from the Solomon Islands with regard to the murder of Captain Donald Guy. A trader, writing from Rubiana under date April 13th, says:

'I am very sorry to have to record the death of Captain Donald Guy. He was killed on or about March 10th, while trading with the natives of a village called Soy. It appears he left his station and went to a place called No No [Nono, south coast of Rubiana], and after trading there spent the night, sleeping in the boat, which had been fitted up so as to be comfortable when away. In the morning he started for home, and when passing one of the small islands, about two miles from No No, a canoe came up to him and told him to anchor, as they had some produce to sell. He did so, and two canoes came alongside – one on each side – one having 15 men in it and the other 10.

'While trading with them one of the men, suddenly, when Captain Guy was not looking, took up his tomahawk and struck him two blows on the head, killing him instantly. There were in Captain Guy's boat three boys, besides a native woman, her child and husband and another man. Two of the boys were killed, and also the woman and child, whilst the two men escaped in a small canoe, and the third boy, jumping overboard, got away into the bush, and reached the station next day.

'When the news of the murder reached Rubiana, Messrs Kelly, Wheatley, and Atkinson, and myself arranged to go to No No at once. We got there next day, and recovered the remains of Captain Guy, which we took to Lillihena station, where the interment took place. All Captain Guy's effects were taken, and the boat, produce, and trade burnt.

'The reason that the natives killed him and the others in the boat was that they wanted to propitiate the devil of two large new war canoes. I have written to the naval authorities, giving details of the massacre, and there is no doubt that those concerned will be properly dealt with.'

Narrative of the Massacre

The following is the statement of the native who was on board the unfortunate captain's vessel at the time of the massacre:

'When the moon was small (March) we went down in the boat to No No to buy copra and ivory nuts. We slept there that night, and next day filled the boat with copra and ivory nuts, and left for Lillihena. There were in the boat at the time Captain Guy, two Malayta boys and myself, also two No No men, William and Neko, also William's wife and child, who were going on a visit to the king of Rapee. On passing one of the small islands in the No No Passage a canoe came off and told Captain Guy to anchor for a time, as they had some produce to sell. Captain Guy anchored the boat on a small reef near the island, the canoe going away and afterwards returning with a larger one, one canoe going on each side of the boat.

'While trading, one man, Cablao, who was standing behind Guy, struck him two blows on the head with a tomahawk. I saw the man pick up the tomahawk, and called out to Captain Guy to look out, but he did not hear me, as there was a big wind blowing, I being in the forepart of the boat at the time. I also saw the two Malayta boys killed by a man suffering from skin disease.

Two men seized me, but I threw them off and jumped overboard. I dived and got away from them, hiding up a tree in the bush. All the men followed and searched for me, but not finding me they all went away again.

'I then came down from the tree, and walked through the bush to Pondockoner, and the natives there took me to Marovo, and then home. I had told Captain Guy before to look out, but he said that it was all right, as he was friendly with the natives, and instead of wearing his revolver had it in the trade chest. His two rifles were also covered up in the locker.

'The chief of No No told me that they had killed the men in the boat to get heads for the two canoes they had just built in Soy.' (*The Auckland Star*, 26 May 1894)

A Punitive Expedition to the Cannibals of The Solomon Islands: Tracking Cannibals – a correspondent sends us a very interesting account of the punitive expedition sent out by H.M.S. *Royalist* against a tribe of head-hunters in the Solomon Islands. The *Royalist* was ordered to the Islands, shortly after the captain of a trading vessel, named Donald Guy, had been cruelly murdered at Rubiana, New Georgia, by the Soya natives under their chief Kaveralaho. (*The Graphic*, 15 September 1894)

3

THE SOUTH SEAS LABOUR TRADE

Labour recruitment vessels, from small schooners and ketches to larger square-rigged brigs and barques, voyaged amongst the islands of the western and central Pacific to recruit (meaning, quite often, to kidnap by force or deceit) indigenous islanders to work on the sugar and cotton plantations in Queensland and Fiji in the middle to later years of the nineteenth century. Insurrections by the islanders recruited on board those vessels were by no means uncommon – and more often than not, bloody. The traffic in indigenous men lured and transported from the islands south-east of New Guinea, Fiji and other western and central Pacific Islands, constituted an often brutal trade in misery known as 'blackbirding'. It was a dirty trade in black human flesh conducted by white men with soiled souls pitted against the constant threat of rebellion by kidnapped islanders. The result was sometimes carnage of gross proportions.

Attack on the *Young Dick* at Malaita

The 162-ton topsail schooner *Young Dick* was built at Goole, on the north-east coast of England, in 1869. By 1875 she ended up trading around New Zealand and east coast Australian ports. In 1884 an Irishman, John Hugh Rogers, resident at Maryborough, on the Queensland coast, bought the schooner to employ in labour recruitment around the Solomons, New Hebrides and nearby islands. Rogers embarked with the *Young Dick* on his first recruiting voyage in July 1884.

It was an inauspicious start to the *Young Dick*'s new life. Rogers was frequently drunk (as were, indeed, most of the rest of the crew). There was a boisterous relationship ('a want of discipline') between him and the crew; his boatswain, Edward Austin, was later convicted of assault on Rogers and 'sentenced to six months hard labour in Brisbane gaol'. But the *Young Dick*'s seventh recruitment voyage, to the Solomons, in 1886, was a truly fractious and ultimately blood-drenched affair from the attack upon her by Solomon islanders on the east coast of Malaita in May that year.

The Massacre of the Schooner Young Dick – Horrible Details

The *Maryborough Chronicle* gives the following details of the tragic events on board the labour schooner *Young Dick* during her recent cruise:

The *Young Dick* left Brisbane on April 7, under the command of Captain Rogers, part owner, with Charles Marr first mate, and John Hornidge second mate and recruiter, a crew of seven Europeans, Polynesian boat's crew and Mr. C.H. [Charles Home] Popham, Government agent [an official government agent was legally required to sail on all labour recruitment voyages]. A course was shaped to the Solomons, and Guadalcaner was reached on the 24th. Recruiting operations were conducted with routine success.

At Malaita

On May 1 the vessel obtained six recruits at Mabo, near Cape Zelee, on the [south] east coast of Malayta [on Small Malaita Island]. Next day, two were obtained and two interpreters landed. On the boat regaining the vessel in the evening, Hornidge, second mate reported that a lot of bush natives had come down to the coast and advised continuing recruiting operations there. Accordingly the *Young Dick* returned to her anchorage and in response to an inviting cooey from the shore, Hornidge went ashore with two recruiting boats as well.

On reaching the beach they only found two kanakas, one of the interpreters who had been landed the previous day, a boy named Rady [or Radi], who had done service in Fiji, and an old man. They invited Hornidge up to the village situate 100 yards from the beach, the country being thickly wooded at this spot. As they neared the village, Hornidge was suddenly set upon by both kanakas, who used their tomahawks with unmistakably murderous intentions. Twice Hornidge was knocked down, but he succeeded in getting away and rushing through the undergrowth to the beach, made for the nearest boat, into which he fell bleeding and faint.

Nothing more was seen of the natives, and the boats, after the crew had fired a few chance shots, returned to the ship. Hornidge was badly tomahawked about the head and face, with a huge gash across his face, another across the vertebrae, four deep cuts in the back, and a bit of his right heel sliced off.

Anchor was weighed and the *Young Dick* proceeded the same day to Port Adams [about 30km north up the coast], where the labour schooner Meg Merilees was lying. The Government agent of the vessel, Mr. Bevan, boarded the *Young Dick* and for the succeeding few days was most skilful and assiduous in his attentions to the mutilated man, and to Mr. Bevan's generous care Hornidge's recovery was mainly due.

The Attack

On May 20, the *Young Dick* being rounded into Sirago Bay [Sinalanggu], on the east coast of Malayta, 16 miles west of Io, Captain Rogers left the vessel with two boats, three European sailors and the black crew, to recruit. The boats had gone down the coast out of sight, when a canoe with six kanakas came from off the shore, which was 150 yards off, and going alongside the schooner invited the hands ashore to recruit a boy who wanted to go to Queensland. This was, as subsequently shown, a ruse to decoy the crew ashore and make easy the capture of the vessel.

Mr. Popham, Government agent, who was too ill that day to go in the boat, told the occupants of the canoe to fetch the boy, and he would recruit him on board.

They left for the shore, and half an hour later the canoe returned with five kanakas, including the king, who was to receive the trade [the barter goods in exchange for the recruit(s)], and the boy who played the part of the 'recruit.' While the king was examining the trade in the deckhouse, and the pseudo recruit was dallying with Mr. Popham in the adjoining cabin respecting the agreement, the natives came off to the ship in dozens by canoes, catamarans [outrigger canoes] and swimming; and clambering up the sides of the vessel crowded her deck. The rule against the admission of native arms on board was neatly evaded, unperceived by the ship's people. Short-handled tomahawks were smuggled aboard in small dilly-bags, or embedded in yams, or artfully concealed in a wrapper of green leaves.

There were on board at this moment the following: Mr. Popham, Government agent, in his cabin; Charles Marr, the mate; Harry Merlin the cook; Beirr the carpenter – in the deckhouse guarding the trade which lay spread on the dinner table; Lagerholm [*sic* – Lagerblom], the sailmaker, on the forward deck; and Thomas Crittenden, able seaman, who was sleeping out his watch below in the forecastle.

The deckhouse is divided into three compartments, running across the afterdeck, with a narrow gangway on each side. The forward portion comprises the separate cabins of the captain and the Government agent; the centre section is the dining-room open at both sides; the third is the mate's cabin and trade-room, opening into the dining-room. As the mate stood at the open door of the trade-room the king demanded more trade, and as Mr. Marr gently refused more and closed the trade-room door, the king gave the signal for attack.

The Massacre

A loud and piercing yell was instantly replied to by a hellish shriek from the crowd of dusky native savages, who thronged the deck space aft, and instantly violent hands were laid on the Europeans. Tomahawks appeared as if produced by magic. Marr was seized by the king and two others, one of whom took the intended victim's thumb in his teeth and nearly bit it off. Marr, who was standing in the recess of the doorway, with his attackers in front of him, fortunately freed his right hand, and giving the king a British blow with clenched fist sent him reeling.

In an instant he eluded the savage clutches, snatched his loaded revolver from the bed, and from the half-closed door opened fire. His first bullet sent one of his attackers, who was aiming a tomahawk at him, to the deck, a bleeding corpse, the next severed another, and the revolver was then brought to bear on the crowds who, on the port side of the deckhouse, were relentlessly tomahawking the carpenter and cook, who taken quite unawares by the attack, were unable to reach their weapons and offer defence.

Meantime the blows in the forward cabin told how Mr. Popham was being hacked to death in the same cruel fashion. Expending the resources of his revolver, Marr snatched up a Snider rifle, jumped across the trade-room for cartridges and continued the deadly fight with the blood thirsty demons, who shrieking, yelling, and brandishing their tomahawks kept pouring into the vessel from canoes alongside. From this vantage ground Marr kept up a steady fire, and more than one savage, as he made his appearance on the taffrail, got his bullet, and fell into the sea to drown.

Unable to face Marr's rifle, the savages of whom there were now fully 50 on board, sought to attack him in the rear, and endeavoured by reaching through the cabin window astern, to tomahawk him. This manoeuvre was responded to by Marr, who seeing that the carpenter and cook were brutally slain within a few feet of him, retired into his cabin, and, closing the door, directed his bullets to the enemy at the window. How the Government agent and Lagerblom met their horrible death can never be accurately known. It is certain that they were attacked at the same moment as the others and chopped to death. Cries of 'murder!' from Mr. Popham were heard, but his agony was short-lived.

Seaman Crittenden's Retaliation

Crittenden, who was awakened from sleep by the savage yelling, ran, clothed only in a light singlet, on deck. The first spectacle which he witnessed was Lagerblom, the sailmaker, struggling violently with half-a-dozen savages on the starboard side of the main hatch. Crittenden immediately returned to the forecastle for his revolver, jumped on deck again, ran aft and found himself also the object of a general attack. He fired several shots with telling effect, the recipients of the bullets leaping overboard as soon as they were struck. A couple of natives clutched his singlet, but that gave way, and his naked body affording no grip, Crittenden freed himself and, making a leap into the forecastle, put on his trousers, filled his pockets with cartridges, took a Snider rifle, and returned pluckily to the combat.

Reaching the deck, he received the idea of conducting operations from the superior vantage afforded by the topsail yard, and hastily making his way up thither, he coolly sat down and opened fire on the seething screeching mob of brutal devils who were rushing hither and thither on the deck below; here chopping the prostrate Lagerblom out of all recognition; there doing the same to a courageous recruit who, having learnt something better than native treachery during a long sojourn at Fiji, was gallantly struggling to defend the ship and his shipmates, and laying down his life therefore; and farther aft, rushing hither and thither looking for white men to slay or valuables to annex.

Shot after shot came from the portsail sail yard with unerring aim, now directed at some prominent slayer on deck, now piercing a canoe alongside and carrying dismay into the savage ranks. Fifteen bullets from the intrepid Crittenden's rifle found their billets, and the savage enemy came to the conclusion that Jack [i.e. 'Jack Tar', sailor – Crittenden] aloft was too much for them, so, with yells of disappointment and fear, they went helter-skelter over the sides, and, with their numberless wounded, hastened ashore.

With only two cartridges left Crittenden descended, and warily proceeded along the top of the deck-house aft to see if any of the enemy were in ambush in the recesses. For a moment Crittenden experienced the strange sensation which a man must feel when he finds himself alone in the face of death. Below him and around him lay the bleeding corpses of his shipmates and no living creature with a white skin visible. But a man's voice from the mate's cabin reassured him, and Crittenden hailing it with the remark that the deck was clear, Marr, whose rifle, by the way, had some minutes before this become injured and useless, emerged from his retreat.

By way of precaution the two men looked into the other cabin for skulkers. In the Government agent's cabin was the dead and mutilated body of Mr. Popham, but some sign of life was visible in that gentleman's great-coat which was hanging on a rail in the corner. From thence sprang a naked savage armed with a tomahawk, but before he could strike his intended blow, Crittenden's rifle was in position and a Snider bullet pierced his eye, passed through his head, and embedded itself in the timber wall, where it still remains, visible testimony to the deed.

No more skulkers were found, but down in the main hatch were the 13 recruits who had been previously obtained and were unwilling witnesses of the terrible scene. The 14th, already referred to, joined in the fight against the invaders and was slain. Those remaining were at once brought on deck, and expressed their willingness to defend the ship – a willingness illustrated by an immediate attack on the dying bodies of the black ruffians which lay about the blood-smeared deck – were supplied with tomahawks and were arrayed to resist a second attack which appeared to be impending. The returning enemy, however, though making a show on reaching the beach of renewing the attack and carrying out their original design on the *Young Dick*, hesitated until the ship's boats hove in sight, and then it was too late.

Aftermath

As soon as the ensign at the fore, the signal for the recruiting boats to return, was hoisted, the two remaining white men, Marr and Crittenden, had leisure to survey the ghastly scene around them, and to search the ship for their comrades. In the meantime the unsuspecting Captain Rogers and his boat's crew returned, having received the most cordial treatment from the natives, all of whom must have been aware of the diabolical work going on, all evidence pointing to its being a preconcerted plan.

His horror on stepping on to the deck, left so clear and ship-shape on the morning, can better be imagined than described. The scuppers were literally running with blood, and when the work of washing down the ship began, the teeth of the unfortunate late tenant were found scattered about the Government agent's cabin.

Above the Captain's cabin door are the deep marks of tomahawks. On his bed, the mate, Marr, found stains of blood which had come from the tomahawk slashed at him through his porthole, and which had just come fresh from butchering the cook and carpenter. In different parts of the ship are the tracks of bullets; holes in canvas, rigging, snapped ropes, and splintered wood bear witness to Crittenden's bombardment.

This fearful tragedy brought the cruise to an end, and the vessel made for Queensland as soon as the land breezes that night allowed of a departure. The *Young Dick* arrived off Woody Island on Tuesday, June 1, having been 56 days out, and came up to Maryborough. (*Queanbeyan Age* [New South Wales], 12 June 1886)

The Murders on the Blackbirding Brig *Carl*

One of the most notorious blackbirding incidents concerned the brig *Carl*, in 1871. The *Carl* left Melbourne on 8 June 1871 'on an alleged pearl-fishing expedition', according to one source, but which was, in fact, a labour recruiting voyage. The atrocities for which the brig's master, Capt. Joseph Armstrong, and Charles Dowden, mate, were subsequently prosecuted, occurred off the Solomon Islands on 13 September 1871. The kidnapped Bougainville islanders, from the New Hebrides, were kept in the vessel's hold and rioted during the night. The crew and others on board fired at them indiscriminately from the deck for hours on end. In the morning the dead were thrown overboard. But so, too, were many of the wounded who were still alive. Something of the order of seventy men, mostly Bougainville islanders, were thus massacred.

Dr James Murray, the principal owner of the *Carl* and organiser of the voyage, was given immunity for testifying at trial and so was never prosecuted for his role in the massacre. His self-serving testimony attracted a profusion of opprobrium from outside observers:

The Murders on Board the Brig Carl

At the Water Police Court [in Sydney] on Friday, August 16, before Messrs. J. Hale, C. Lester, and J. Stewart, Joseph Armstrong was charged with having wilfully, feloniously, and of his malice aforethought, killed and murdered a man whose name is unknown. Mr. John Williams, Crown solicitor, prosecuted. Mr. Lowe appeared for the defence.

Mr. Williams informed the Bench that the charge of murder would be withdrawn as against Solomon McCarthy and William Turner (who in the first instance were charged together with Armstrong, with murder on the high seas), but that they would be still retained in custody on a charge of kidnapping.

Dr. Murray's Testimony

Dr. James Patrick Murray deposed:

'I have lately come from Sandhurst, Victoria. I arrived in the City of Adelaide this morning. In 1871 I was the owner of the brig *Carl*. She sailed from Melbourne in the early part of 1871, on a voyage to the South Seas. Captain Flynn was then the master. Prisoner Armstrong was mate of the vessel. We proceeded with passengers to Levuka, Fiji. We arrived there in about three weeks from the time we started from Melbourne. I labour under some difficulty in recollecting dates. I have lost the memoranda of dates, but I think I could get some tomorrow. I did not expect the case to come on this morning.

'When we got to Levuka the passengers were discharged, and Capt. Flynn was discharged. Prisoner Armstrong then became master of the vessel. She was chartered for the labour trade by authority of the consul. The labour was to be collected on my account. I proceeded in the vessel. I remained in Levuka upwards of a week. The brig then sailed for the New Hebrides, the prisoner being the master. It took about four days and a half to get to the Hebrides. We took in water at the island of Tanna. From there we sailed to Sandwich [Efate] Island. We did not get any labour at these places. We then sailed to the Island of Apia [probably Epi], one of the Hebrides.

'We stayed for some little time there getting yams, and then sailed to the Island of Malakolo [Mallicolo], about 30 miles distant from Apia. We anchored outside a certain place. The boat was sent to look for better anchorage. I was in the boat. Whilst looking for better anchorage the boat was fired upon with arrows. At this time a number of canoes were trading round the vessel. We saw these canoes round the vessel when we returned to the ship. Partly in retaliation for the firing, we made an attack upon these canoes. We fired at them. Most of the natives jumped out of the canoes. One remained in one of the canoes fighting; another was wounded.

'The second boat of the ship was then lowered and the natives were picked up out of the water by either one or other of the ship's boats. On reconsideration I am not sure whether the second boat was lowered or not. Our boat picked up 12 or 13 natives. They were taken on board the ship, and put in the hold. They were pulled up the ship roughly by the crew of the brig. When they were got on board they were placed in the hold. Those men did not resist. We sailed away directly we got the men in the hold, and went to the Solomon Group. The ship was anchored not more than two or three cable lengths from the island of Malakolo. The natives who were not picked up escaped to the shore. Some were wounded. Prisoner was assisting in the general effort to take the natives.

'We sailed for the Solomon Group. The voyage thither took eight or nine days, or perhaps less. We sailed to the island of Santa Anna, the southernmost island of the group. We had been in the channel about an hour, perhaps, when canoes came to us from Santa Anna, with natives on board. The vessel was under sail at the time. The natives commenced to trade with us. They exchanged cocoanuts, tortoise-shell, and such things. Two of the natives came on board. The majority remained in the canoes. The canoes came close alongside. Heavy pieces of iron were thrown into the canoes by the crew and captain. Some of the canoes were by this means upset.

'The ship's boats were lowered, and the natives were picked up by the crew of the vessel. About 12 or 13 were picked up in this way. The natives were pulled out of the water into the boats, and from the boats they were lifted into the ship. The ship might have been about a quarter or half a mile from land at this time. The canoes and natives that were not taken went to the shore. When the natives were got on board they were put in the hold. The natives who had previously been placed in the hold were allowed on deck. They were usually kept in the hold a couple of days.

'After the men were got on board the brig sailed away to an island north of Santa Anna, but still in the same group. There were no natives taken there. We went from there to the island of Isabella, another of the same group. The canoes came out as before, and commenced to trade.

'Whilst trading, they were upset in the same manner as the others were upset, by the captain and crew of the brig *Carl* throwing iron into them. Directly the canoes were upset, the ship's boats were lowered, and manned by a crew from the vessel, and all the natives that could be picked up were so picked up. About 10 of them were picked up. The canoes were, generally speaking, small ones, having three or four men each. The ship was under sail all this time. The natives came on board from the boats almost voluntarily. They were put in the hold, and kept there for a day or two. They were liberated in a day or two if they did not exhibit any inclination to fight.

'We sailed away to Bougainville, the northern-most island of the group. The voyage took us a few days. The island of Bougainville is densely inhabited by warlike natives. The natives of the other islands were not so warlike. We sailed along the east coast of the island.

'I omitted to say that before going to Bougainville we called at the Florida group. We obtained a few men there; not more than four or five. We got them in the same way as the others were got, by the upsetting of the canoes by dropping pig iron into them. In throwing the iron, care was taken that none of the natives were hurt. I saw the pig iron taken from the side of the vessel and thrown over. It was placed on deck for the purpose of throwing into and sinking the canoes. One of the crew would take up the iron and stand on the taffrail of the ship and throw it into a canoe. I did not actually see the iron strike a canoe. I did not look over the side of the vessel, but I heard the smashing occasioned by the throwing of the iron. The iron was used for ballast.'

Bougainville Uprising

'Having got to Bougainville canoes came out very plenti-
fully. We went very near the land when coasting along
the island. We were about a week or 10 days off and on
at Bougainville. We were getting natives for four or five
days. We got about 80 natives from this island. They
were obtained by their canoes being upset by the crew
of the brig throwing iron into them. When the canoes
were upset, the crew of the brig manned the boats and
got the natives on board in the same way as the others
had been. When they were got on deck they were placed
in the hold. These Bougainville men resisted very much,
but the crew and some other white men on board assisted
to get the natives into the hold. They resisted the capture
altogether. At night time the natives were all put into the
same hold; but the natives from the different islands did
not mix with each other.

'We had not the men on board more than 48 hours,
when an alarm was given by the evening watch. The day
before there was some talk of a disturbance; but it was
not noticed. But on this evening, about 7 or 8 o'clock, an
alarm was given that the natives in the hold were rising.
The alarm was given by the man on the watch. The brig
was under full sail at the time. After the alarm had been
given, I could hear the natives battering at the main hatch
with poles, and fighting with the other natives at either
end of the vessel. The bunks of the natives were made
of green saplings and poles. These the natives had torn
down and armed themselves with.

'They made javelins of some of the saplings, and threw
them up the hatchway. The hatchway was covered with
open beams; but not sufficiently wide apart to admit of
a man getting through. The openings were, perhaps, six

inches square. The openings were for the purpose of ventilation. These hatches were made on board ship after she had sailed from Levuka.

'Every effort was made to pacify the natives. No white man on board knew their language. None of the natives from the other islands could converse with those from Bougainville. The Bougainville natives and the others kept aloof from each other. We shouted to them, and endeavoured to intimidate them by firing pistols over their heads. We did our best to quell the disturbance. The disturbance lasted for about a quarter of an hour. The Bougainville natives endeavoured to set fire to the ship by rubbing cocoanut shells together. I believe that caused the natives to fight. The other natives endeavoured to extinguish the fire.

'After the expiration of about a quarter of an hour, the natives were fired upon. The fire was directed to the natives under the main hatchway. Guns and revolvers were used. Everybody fired. I am not sure whether Captain Armstrong fired. I think he was at the wheel. I do not think he fired. The firing and fighting lasted all night. When the natives stopped in the least, every effort was made to pacify them. The natives succeeded in loosening some of the bars of the hatchway.

'The fighting was kept up at intervals all night. The firing could not be said to have ceased until the morning. The firing was carried on voluntarily by the white men. No positive orders were given by any one. The general alarm being given, every one took their firearms and proceeded towards the main hatch. Some of us carried arms with us, but most of the arms were kept in the cabin. I think some of the arms were loaded.'

Dead and Wounded Dumped Overboard

'In the morning the hatches were taken off, and the killed and wounded were taken out of the hold and put on deck. I think some of the crew went down to bring them up. The captain was giving directions. About 70 dead and wounded natives were brought on deck. All the Bougainville natives, with the exception of 10 or 12, were either killed or wounded. The dead natives were thrown overboard. I could not say definitely who gave the directions.

'The wounded natives were also thrown overboard.

'I never could ascertain whether positive orders were given for them to be thrown overboard. I think it was done with the general will of the whites. I endeavoured to get their lives spared, and suggested that they should be put on an island, but the general feeling was against doing that. There were about 50 killed, and about 20 wounded were thrown overboard whilst they were still alive.

'My attention was not directed particularly to prisoner Armstrong. I saw him with the general mass. I could not swear positively what he was doing at the time the dead and dying were thrown overboard. I paid no attention to him, and do not know what he was doing. I was desirous of saving the lives of the wounded natives. I appealed to the mass, not to Armstrong specially, as master … The throwing of the wounded overboard was the joint action of all. I could not swear positively whether the captain was engaged in throwing them overboard. I could not speak of any one particularly.

'The wounded were first of all put on the deck. The dead were thrown overboard as they were brought out of the hold. I did not look at the wounded as a medical man, but I looked casually at some of them. It took me a few moments. They must have been on deck a quarter of an hour or 20 minutes before they were thrown overboard. I would not say that the wounded were not brought up on deck first, and the dead brought up afterwards and thrown overboard. The wounded and dead were not mixed. There was no discussion as to whether the wounded should be thrown overboard. It was a spontaneous movement.

'I heard the wounded were to be thrown overboard, and I went forward that I might not see it done. It was the general feeling that that was the best way to dispose of them. There was a general cry for them to be thrown overboard. The crew and the other white men were assembled round the after hatch at the time. The whole of the white men, including the captain, were together. The friendly natives were all forward. I saw some of the wounded thrown overboard. They made no resistance. Some of them were tied. They were tied when they were brought up. Their legs were tied together. I could not say how many of the wounded were tied. I do not know for what particular object they were tied. They did not resist.

'Some of the Bougainville natives, who were neither killed nor wounded, were not found. They were hiding. Some of them were on deck. They were treated like the other natives, as they had ceased resistance. I do not think the passengers took any part in throwing the wounded overboard. I said it was no use throwing the poor wretches overboard, that it would be better to place them on some island, where they would have a chance of recovery.' (*The Argus* [Melbourne], 22 August 1872)

'The general voice was to heave them overboard ...' [Trial notes continue.]

George Heath's Testimony

Another seaman on the *Carl* during that wretched cruise, George Heath, was some months later 'apprehended on board the *Brust*, French man-of-war, and was duly committed for trial by the Water Police Magistrate at Sydney on the 8th instant [8 November 1872]'. Heath corroborated Dr Murray's earlier testimony about how the *Carl*'s crew used pig iron, tied to lengths of rope, to upset islanders' canoes, kidnap the men from the water, and put them in the hold. He then described what happened after the night the *Carl*'s crew, and the passengers on board who all seemed to have a financial interest in the *Carl*, shot down into the hold to quell the mêlée there:

> It was daylight then. Prisoner [Capt. Armstrong] was not with them. The gentlemen [passengers on board with financial interests in the *Carl*] came on deck, and after breakfast some of the natives came on deck, and those who could not come up were dragged up by means of ropes. Some of the crew and passengers went down below with the ropes. Some of the natives were dead, and others wounded. The dead were thrown overboard, and some of the wounded also. Ten of the wounded, however, were kept by Dr. Murray, who thought they would recover ...
>
> The natives were put overboard by the passengers and crew. Prisoner assisted, and said it was no use to keep them on deck, and that they must be put overboard. He could not say whether he helped to put them overboard, but they were put overboard. Some of them were alive at the time, but were badly wounded in the legs, back and arms. Some of them had three or four shot wounds.
> (*Rockhampton Bulletin*, 23 November 1872)

Repercussions

Capt. Armstrong and mate Dowden were found guilty of murdering the *Carl*'s captive insurrectionists; their sentence of the death penalty was later commuted to life imprisonment. (Five other seamen were convicted of lesser criminality.) Dr Murray escaped the punitive arm of the law but was lashed by the vituperation of public opinion. The atrocity itself, as well as the way the islanders were kidnapped, roiled the bile of ordinary people who were outraged at the deceit and barbarity of it all. A newspaper editorial in December 1872 spat venom at Dr Murray in particular regarding the events on the *Carl*'s 'slave cruise':

The Carl *Outrages*

Three or four months have passed since particulars were published by us of the revolting acts of kidnapping and murder perpetrated among the South Sea Islands by the men on board the brig *Carl*; but no doubt the peculiar atrocity of the circumstances will render them still fresh in the minds of our readers. It is a satisfaction to find that some of those who took part in the barbarously treacherous capture and the cold-blooded massacre of the helpless un-offending islanders have been called to account at the bar of justice for their share in the crime.

Five of the sailors who were on board the brig during her slave cruise have been tried in Sydney, and found guilty of having 'unlawfully assaulted, wounded, and ill-treated a man upon the high seas,' that being the cautious form of the indictment. Joseph Armstrong and Charles Dowden, the captain and mate, have been found guilty of the more serious charge of murder and sentenced to death. That sentence has since been commuted to imprisonment for life, the first three years to be spent in irons.

The evidence adduced at the trials does not in any degree soften down the circumstances of the outrage as first published. On the other hand some incidents have come out which give the affair a yet more fiendish aspect, and deepen the feelings of abhorrence and indignation with which every ordinarily humane person must read the account.

The principal witnesses were Dr. Murray and Reiby Wilson, passengers, and George Heath, a sailor. One of the kidnapped islanders, a man named Jage, also gave evidence through an interpreter. A girl taken from another island was put into the witness-box. She was called Nikomai, and appeared to be about 16 years old, but as the Court were unable to discover whether she was capable of giving trustworthy testimony her evidence was not taken. Parts of a log kept through the cruise by Bennett, one of the sailors, was also read.

Tactics

The facts sworn to are minutely confirmatory of the statements originally made. There is the same precise account of the duplicity and tricks employed at the various islands visited to induce the natives to approach the brig for trade. Equally circumstantial descriptions are given of the confiding islanders who came on deck being forced down into the hold and made prisoners. Details are given of the canoes of others being smashed by dropping into them pieces of iron or a small cannon, attached to the brig by a cord, so as to save the destructive missiles for future similar use, and carry on the horrid system of violence as cheaply as possible.

Sickening details are renewed of the terrified islanders being pursued as they struggled in the water and heartlessly kidnapped, and if they were troublesome to catch, of their being struck on the head with clubs or bags of shot. All who could be laid hold of by any means were dragged without thought of mercy or gentleness to the brig's deck and thrust below the hatches. About 150 islanders were thus ruthlessly torn from their native homes and kindred.

Nor is the horror of the massacre of the Bougainville men, of whom a larger number were entrapped on board, diminished one jot by this further testimony. There is the cool statement of their having become 'troublesome' when the brave fellows tore down the poles of their bunks and made a determined attempt to regain their liberty. The farce is recorded of the attempt to pacify them by speaking in a language they did not understand.

Then follows a narrative of how the courageous natives were shot down like so many wild cattle by their brutal captors. To render the murderous work more effective lights were flung down into the hold and a lantern held over it, by the assistance of which surer aim was taken. The dead were afterwards thrown overboard, and the wounded, to the number of 16, while still living were cast into the deep with them. In all between 60 and 70 human beings were atrociously and wantonly murdered. The iniquity of the whole transaction is equal to anything recorded in the blackest annals of the South African slave trade.

Some points in the evidence excite especial indignation. In one or two instances those who assisted at the tragedy, but who had been accepted as witnesses for the prosecution, spoke as though they were conscious of no rights of humanity appertaining to these outraged men.

Because they were people of another colour, and living in a lower state of civilization, they evidently regarded the natives as so many animals to be treated according as convenience dictated. Although they were depriving the islanders of their freedom, the statement that they resisted and were violent seemed to these men a justification for all the unlicensed force they chose to use.

Because the enraged Bougainville men, in their determined attempt to get free, threatened the safety of their white gaolers, that appears to be put forward as a sufficient explanation and excuse for the act of butchery that was committed, as though having placed yourself in jeopardy by first taking a fellow creature's liberty, to kill him in self-defence were a virtue.

In view of such facts we feel that the verdict of assault returned against five of the accomplices was an extremely lenient one, and that so long as hanging is a recognised punishment of the land, that fate was richly deserved by the two men upon whom sentence of death was pronounced.

Dr. Murray's and Passengers' Guilt

But the evidence as a whole does not limit the guilt of this outrage to the seven convicted prisoners. From the admissions of some of the men themselves, and the statements of the witnesses, it comes out that Dr. Murray was the principal owner of the *Carl*, and that the four passengers – Messrs Mount, Morris, Scott, and Wilson – were partners in the speculation to which she was applied. Both crew and passengers were concerned in the lawless labour excursions undertaken by the brig, and the latter are undoubtedly the more guilty.

By Dr. Murray the trip was planned; for his profit primarily, and that of his associates secondarily, the cruise was made. In the capture of the islanders the passengers played an active and reprehensible part. The man Mount on one occasion, with the sanction of the rest, dressed up as a missionary in order to induce the natives to come on board. A more shameful piece of deception than this is difficult to imagine. He was also captain of a boat regularly manned by the passengers alone to assist in picking up the natives whose canoes had been swamped.

During the firing on board Morris loaded the guns in the cabin. The passengers are said to have joined in the shooting, indiscriminately with the crew; although Scott is represented as doing less in that and being principally employed in keeping guard over the hold with a drawn cutlass. Their voices were also raised for throwing the wounded overboard with the dead. These men are therefore participators in the crime.

As being in the position of employers, too, their responsibility and guilt are greater than that of the crew, who, although criminal, acted in a measure under their directions. In the interests of justice they should answer for their share in the outrage as well as the prisoners already sentenced, and it is therefore satisfactory to learn that Mount and Morris have been arrested in Victoria and committed for trial for the part they took in the matter.

Arch-villain Murray

His own evidence and that of the other witnesses make Dr. Murray's conduct appear the most criminal of all concerned in this detestable performance. As already stated he was principal owner of the *Carl*. He it was who engaged the crew, evidently for the purpose of a kidnapping cruise, his own statement being that he stipulated to pay the captain and men head money for every native obtained. He admits having been a leader on board, with authority to say what should be done, and that he might have prevented some of the acts perpetrated.

But while he was to be principally profited by the proceedings he assented to the trickery and violence used. It was he who called the men to arms before the massacre, in which he took part, according to one witness, while singing the song 'Marching through Georgia.' His own statement is that he protested against the wounded being flung into the sea while living; but his protest must have been but a weak one, for after a few minutes' absence he was amongst the group committing that double murder.

The statement of such villainy in a man habituated to the refinements of civilized life, and belonging to a profession more distinguished than perhaps any other for active philanthropy, would be incredible were it not so abundantly attested. It is true he appears to have suffered severely since that time. He was wounded at Mallicolo by one of the natives, and left the brig suffering from an illness which threatened to be fatal. The remorse which seized him whilst at death's door is alleged to have led him to seek out Mr. Marsh, the British Consul at Levuka, and lay all the circumstances before him that the law might take its course.

'Prince of malefactors'

In doing this, however, he evidently took steps first of all to ensure his own safety – a fact which throws utter discredit upon the honesty of his self-alleged repentance, and proves him to possess, amongst other illustrious vices, hypocrisy and cowardice of the most contemptible cast. As it is, not only does he – the prince of malefactors – escape, but his evidence is used to convict his far less culpable comrades in guilt. There are some places where even the guarantee of security given him as Queen's evidence by the Consul at Levuka would not shield such a man from a punishment adequate to his offence. We repeat that the course he has taken, coupled with his statement that some of his accomplices had sought to murder him, shows pretty conclusively that his compunction arises from fear of the consequences of his actions rather than from a true wish to make atonement for them.

Viewing all the facts of his deep and direct complicity in the crime perpetrated, the force of Judge Fawcett's words, uttered before passing sentence upon Armstrong and Dowden, cannot but be felt. 'It is a stain upon the Government, upon the community, and upon the administration of justice, that the ringleader of all these atrocities – the chief mover and instigator of all these acts – the man Murray – who had employed the unhappy prisoners to act against the islanders in the way that he described, should nevertheless escape.'

The only thing which justifies the commutation of the sentence of capital punishment of the captain and mate is the fact that the inhuman monster under whom they acted gets off untouched by justice. (*South Australian Register* [Adelaide, South Australia], 9 December 1872)

Around the same time, an anonymous letter-writer to a Melbourne newspaper expressed even greater damnation of Dr Murray's villainy, amongst other points of fact about the labour trade, sparing no sympathy for the wretched man's 'Satanic' soul:

Permit me, in conclusion, to offer a valuable suggestion to Dr. Murray, which, if his recent account of himself be true, cannot fail of being eagerly and joyfully acted upon by him, inasmuch as it points out to him how to make the only possible atonement for his villainy. As sure as we live, the natives of the island when he stole those miserable wretches whom he shot, and then threw overboard before the breath was out of their bodies, will kill the first white man upon whom they can lay their hands.

I therefore take the liberty of suggesting to Dr. Murray that he prevent the sacrifice of a missionary, a scientific traveller, a whaler, or an honest trader, by hastening with all speed to that island, and giving himself up to be killed and eaten, first carefully explaining to the natives that he is the murderer of their kinsfolk. If he be really converted, as he says he is in that pitiful whine which he sent to Sandhurst, he will not fear to leave a world where he can expect nothing but the execration of all honest men; and it is just possible that he may find another world which will be willing to receive him, though I cannot imagine how even Satan himself could have anything to do with him.

I have not a very good opinion of the devil, but I should have a very much worse opinion of him if he did not turn his back upon Dr. James Patrick Murray.
I am, Sir, your obedient servant. VITL.
(*The Argus*, 10 December 1872)

Homeward Bound
Twenty-seven of the blackbirded men from the *Carl* were eventually returned home after eighteen months' 'captivity' working in Fiji, 'smarting under the lash of cruel plantation owners' there, transported by HMS *Alacrity* to 'the Kingsmill or Gilbert group of islands', in June 1873.

Landing the *Carl* captives. From a sketch by an eye-witness. The picture ... represents one of the scenes in the last act of the infamous *Carl* tragedy, viz., the return of some [27] of the captives to their homes in the Kingsmill or Gilbert group of islands, situated on the equator [by H.B.M. schooner *Alacrity*]. (*Australasian Sketcher*, 29 November 1873)

The *Dancing Wave* Massacre

In 1876 another labour recruitment vessel, the schooner *Dancing Wave*, was centre stage of an uprising by Solomon Islands labourers who slaughtered most of the crew of five. The only white survivor, a seaman named William Broad, escaped to a vessel near the scene, the barque *Sydney*. (The other survivor was a Solomon islander boy from Makira, on the island also named Makira, or Christoval Island.)

After a three-day pursuit of the *Dancing Wave* by the *Sydney*, she was found ransacked, 'bespattered with blood' and abandoned by the Solomon men. The *Sydney*'s captain claimed her as 'a prize'. He put his mate on board to navigate *Dancing Wave* first to Makira Harbour and thence eventually to Sydney, in the then New South Wales colony in Australia:

Massacre Of The Crew Of A Labor Vessel At The Solomon Islands – *the* Dancing Wave

By the schooner *Dancing Wave*, which arrived at Sydney early yesterday morning, we have received intelligence of one of the most bloodthirsty massacres recorded for some time past. Mr. Richard Davis, who was formerly chief officer of the barque Sydney, has kindly furnished us with the following particulars of the event:

The *Dancing Wave* sailed from Sydney on a labor cruise, her ultimate destination being Somerset. She proceeded to the Solomon Group, and had engaged a certain number of the natives of Florida Island. On the 22nd April, at 10 a.m., the labor was all on board, and Captain Harrison was taking down their names, when suddenly there was a general rising among the natives on board, and instantly the crew, with the exception of one man, were tomahawked. The captain went into the cabin and died at once. The chief officer and steward, who had taken refuge in the cabin, being badly wounded, shot themselves to avoid more torture.

William Broad, the man saved, jumped overboard, and, getting hold of the ship's boat, made for Savo Island [off the north coast of Guadalcanal Island]. Broad was placed on board H.M.S. *Sandfly*, at Makera, and she at once made for the scene of the massacre.

The following are the names of the murdered men: Capt. A. Harrison; Mr. J. Dare, chief officer; Thomas

Hellier, steward; Sanderson, Nicholson, and Thompson, seamen. (*The Evening Post* [Wellington, New Zealand], 15 July 1876, from the *Sydney Morning Herald*, 5 July)

Capt. McDonald, master of the schooner *Star of Fiji*, gave a detailed first-hand account of the massacre on the *Dancing Wave*:

The Dancing Wave *Massacre*

The *Dancing Wave*, chartered by a pearl-fishing company, in Sydney, to recruit labour for their pearl fisheries, and commanded by Captain Harrison, who was well-known in Fiji, having been mate with Captain Brown for a considerable period, and with him at the time when some of his crew were murdered, arrived in Makira Harbour, Solomon Group, in May, and engaged an American negro, named Freeman, as recruiting master, also a boy belonging to Makira.

She left for the island of Guadalcanar, recruited 12 labourers, and stood for the small group of islands – the Floridas – came to anchor and began recruiting. The men on board all spoke English. As each man consented to accompany the vessel, he received a tomahawk or knife as an acknowledgement of his engagement. Freeman, the recruiting master, saw that instead of passing these to their friends they kept them themselves, and thereupon told the captain that these were not the sort of men to recruit, and that he had better arm the crew. The captain replied, 'Oh, you need not be frightened, they are all missionary scholars and returned Queensland labourers.' Freeman then said he would recruit no more until he had his shooting irons, and shut the trade box; but instead of going down to the cabin for them, he went forward.

The carpenter was sharpening tomahawks, and the mate, who was standing close by, said, 'He is right, you are sharpening that tomahawk for the last recruit, and he will, perhaps, cleave your skull with it.'

This was scarcely uttered when, with a yell, the natives, who had, in the meantime, evidently well placed themselves, sprang upon the crew and commenced hacking them frightfully with the tomahawks, while one seized that last ground sharp, from the hand of the carpenter, and planted it in his head.

The captain had fared no better; for as he was writing a name in the book he was struck down. He, with the mate, steward, and one of the crew, managed, amidst the blows that were showered upon them, to get down to the cabin, where the captain expired; the steward got a revolver and shot himself; the mate said, 'I am dying, and I will do the same.' The seaman got a rifle, loaded it, and fired through a port hole. Immediately after, he heard the report of another gun or revolver, and on turning round saw that the mate also had shot himself; he then lost all self-possession, and going on deck, jumped overboard.

By a strange coincidence, the shot thus fired killed the chief in command of the murderous assailants, who thereupon used all speed in getting clear of the vessel. While in the water he heard the Makira boy, who was up the rigging, call to him that all the natives had fled, whereupon he came back on board, and found that the only natives remaining were 10 of those recruited at Guadalcanar, the other two having been killed; these men had taken no part whatever in the cowardly and fatal onslaught.

He slipped the [anchor] cable, and getting a sail up made for an island called Suva, where the barque Sydney was at anchor, but the Guadalcanar natives demanded to be taken back to their own island, and took charge of the ship. At this determination on their part the seaman became alarmed, and jumped into the boat; the Makira boy followed him, and they pulled away to Suva. The captain of the barque sent a boat after the *Dancing Wave*, but a breeze sprang up and they were unable to catch her.

When the boat returned, the captain got the barque *Sydney* underweigh, and chased the schooner [i.e. *Dancing Wave*] for three days, at the expiration of which time they discovered her lying wind-bound at Guadalcanar. They found everything in complete disorder, the vessel having been thoroughly ransacked by the natives before they left her, and stains of blood everywhere.

She was taken as a prize, and placed in charge of the mate of the barque, who conveyed her to Makira harbour, where the man-of-war schooner *Sandfly* was lying at anchor. Captain Bell, who is in command, said he could do nothing in the matter as against the natives, as he had no authority to go to the island and take them prisoners. If they were on board, the only thing he could do would be to convey them to Sydney.

The seaman, who was the sole survivor of the *Dancing Wave*, was wounded in several places, having received a blow on his head, a large gash on each shoulder, and an injury with a bolt on his spine. (*The Argus* [Melbourne], 22 August 1876)

What the *Sydney*'s Capt. Woodhouse and crew found on board the *Dancing Wave* when the *Sydney* finally caught up with her was recounted as follows:

Having come up to the schooner, Captain Woodhouse, accompanied by 12 of his crew (principally natives), boarded the *Dancing Wave*, and found that the vessel had been ransacked from stem to stern; the natives had murdered the captain and all his crew excepting William Broad and the man Harry, and had pillaged the whole place, carrying off everything that they could lay their hands to, and destroying life as well as property. The decks and the cabin floor were all bespattered with blood and other human remains; and, in the saloon, pickle and pepper bottles were found to have been emptied, and their contents cast upon the floor, mixing themselves in heterogenous masses with the blood, &c.

Near the mainmast the head of one of the native crew was found.

As soon as Captain Woodhouse could make it convenient, he had the decks washed, and removed, as far as possible, all signs of the fearful outrages that had been perpetrated on board her.

Cannibalistic Natives

It may not be uninteresting to our readers to know that the inhabitants of the Solomon group are cannibals, and that Mr. Davis informs us that when bartering with the natives he has always exercised the greatest possible caution, as they can never be trusted, and that at the moment at which they may appear to be on the most friendly terms, is the very moment at which they may be expected to turn round and make free use of their weapons.

As an illustration of their treacherousness, he relates that last year, in the *Kate Kearney*, when he was chief officer of that vessel, she was at a place called Guize, and one day when they were landing a chief who had been on board the ship, the islanders suddenly turned round and murdered four out of eight of the native crew that were in the boat. The

Massacre of the crew of the *Dancing Wave* at the Solomon Islands.
(*Australasian Sketcher*, 5 August 1876)

crew are said to have given no provocation whatever, and
without the slightest warning they were brutally assaulted
by the men on the beach. The men who had disembarked,
seeing themselves molested, immediately made for the boat,
at which time four of them were killed. The remaining four
swam to the ship, which they reached in safety.

The time at which they appear to be most treacherous
is at the death of a chief, at the death of a chief's wife,
or at the launch of a canoe, when human heads are in
much request for adorning their 'taboa [taboo] house,'

in which a female is prohibited from entering under pain of death. (*The Evening Post* [Wellington, New Zealand], 15 July 1876)

More Murder in the Labour Traffic – The *Hopeful*

By the early 1880s atrocities in the blackbirding of Pacific islanders were inciting repugnance amongst politicians, government authorities and the general public in Queensland. Abuses of the forced trade in indentured labour of Melanesians were a stain on the Colony's reputation, more so since the legislation in the business seemed to fuel and abet such abuses. Things came to a head with the so-called *Hopeful* trials of 1884.

On 28 April 1884 the labour schooner *Hopeful*, owned by the big South Seas trading firm of Burns Philp, sailed from Townsville, Queensland, on a blackbirding cruise around the south-east coast of New Guinea and off-lying islands. Her master was Capt. Louis (or Lewis) Shaw. Harry Scholefield was the government agent responsible for the men 'recruited' by the *Hopeful*. First mate was a man named Thomas Freeman. Second mate, with responsibility for the actual 'recruitment' of labour, was Neil McNeil. The boatswain was Bernard Williams. The cook/steward was a black man, Albert Messiah. Two other seamen, Edward Rogers and James Preston, completed the crew.

On 13 June, off Harris Island in the D'Entrecasteaux group, the crew of the *Hopeful* pursued, kidnapped and shot and killed some (at least two) islanders in canoes whose only apparent aim was to trade yams and coconuts in exchange for tobacco from the white man.

After the *Hopeful* returned to Queensland, news of the killings spread. McNeil and Williams were put on trial in Brisbane, in December, for the murder of two islanders. Captain Shaw, agent Scholefield, and Freeman and Preston were tried on the lesser charge of kidnapping eight islanders (though many other men – well over 100 – were also taken into the *Hopeful*'s hold by the end of the voyage).

Royal Commission

The Queensland government's Royal Commission report on blackbirding, in 1885, revealed the degree of savagery perpetrated by one of the *Hopeful* defendants, boatswain Williams, in his pursuit of the islanders' canoes:

> In the meantime Williams had been encouraging his crew to pull smartly, so as to catch up with the canoe containing the six or seven natives. The latter made for a reef which had only a foot or two of water on it, but before reaching it the canoe was cut by Williams, and the natives, as usual, took to the sea. A rifle was fired, and one islander shot; five and a small boy were picked up by the boat.
>
> One of the rescued islanders jumped overboard from the boat, whereupon Williams followed him with a large knife in his hand. As the islander was coming up on the reef Williams cut the poor wretch's throat, who sank into deep water.
>
> The boat was then pulled up to the reef, from which Williams leapt into it. The two boats then joined company, and the little boy, being of no use as a recruit, was cast adrift on two cocoa-nuts, which were tied together and placed under his arms. The little fellow was seen to slip from the cocoa-nuts, and was drowned in the surf.
> (*Shipping Gazette and Lloyd's List*, 23 June 1885)

The black cook, Albert Messiah, gave the following narrative of the incident, against which evidence Williams and McNeil 'were, without doubt, convicted,' as were the others on the kidnapping charge:

Murder in the Labour Traffic – The Hopeful

On the afternoon of Friday, the 13th of June last, the vessel was standing off an island called Moresby Island, off the coast of New Guinea. He believed that was the name of the island, but he was not perfectly sure, as he only gathered the name from the boys. On that date they were three or four miles off, standing in towards the island, when three or four canoes came off. One large canoe contained some 12 or 15 boys, while the others contained three or four boys each. The whole of the canoes came on the starboard side of the vessel, and brought cocoanuts, yams, and fish for trade.

At this time the vessel was setting sail preparatory to standing off the island. While witness was engaged cleaning lamps, at the galley door, the accused McNeil passed witness, going forward, carrying Captain Shaw's Winchester rifle. After a lapse of about five minutes he returned, and as he was passing witness he said, 'We are going to ram them up.' McNeil then went aft, and sang out for the port boat to be lowered. Witness then saw the men Rogers and Preston coming out from the forecastle, each with a Snider rifle in his hand, and a pouch suspended round his waist.

Two of the boat's crew, Charley and Harry, were at this time in the boat, and Rogers and Preston, with McNeil, got into the boat, which was then lowered on the lee side of the vessel, which was then standing off the land. When the boat was lowered into the water, the canoes had just shoved off from the starboard side. The natives, however, at that time could not have seen the boat lowered. As soon as the McNeil boat was lowered, the painter was cast off, and the boat dropped astern. The boat was pulled round to the large canoe, in which there were 12 or 15 boys.

As the ship's boat pulled alongside of the canoe, witness noticed Rogers and Preston go forward to the bows and catch hold of the canoe, which was then about 30 yards from the vessel, which was under way, but the wind was very light. When the ship's boat joined the canoe, one of the boys in the canoe stood up holding a sucking pig in his hands, but shortly afterwards dropped the pig and picked up a paddle, which he held above his head, in a striking attitude.

Witness then heard McNeil say to some one of the two on the bows of the boat, 'Drop him.' Preston then put his Snider to his shoulder, but did not fire. About two minutes afterwards, Freeman, the mate of the *Hopeful*, who was standing on the other side of the poop to witness, took aim with his Snider and fired in the direction of the boats; he did not see any one in the canoe fall.

First Fatal Shooting

The next thing witness saw was the prisoner McNeil drop his steer oar and slip to the side of the boat, and, putting his rifle to his shoulder, fire. The islander who was standing up in the canoe with the paddle in his hand staggered back and fell. McNeil was then about five yards from the islander, and Preston and Rogers had hold of the canoe. When McNeil fired, all the islanders jumped overboard with the exception of the man who was shot, who was lying across the thwarts of the canoe, and a child, about five years of age, who was crying.

McNeil then called out, 'Lower away the second boat,' and he then shoved off from the canoe and started off, leaving the islanders swimming in the water, and pulled after the other canoes, which had gone away. The second boat was immediately lowered, containing the accused, Williams, Charley (German), Dingwell (carpenter), witness, and Jack, and they then went after the boys who were swimming in the water. It might have been a quarter of an hour before they got to the boys. The boat in which witness was, picked up six of the boys, and then pulled to where the large canoe was drifting.

While doing so one of the boys they picked up jumped overboard. The boat was again turned round in pursuit. When they made an effort to catch the boy he dived two or three times; and Williams, who was standing in the stern of the boat, called out, 'If you don't come back I'll shoot you.' Witness said, 'For God's sake don't shoot him, turn the boat round and try and save him, and if we can't we'll go back to the ship.'

Second Victim

After this witness saw Williams with his Snider in his hand, and, as soon as the boy came again in sight, Williams fired. Witness did not believe the first shot struck the boy, as he kept on swimming. He then heard Williams tell Jack (South Sea Islander) to fire at the boy in the water. Jack did so, but missed him. He next saw Williams take out a cartridge from his pouch and put it in his rifle. Williams again fired at the boy, and witness noticed something go off as if part of the man's head. Witness did not see the boy who was shot by Williams come to the surface again. When Williams fired the last shot they were about nine yards from where the boy was swimming in the water. Witness said to Williams, 'You have shot that man,' and he replied, 'He has only dived.'

The ship's boat was then pulled towards where the large canoe was drifting, when witness saw the body of a man, apparently lifeless, lying across the thwarts of the canoe. The child was still sitting crying in the canoe as before. When they passed the canoe another of the islanders in the ship's boat jumped overboard. He was a deformed old man, and was allowed to swim away, as Williams remarked that he would not pass the doctor. Both the men who were shot belonged to the large canoe.

They took four of the islanders on board and returned to the vessel about half-an-hour before McNeil's boat, which also brought four boys on board. Witness said to the captain, 'Barney [Bernard Williams] shot a man in the boat.' The captain replied, 'Steward, if you want to be in this trade you must be blind and see nothing.' (*Shipping Gazette and Lloyd's List*, 20 December 1884)

Boatswain Williams claimed that: 'Messiah's evidence is as fake and foul as was ever uttered, God knows. He says he saw the act which he never saw.' His indignation proved in vain. Capt. Shaw and agent Scholefield were found guilty of kidnapping and sentenced to life imprisonment, 'the first three years in irons'. Freeman was sentenced to ten years (two years in irons) and Rogers and Preston to seven (one year in irons).

McNeil and Williams were convicted of murder and sentenced to death by hanging, 'to be carried out on the 29th inst. [December 1884]'. The historical precedence of lightening that capital punishment, with the even greater weight of a public outcry for clemency, ultimately saved the men from the noose:

> Still there is the fact that the extreme penalty of the law has not hitherto been enforced, and that, in the heat of chasing these natives, there is little doubt that McNeil and Williams regarded their acts as something less than murder. It has been for this reason, and because it is a new departure to hang these men for such an offence [none had been hanged in the past], that so powerful an effort has been made in Queensland within the past fortnight to commute the sentences from death to penal servitude for life. (*Shipping Gazette and Lloyd's List*, 20 December 1884)

Clemency and Abolition

The vociferous appeal for clemency, to commute the death penalty to life imprisonment, came from the public's indignation that two *white* men should hang for carrying out a legitimate trade in labour that was sanctioned by law – and, more tellingly, upon the evidence of a *black* man, cook Messiah. A press opinion by the *Queensland Times*, before the death penalty on the two men was commuted, implied that the offensive nature of the labour trade itself 'should cause us to do all we can to save these men from a doom which in some respects very nearly approaches a vicarious one'.

It suggested that criminality in the *conduct* of the trade was a natural consequence of the legally sanctioned trade itself. Not that its criminal conduct was an excuse for murderers and kidnappers who were complicit scapegoats of the trade, but rather that it was a criterion for its abolition altogether, to eliminate the complicity of the abusers' criminality – and, not least, the common man's conscience – in it:

> ... when men get beyond the pale of civilisation, goaded
> on by owners who are themselves not very scrupulous as
> to how labourers are obtained, and incited, perhaps, by
> promises of reward proportionate to the living result of
> the trip [i.e. the number of labourers 'recruited'], they
> acquire a sort of enterprising recklessness which might
> be foreign to their nature were it not for the ... hot bed
> in which they are placed. In other words, the recruiting
> system is inimical to honesty; it tends to the growth of
> moral exercises. (*Queensland Times*)

Conclusion

Although the death sentence for McNeil and Williams was, with some reluctance by the authorities, commuted to life imprisonment, the public outrage over their conviction continued. A lengthy petition presented to a newly elected government in 1888 forced the issue: apart from Scholefield who had died thirteen months into his sentence, all the *Hopeful* prisoners, including the two convicted murderers, were released from jail in 1889.

The consequence of the *Hopeful* trials, the public outcry arising from them, and the 1885 Royal Commission, was that the indentured trade in labour from New Guinea waters was abolished in 1890. The Pacific Island Labourers Act of 1901, which prohibited the introduction into Australia of labourers from all Pacific Islands after 31 March 1904, effectively closed the book once and for all on those wretchedly blood-curdled chapters of that wretchedly malignant enterprise.

THE END

Also in this series

978 0 7509 9085 1